D1525412

WHITE
PICKET
PRISONS

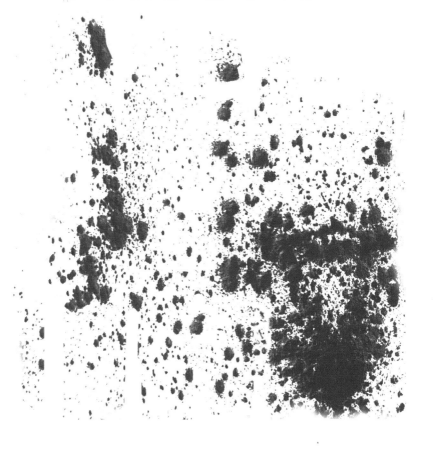

Also by Kelli Owen

Floaters
The Hatch
Wilted Lilies
Deceiver
Grave Wax
Buried Memories
Survivor's Guilt
Crossroads
Live Specimens
White Picket Prisons
Black Bubbles
The Neighborhood
Waiting Out Winter
Six Days

WHITE
PICKET
PRISONS

Kelli Owen

Gypsy Press

www.kelliowen.com

For Brian Keene…the best "big brother" a girl could want.

ACKNOWLEDGEMENTS

Thank you to Mark and Amanda, as always. To Bob Ford for accepting this on top of tax season, ves'tacha. To Paul Goblirsch for being his awesome self. To my amazing prereaders: Tod Clark, John Foley, Nikki McKenzie & Dave Thomas (DT76), and the incredible shark expert, supreme cook and final eyeballs, Dave Thomas (Meteornotes). To Matt Blazi for letting me torture him throughout the writing of this. To Camille for the willing use of her name (you're younger in real life, but just as hot), to several who didn't know I was using theirs, and to the countless people on Twitter and Facebook who answered the call for names to help me populate an entire village. And to Michigan—with apologies...

"When the Gods wish to punish us, they answer our prayers."

~ Oscar Wilde

CHAPTER ONE

Bobby "Squeak" Charles walked through the double doors of the courthouse a free man. The sight of Squeak caused blood to flush Mark Baker's jaw, the internal heat of frustration and anger flowing through his system to the clenched fist he would never swing. Mark's service pistol was on the dresser at home, and he found himself torn between relief and disappointment.

Injustice is not an inanimate thing, Mark thought as he watched six months of work waltz into the open air without cuffs. *It's a persona. A personality. And occasionally, a person. It's every defense attorney who's ever won a case they shouldn't have. It's every judge who ever let the guilty go. It's loopholes and assholes.*

And my fucking life.

The wrinkles in Squeak's borrowed suit were obvious in the natural light of the afternoon sun, extra fabric hanging off his skeletal frame like cheesecloth over a mason jar. Mark wondered who in Squeak's circle even had a suit for him to borrow, but decided it was more likely provided by his defense attorney. Lauren Patterson was a first-class bitch when it came to defending her clients and shredding both witnesses and evidence, but she had a heart outside the battle of the courtroom, and he wouldn't put it past her to have fed Squeak as well as dressed him to make him appear healthier and more respectable than the druggie street thug he was in reality. Damn her. She was good at her job.

But so was Mark. Squeak would fuck up again and Mark would be right there when he did. He watched as Squeak bounced down the steps, a free man, and felt the anger rolling through him anew.

"Fucking loopholes…" he cursed under his breath, but loud enough for Squeak to hear him. The junkie turned his head to the pillar Mark was leaning against and grinned. A big stained grin. His missing tooth created a black hole in a pugnacious smile, which chilled the blood of younger thugs and civilians wandering the wrong part of town. It didn't affect Mark the same way. He wasn't inclined to cross the street to avoid the dirt bag, or avert his eyes from making contact. Instead, Mark's eyes narrowed and he nodded to Squeak, silently daring him to fuck up again, or better yet, start something right there on the courthouse steps.

Squeak curled one corner of his lip up in a mock grimace, "Better luck next time, Baker." He turned and continued bouncing down the steps without seeing Mark's reaction.

Mark shoved his hands into his pockets, wishing he had his gun. Wishing he had the authority to just do what the courts didn't. Wishing there was some loophole to save him if he went ahead and just took the dealer off the streets, off the planet, permanently. He growled in frustration. There wasn't. He knew that.

He turned and walked toward the side parking lot. His day was done. No way was he heading back to the station now. He'd had enough of crime without punishment for one day. As if to urge him in the right direction, his stomach growled and he remembered Gina was making her enchiladas tonight. A plate full of spicy happiness filled his mind and pushed the thoughts of Squeak back to the darker corners where they belonged.

--==●==--

Mark heard music emanating from his duplex apartment as he reached for the door and paused, grinning. He stood outside the door for a moment and listened to Gina warble out the last chords of the latest pop song she'd fallen in love with, something by someone who used to be in a band and was now solo and better according to her, but whom Mark could never remember the name of—solo or band.

He gently opened the door as the next song kicked in and he recognized Guns N' Roses immediately. He slipped inside the apartment, careful not to let the sunshine give away his presence and leaned against the door watching his girlfriend gyrate around the kitchen to "Welcome to the Jungle." Gina alternated whistling, humming and singing, as she spun from a frying pan full of spiced hamburger to the cutting board on which she massacred various herbs and scallions. Occasionally she would stop all action and swoop like a snake toward the floor and back up, popping a hip with the beat as she impersonated Axl's famous move.

He grinned while he watched, feeling the day wash off him like dead skin and felt his heart lighten and his love of life rejuvenate. Watching Gina unawares was always good for the soul. It reminded him to stop and enjoy life. To dance while cooking and sing while cleaning. He absently began to whistle in tune with the song and Gina spun in a panicked move, knife held up to defend herself. They met eyes, both wide from surprise, and laughed.

"Bastard! How long were you standing there?"

"Long enough."

"I hate it when you do that." She put the knife on the counter and sashayed toward him. "You know that?" Her cupid lips askew as she smirked.

"Yeah, but I love watching you and I'm going to keep doing it as long as you keep putting on a show, so learn to live with it or give up the stage." He wrapped a hand behind her, planted it flat on the small of her back, and pulled her the last few inches to him. He leaned down toward her face and locked her eyes as his lips brushed across hers. Half a foot shorter than him, she felt tiny in his arms, but he noticed the baby bulge beginning to make a bigger gap between the two of them when he pulled her close like this.

He felt her grin beneath his lips a moment before she bit his lower lip and pushed him away as if she could ever overtake him. Gina spun and returned to the cutting board. "Enchi-mee-ladas in forty-five."

"Excellent." He sat on a kitchen chair and began untying his shoes.

"So? How'd it go in court today?" Gina began assembling the enchiladas and asked the question without turning toward him. She didn't see his grimace but his pause in answering let her know it was there. "That good, eh?"

"Fucking bullshit, that's what it was." He flipped his foot and let the shoe fly toward the corner by the door. "Yet another case of too much of this, not enough of that, tiny protocol slip here, forgotten warrant there. I had a fucking warrant. It said residence. It should have covered the fucking shed out back, Goddamn it."

"Breathe, baby. That rage is not good for you..." She cooed as she flipped a wrapped enchilada into the pan. "Or me. Remember, I have to live with you. Not to mention Junior here..." She patted her tummy with the side of the spatula.

"It's bullshit, Gina. There are dead kids because of this piece of human shit. I work my ass off to get these fucking thugs lined up just right, to take them down like filthy dominos. And the system is on their side. The system hasn't seen firsthand the cast-off children left in the wake of these drug dealers. The system has never had a deal or a bust on its lawn. The system lives at the edges of civilization with large yards and locked gates. They don't truly understand the underbelly found in royalty around here. Fuck, what was the first warning I gave you?"

"If the street has a royal name, don't be on it." Gina's tone was a mockery of a parental warning spoken so often it had lost its intimidation.

"I'm serious. I was then and I am now..."

"Oh I know you are, honey. I avoid the parts of town you want me to avoid. I understand what these punks leave in their wake. And I understand your frustration." She grabbed a handful of chopped greens and tossed them into the bowl of shredded cheese. "But you have to understand right now, right at this instant, the thugs are winning, because they've got you so riled up you can't think straight. You can't function properly. You don't sleep, you don't eat like you used to, and you hang on every squawk that comes from that damn scanner. It's not healthy. You need to do your job and rely on others to do theirs."

"I hate you."

"I love you, too." She poured the last of the sauce across the pan of rolled enchiladas and turned to face him, leaning back against the counter. "You know I'm right. You're very good at what you do. That's the best you can do...your best. If the next animal in the food chain fucks up the kill you offer them, that's not your fault. You do your job, let them do theirs. And if they fail, the universe will pick up the slack." She grabbed her coffee mug and walked toward him. "After all, how many street-level dealers do you know of who die peacefully of old age outside of jail with a family who still loves them?"

Mark opened his mouth to speak. It was the same battle they had whenever court went poorly and he was going to win this one, but she kept right on going.

"None. That's how many. They get what's coming to them. Sometimes it's your doing, sometimes it's their own. But they get it in the end and that's all that really matters." Gina kissed his head, and headed to the living room. "Now go take a shower before dinner, you smell like alligator spit."

He laughed. He'd never understood the reference but always found it amusing when she proclaimed his similarity to zoo animals. Mark was certain she'd never actually smelled alligator spit, and even more certain he didn't smell like it, but it made him smile, which is what she was after. Damn her. Spunky little girl won again.

Mark flicked his remaining shoe to the corner and headed to the bathroom without another word to her. To himself, he had plenty. *I am not above the law. I am the law. Unfortunately, I'm not the top of the totem pole or the highest wrung on the ladder, and as Monday morning courtroom antics have reminded me: sometimes, even when I do my job, it's not enough.*

CHAPTER TWO

Where are you going?" Gina's groggy voice startled Mark and he looked toward the bed. In the wash of light escaping the bathroom, he saw her squinting in his direction, an arm outstretched and hand splayed flat on the spot where he should be. Instead, he was leaned against the wall quietly pulling a sock onto his foot.

"I couldn't sleep."

"Yeah, yeah…but where are you going?"

"Nowhere special, hon. Just go back to sleep."

She leaned up on an elbow and opened her eyes more fully. "Bullshit. Remember why this works? We communicate. Now what the…"

"You're right. Sorry." He stepped toward the bed. "I was flipping channels downstairs when the scanner went off. They grabbed Bobby Charles in the yards."

"Oh Christ, really? Really?"

He couldn't tell if the annoyance was at him, the scanner, the thug or the fact he'd woken her because of the job—again. "Baby, I have to make sure they don't fuck it up." He leaned in to kiss her and she backed away. "If I can put him back behind bars, even for a few days, it negates his victory earlier today."

"No, it just makes you obsessed." She pouted and he could see the thoughts churning in her soft brown eyes.

"You know the uniforms won't do what they should. Especially the damn night crew."

"I know you're frustrated, but Jesus, give it a rest. Just for a day. Twenty-four whole hours without the fucking dealers and street dirt breaking into my life and tearing you out of it, out of our bed, in the middle of the night."

"Gina, it's Bobby Charles though. It's still fresh. It's…"

"Fine. Go. You're not going to sleep if you don't and if you think I'm mad you'll just act all weird tomorrow. Go. I'll sleep all by myself on your side and pretend the smell is really you…"

"Gina…"

She smirked and rolled over. "Sheesh. I'm just giving ya shit you big lug. Go catch your bad guys. Make the streets safer for me and Junior."

He put a knee on the bed and leaned in to smell her hair before brushing it out of the way and kissing her shoulder. "I love you, Gina Beana."

"And I'm IN love with you."

"Lunch tomorrow before your shift?"

"Mmmhmmm…" She murmured and began drifting off again immediately. Mark slipped out of the bedroom, flicking the bathroom light off as he did so.

--==•==--

"Are you fucking kidding me?" Mark pulled up to the scene in a rage. The radio chatter had been a mess and he expected Bobby Charles to be gone already by the time he got there. He pulled his unmarked in behind a squad car in the factory parking lot and slammed it into park, his driver's door open before the keys were out of the ignition.

"Where's Ray?" Mark barked at the nearest uniform. A young cadet stuck on night shift and ill prepared for the foulness of late-night city shenanigans pointed behind him at a cluster of bodies.

Mark pushed past the boy fiddling with scene markers and shouted over his shoulder at the officer squatted on the ground to the left of him, "Make sure you shoot evidence from several angles and put tape there so we can size it correctly later. And for fuck's sake, don't move anything until someone higher than you on the food chain says you can fucking move it!"

He heard mumbling behind him but could neither make out the words nor find it in his heart to care what they'd been. Bobby Charles was here somewhere, in cuffs he hoped, and he needed to make sure fucking Patterson wouldn't have any loopholes to jump through this time.

"Baker, what the fuck are you doing here?" The captain spotted him before he got to the circle of men.

"Why didn't you call me, Ray? You know Squeak's mine." Mark's stride increased and he closed the gap between them. "For fuck's sake…"

"Captain, Baker. I'm your Captain." The balding man plucked his cigar from his mouth and waved it between pinched fingers at Mark. "Don't you fucking start with me. I know you had a bad day, but this isn't tied into your drug case. We got a dead girl and your boy Squeak here called it in."

"He called… He what?!" Mark bellowed. "No he did not. He wouldn't. It's not his style." Mark looked around him, noticing the sprawling body of a poorly dressed girl and a shaken Squeak sitting on a curb talking to a uniform as the officer quickly jotted down a statement. "I call bullshit." Mark turned and headed toward Bobby Charles.

"Baker, I am not fucking kidding. You fuck with this scene, or your boy, and your ass is going on vacation."

Mark froze. *Fuck.* And turned back to his commanding officer. "Just let me talk to him. I know him. I know how he works. I can tell you if he's lying."

"He always lies, that's the beauty with his kind. Just take what he says and flip it to find the truth."

"Ray…"

"Baker…" The captain mimicked him and he put the cigar back in his mouth and resumed chewing on the end rather than smoking the stub. "When we're done you can have a word. Until then you can sit your pretty ass in your car, take a walk, or find some way to be helpful…without harassing my crew."

"Fine." Mark scanned the parking lot. "Where the fuck did he call from? It's not like there's a phone booth handy, and he sure as shit didn't use his throwaway and hand over his number to us."

"Good question. Write that down for later and get the fuck out of my way." The captain pushed past Mark and headed toward the body on the ground near the corner of the building.

Mark squinted toward the girl, trying to see if he recognized her, but couldn't make out her features in the shadows. "Can I take a look at the vic?"

"Sure, whatever. Just don't touch anything or talk to anyone until we're done." The captain's words were garbled around the chewed end of his cigar but years of practice helped Mark understand them perfectly. "And stay the fuck away from Squeak."

Mark offered a cursory glance to the boys in blue, the lot itself, and made eye contact with Squeak—letting him know he was there— as he made his way to the girl on the pavement and glanced over the shoulders of the bus crew.

Young. Early twenties, tops. Probably attractive once, though not recently. The girl was far too skinny for the leggings and baggy sweater she wore. Her shoes didn't match her outfit and seemed an ill-fit for her feet, making Mark wonder if she'd found them or stolen them. The sleeves of her thinned sweater were pushed up to show track lines and Mark turned to glare at Squeak at the sight of them. Her hair was most likely blond but filth and dim lighting made it appear darker. Her face was without makeup and a jagged scar ran along the bridge of her nose.

"Rosie?" He stared at the scar and thought of every description he'd ever gotten of Bobby Charles' twin. "Squeak, is this Rosie?" He yelled at the small-time dealer and watched him drop his gaunt face into his hands. It was Rosie.

And it explained why Squeak called it in.

On the street, family was rare. Close family was unheard of. But the legend of Squeak and the twin he shielded from everyone's eyes had been around as long as he'd been on the nitwit's tail. Even Mark had never seen her. But he'd gotten enough reports to know she used and had a scar along her nose from the night she fought back with a broken beer bottle, the last night her daddy touched her.

This was not his crime scene. This wasn't Squeak's drugs. But he could use it to break Squeak. He could use it to make him squeak.

Mark walked over to the captain and interrupted instructions to the young night cop taking pictures, "I'll wait at the station for him. Bring him in for me."

Rosie was dead. Squeak could very well be next. And if the idiot was going to get his clock punched, Mark wanted as much info out of him as he could get first. "The body is his sister. Keep an eye on him."

Commotion behind him spun Mark on his heel. Squeak had stood from the curb and either pushed or attacked the cop taking his statement. "Sit the fuck down!" was met with "Fucking make me!" and the two went into a tight locked close-combat struggle. Before Mark could react, before the captain could intervene, Squeak pulled back from the officer, brandishing the officer's service pistol in front of him.

Guns were drawn universally in the lot and several shouts drowned each other out, as multiple voices demanded Bobby Charles put the gun down. Squeak's eyes were wide and wet as he scanned the uniforms around him pointing their weapons at him. He turned to Mark and locked eyes, stolen pistol at his side. Mark had his drawn and a bead on the thug's kneecap.

"It ain't right, Baker." Bobby Charles' voice broke and he started to lift the gun. Mark realized it was more of a gesture than a threat, as the dealer often talked with his hands, but moved his sights from the man's knee to his weapon-wielding elbow.

"Put it down, Bobby." Mark took a cautious step forward. "You don't want to do this. Hell, you beat me, remember. You're a free man. You wanna fuck that up?"

"He already has." One of the other officers commented and Mark turned to glare at them. Squeak took the chance and raised the gun up fully.

"Bobby!" Mark yelled too late and a shot rang through the buildings like a ricochet. Squeak crumpled as his knee went out beneath him, another officer having taken initiative, but held tight to the weapon in his hand. The cop in front of Squeak saw the dealer lose concentration for a moment and kicked him hard in the gut, knocking him backward onto his shattered knee and the unbalanced foot of the other leg.

"It ain't right." Squeak lifted the gun, tears in his eyes and pulled the trigger. The loud pop reverberated between the buildings for longer than it took Squeak's limp body to hit the pavement. The spray of pink and speckles of bone bits blew to the side and covered the officer standing next to him.

"NO!" Mark sprinted forward and pushed the young officer

out of the way. "No, no, no…" He looked down at the dealer and watched the blood pool under his head. Anger seethed behind his eyes as he calculated the months of work lost in a moment. The lost opportunity this tragedy could have helped him procure. And he spun on the officer.

"You stupid, stupid son of a bitch!" Someone grabbed his arm and pulled him back as the officer's eyes widened in fear.

"Down, boy." The captain's voice was a creepy calm, which usually meant he was somewhere three miles north of pissed. "We got a mess to clean up and you're not officially here. Just go home. Stay off the paperwork."

"That fucking rookie…"

"I know. And it's my problem, not yours." The captain tightened his grip on Mark's arm until Mark focused on his face and his eyes cleared. "You got enough bullshit going on. Now get the fuck out of here."

"Yeah. Whatever." Mark jerked his arm free from Ray and walked toward his car. "Fucking waste. Just a fucking waste…" He slammed the door shut and sat there for a moment. The reality of his best drug dog being dead was just sinking in. He hit the steering wheel in frustration and wished he hadn't given up drinking. A shot of tequila never sounded so good and he debated hitting the bar rather than going home.

Mark turned the key in the ignition. The car came to life with the radio still on and the dying refrains of "Welcome to the Jungle" bled from the speakers.

"Fuck." He dropped his head to the steering wheel. "She's right." He thought of Gina, lying in their bed alone, and the words she tried to drill into his head. He needed to be there for her emotionally as well as physically when he wasn't on shift. He needed to let go of this bullshit after hours. It got him nowhere except out of his bed. He sighed and pulled out of the lot.

CHAPTER THREE

Mark drove straight to Harp and Fiddle out of habit. He pulled up front, put the sedan in park and froze. He watched the customers through the large glass windows—drinking, laughing, dancing to some local Irish band playing and wanted to be part of it. Or at least a peripheral participant. He never danced and he rarely chatted with the bartender, let alone the clientele, when he was a drinker. He sat at the end of the bar on a tall stool at the corner and drank his Jack Daniels in silence—contemplating the current case, his lack of a social life and wondering if this was all there was.

As the night air cooled, the windows of the bar steamed from the crowd and food being prepared inside. Mark didn't miss the hangovers. He didn't miss the antisocial drinking. But he did on occasion miss Molly's hot wings. If it wasn't so cliché, he'd have asked the bartender out a number of times, but it just wasn't him. Or his frame of mind at the time. And he never ran into her away from her bar rag, his Jack Daniel's and their mutual understanding to keep both moving without a word. She was a good kid. Older than her years, yet younger than a hard life had tried to make her. He nodded to her, though she couldn't see, and pulled away from the curb.

Mark had no idea how or why he ended up on George Street, and honestly wouldn't have known immediately which street he was even on until he realized he had pulled over under the giant neon cross outside Yorktown Mission.

"Benny…"

He took a deep breath and turned the ignition off. He stood in the open door of his car and looked up at the building for a few moments. Then shut the door with a click that echoed on the quiet street, pushed the lock button on his keys, and dropped them in his pocket.

The neon cross buzzed in the still air, sounding like thousands of angry insects. The brick building didn't resemble a church by structural definitions, and technically wasn't, but it was as close as he'd come to one in quite a while. Crammed into the middle of the block, between a barbershop and a beauty salon, it appeared worn down, ancient even, and out of place. The heavy metal doors and bars on the windows were not welcoming against the cold brown brick. The script "God is Love" on the white banner above the door attempted to portray the acceptance the steel doorway and bars dissuaded. If he didn't know better, he would have thought they were closed to the refuse prone to wander this time of night, but he knew Father Benjamin would be in there. Reading or cleaning or praying or doing whatever it was he did when he had no downtrodden to lead to the light.

Mark walked around the car to the entrance. A loose piece of cellophane from a cigarette pack floated across his path, dancing on the light breeze snaking its way down the street like it was funneled between the buildings directly at him. He returned his gaze to the neon cross above him, flickering against the dark sky, and shook his head. He wasn't in the mood for subtle hints from the universe.

He tested the doors and his theory held true. They opened easily and he walked into the dimly lit building, spotting Ben sitting on the steps at the front of what would be considered the sanctuary. Ben looked up from whatever he'd been reading, Mark presumed it was the Bible, and squinted into the darkness.

"Good evening, my child." He stood and prepared to greet the intruder as he always did, beginning as if scripted and sounding very much like the practiced spiel of a telemarketer. "And why has the Lord led you to me tonight?"

"Hey Benny." Mark's voice carried farther than he expected and seemed as if he'd shouted the greeting harshly.

"Mark? Hey…" Ben sped up his pace and met Mark halfway down the aisle with a hand held out in front of him. "How are you? How's Gina? It's kind of late for you to be here, isn't it?" The questions came fast as Ben eyed Mark up and down, inspecting him for wounds, blood or weapons.

"She's good. We're good." He pushed Ben's hand out of the way and hugged the man he'd known since ninth grade at York Catholic. "And I always come see you late, you know that, Benny."

"Father Donnelly," he corrected with a smile. "Just try to say it once a year if you could."

While Ben's smile was generally infectious, the most Mark could muster would be considered a snarl, as one side of his mouth curled up in an acknowledgment of Ben's attempt at humor.

"So? What beef do you have with God tonight, then?" Ben motioned to a row of folding chairs, sitting in the chair across the aisle himself.

Oh, I've got a beef, Mark thought. *A couple.* But he didn't immediately speak. He huffed out a long breath, still absorbing what had happened tonight and the fact Ben knew he was there with a beef made him thankful his friend knew him well enough.

He should. They'd been through enough in the last twenty years.

York Catholic hadn't been a breeze for Mark. A Protestant put in Catholic school by a mother who'd decided it would be good for him was generally an outcast from the first day. Mark hadn't been. He'd been accepted by the kids just fine. The staff, however, usually wanted to slap him silly with a ruler or a switch or whatever might be handy and acceptable to Jesus for punishing troublesome teens. Mark wasn't required to take religion class and was never asked to play altar boy. Benjamin Donnelly had been both, and usually in just as much trouble as Mark. They became friends almost immediately and spent ninth grade trying to outdo each other without getting caught.

The day Benny threw the cherry bomb into the toilet of the girl's first-floor bathroom and shook the statue in the hallway, everything changed. Mark didn't think Benny's being Catholic was going to get the nuns to turn their heads this time. He stepped up and took the blame, expecting a couple of days' worth of suspension and a month of grounding from his parents.

Instead, he was expelled. While he was relieved to be out from under the thumbs of the nuns and Father Matthews and God, he wondered in hindsight if it would have been better to let Ben take the fall, but couldn't convince himself they wouldn't have done the same to him. That would have destroyed Benny—having already decided he wanted to work with the church in some capacity someday—and Mark swallowed the blame and punishments it carried.

Mark ended up in Suburban High School, grounded for the rest of the school year, and worried he'd never see Benny again. But Ben climbed the tree to Mark's room a couple times a week and talked to him from the branches, filling him in on the latest troubles and tales from the school Mark had hated but somehow missed. Fate moved Ben's family into the neighboring development the following fall, and they saw each other whenever they weren't in their separate schools.

Even though they'd gone different routes after graduation, Mark to college and Ben to seminary, they kept in touch. When Mark made detective they celebrated. When Benny took over the Yorktown Mission, they celebrated. Benny had been Mark's best man when he married Kim. And drank alongside Mark when she left him. Mark had been there when Benny's mother died suddenly of stomach cancer. And giggled as Ben's father opened the sampler packages Mark and he had gotten from Excitement Video for the newlyweds, when Ben's father remarried a couple years later.

Over the years they saw each other less, due to life being busy or conflicting plans, but they still talked at least weekly and saw each other at least once a month. Mark had to admit Ben had been right when he asked what Mark's beef was, since he'd only come to the mission lately to complain. A part of him felt sorry for the habit forming. The other part of him—the part that had watched Squeak off himself and had barely escaped the Harp and Fiddle—had other ideas.

"Oh I've got a beef alright," he finally said, narrowing his eyes at his old friend. Mark didn't see Benny. He didn't blame the low lighting or the anger, he knew pointblank what he was doing. He was using God's conduit to relay a message. "Your God can go fuck himself."

"*My God*? I see…"

"I wonder if it was the nuns that expelled me or God himself some days, Benny." Mark finally sat down, or rather dropped his weight, his consciousness and his anger, into the end chair across from Ben. "You work your ass off to help them find Him. I mean really, Benny, what time is it? And you're still here, stubbornly waiting for the one you don't want to get away. But does it work? Do they come back? Do they clean up their shit and find God and a better life?"

Benny opened his mouth but Mark cut him off and continued.

"And me? Christ." He huffed out a breath and took a deep inhale of stale wood polish and frankincense-laced air, "I work hours and hours, more on duty than off, to get the scum off the street. To make the streets safer. To clean up the neighborhoods. To punish those that deserve it far more than those innocent bystanders that fall victim to criminals and God alike. And what happens? What happens, Benny? The fucking system, the authority figures, the political arm of fucking God, lets them go. Just lets them walk back out into the sunshine… The sunshine no longer enjoyed by the kids that died on their drugs, or the mothers lost to their gang wars. The innocent suffer. The guilty go free. It's fucking bullshit and I'm fucking sick of it."

"Mark…" Ben held his hand out across the open space between them, attempting to place it on Mark's knees but not quite reaching and instead swinging it toward the front of the church, pointing at the cross in an afterthought. "He sees the crimes. He punishes. But He punishes on his terms, in his timeframe. It is not for you to decide when and how His work is to be done—"

"His work? You do His work, and you damn well decide when you're going to do it—"

"You know what I mean. You know the difference." Mark shook his head. "I speak of Him. You demand of Him."

"You're damn right I do. I'm sick of this. Sick of all the times I prayed for Kimmy to get pregnant. Unanswered. Prayed for your mother, by your side. Unanswered. Prayed for this criminal or that to get what they deserve as I held the hand of their victim while the heart monitors flatlined. Unanswered."

"So what happened? You know the rules and you're swearing like a truck driver in here, so it must be pretty bad or pretty fresh or both." Benny raised one eyebrow at Mark as if he hadn't heard the words, only the tone and vulgarities. A mother with her hand on a hip waiting for an apology.

"Fucking case. Sorry. A case." Mark exhaled through his nose, lips pursed tightly as he thought back to the day for a moment. He stared at the floor as he spoke. "First the bastard got set free by Judge Eaton, thanks to fucking Lauren—again. And then tonight he goes and creates chaos at a crime scene and ends up offing himself and looking like the victim. It's just fucking wrong." The threadbare brown speckled Berber carpet had seen much better days. Long lines of missing threads, where heavy furniture had either sat or been dragged across too many times, showed the battered wood underneath. Not worth scraping and sanding and exposing, but wood nonetheless. He looked up at Benny. "I meant it. Your God can fuck off."

"Mark…" Ben's word faded off and he squinted for the tiniest fraction of a moment, recognition or realization caught in the dim light and sparked from his eyes. "You keep saying *my God*. When did you stop believing?"

"I never said I stopped believing."

"I mean, I understand." Ben sat a little taller, trying a new tactic. "You see some awful things on your job. It can wear you down. Pastor Warner says you haven't been to United Methodist in years and thought maybe you'd switched churches. I knew better, but didn't tell him—"

"I didn't stop believing…"

Benny continued past Mark's protests, "And you're angry. All the time. You only come into His house to yell at Him. And not for nothing, but that's usually through me."

"I just have too many questions to bother asking anymore, Benny." Mark's eyes flitted around the sanctuary as he considered his answer. Two new sets of pews had been procured since his last visit, and Mark just noticed those two rows of folding chairs were missing. The lectern mimicked a pulpit better than the old wooden stand that had stood in its place for as long as Mark could remember.

"I just want the criminals punished, Ben." Mark finally found the words he was searching for and dropped the informal nickname for his friend as his voice became calm and serious, rather than loud and angry. "I want the punishments to fit the crime. I want the Old Testament—an eye for an eye. If people were punished they would treat each other better. Period. It's that simple."

"Is it?" Ben's mouth was still open with more to say, but the telltale grinding of metal on metal made them both turn to the doorway as someone pushed into the dark mission.

Immediately, Mark's nostrils flared and his eyes widened. It was Poonut. The closest thing Squeak had had to a friend on the street and his sometimes partner in crime. Mark moved to stand and approach but Benny grabbed his arm.

"Mark. Rules."

"Ben…"

"I don't care if they're your case, your enemy, your whatever… In this house, they're mine." He met Mark's eyes and stared with a straight-faced seriousness, reminding Mark of his days in Catholic school. He wondered if they actually taught that look in seminary.

"Fine. Fucking keep him." Mark twisted out of Benny's grip and rushed out of the building, physically pushing past Poonut on his way. He tried to slam the door as he went through it, but the hydraulic arm on it prevented his anger from venting through noise and quietly pushed the door to a close.

He'd ended up spending the rest of the night at the station, going over the files on Bobby Charles and deciding where to turn now with his prime rat out of the picture. He had plenty of contacts, plenty of leads, he just didn't have any solid dirt on any of them. He'd be essentially starting over on the Queen Street busts. It sucked

CHAPTER FOUR

Mark checked his watch as he pulled into the driveway. He was twenty minutes late and hoped Gina hadn't made something hot—she'd just be upset he was eating it cold. He bound up the back steps of their apartment two at a time. Mark took a deep breath, exhaled it slowly on their stoop, and let the details of his day, his desk, wash off his mind as he opened the door.

"Glad you could bother showing up." Gina sat in a kitchen chair, legs crossed with the top one swinging wildly.

"Sorry, hon. I wasn't expecting traffic on the back streets to be bad."

"Blah blah, whatever." She stood and briskly walked to the counter to fetch two plates. "Sit down. Eat." Gina returned to the dining area, slammed them onto the table—jostling their sandwich contents—and plopped back into her chair in a huff. "And tell me who the fuck Sarah is."

Mark looked at her in confusion and realized her eyes were dry but her mascara was smeared. He furrowed his brows and questioned her with an expression, unable to speak in the echo of her unusual tirade.

"Sarah." She spit the word as she pulled an envelope from her back pocket and slapped it onto the table next to him, nicking the plate hard enough to displace his toast from the top of his sandwich. "As in some whore with the balls to write to you at our house. Where you live with *me*. Where your *pregnant* girlfriend gets the fucking mail!" Her voice rose in a crescendo and cracked. She took a jagged breath, "Sarah. Your whore. Your ballsy whore that better hope I never find out her fucking address!"

"What? I don't know a…" He looked at the envelope. His name and address were hurriedly printed in block letters. The return address was nothing more than a name—Sarah. He recognized the backward swirl of the *S* immediately.

"Oh wow… Sarah." He stared at the envelope with disbelief.

Gina sat upright and stared at him. "Really? You're just going to admit it like that? What the fuck? Do I mean anything to you? What are we doing here? Is this a game? How long have you been whoring around on me, you fucking asshole?"

"Gina, no." He raised his voice to cut her off but not to a shouting level. The stern daddy-means-it tone shut her up immediately and he knew if he didn't back it up with something immediately, she'd begin crying or trembling at the mere idea of them fighting. "My sister, Sarah, silly. My sister…"

He let the words fade as he returned his attention to the envelope, if it could be called that. It appeared to be nothing more than a piece of paper folded correctly and glued together haphazardly.

"Your…sister?" Gina's eyes flitted from the envelope to Mark's face and back again. "Sister?"

"Yeah, that's her writing."

"Oh my God." Gina moved her crossed arms from her chest to the table and flopped her head onto them. "Oh my God. What the hell? Ta fuck is wrong with me? I trust you. Why would I…?" Tears welling in her eyes. "Baby, I'm so sorry. I'm a fucking retard. I totally forgot about your sister. You don't ever talk about her. Ever. And I lost my shit… I…" Gina rolled her eyes into a flutter and sighed. "I blame the damn hormones."

"It's okay." He didn't look up from the envelope but smiled, "I do, too."

"Smart-ass." She reached over and put his sandwich back together, and brushed her hand across his gently as she retracted her own. "So, your sister. I thought you guys didn't talk anymore."

"We don't." He touched the envelope with caution, as if he expected it to explode should he pick it up too quickly. "I mean, we haven't. Not for years."

"Well? Are you going to open it?"

"I… I don't know." He finally met her gaze and she was taken aback by the expression in his face. He looked hurt and scared. Like a little boy.

"I'll tell ya what." She put her hand on the side of his face, cupping his cheek and chin in her tiny hand. "Let's eat. Afterward you can decide what you want to do."

"Sounds like a plan." He pushed the envelope to the side and pulled the plate forward. "Looks good now that it's back together. What did ya make me?"

"Ah well, there is only one sandwich for my boy."

"Excellent." He smiled knowing she'd never forget one of their very first conversations—his love of the simple BLT. "Extra bacon?"

"But of course!" She picked hers up and took a bite from the center, leaving tiny dots of mayo on either side of her mouth. After a few moments, she shoved the half-chewed bite into a corner of her mouth, held there expertly by her teeth. "So? Did you get Bobby Charles last night? You didn't come home…"

He ground his teeth through the bite he'd taken and flared his nostrils. Unlike Gina, he'd never mastered talking with his mouth full and had to finish before he could speak. The idea of rehashing the previous night dried his throat against the cold toast and he forced the masticated food down over the lump of his Adam's apple.

"We got anything to drink?"

Gina hopped up and spun to the kitchen. "Sure babe, whatcha want? Coffee, water, milk, O.J.… I think there may be a Coke left in the bottom drawer?"

"Water's fine." He contemplated whether he wanted to take another bite or talk about Bobby Charles. The BLT was obviously the better option and he took a large bite to purposely occupy his mouth for a bit longer so he wouldn't have to answer her previous question.

Gina returned with two glasses of water and he grabbed his, washing down the bite in his mouth with it and diluting the bacon flavor.

"So? An all-nighter can't be a good sign." She took a sip of her water and grimaced.

"Your tooth?"

"Yeah, stupid thing is getting really sensitive. I'll have to call Dr. Heimbuch later."

"You do that…" He looked from her to the sandwich and back.

"If you don't want to talk about it, Mark, I get it. Just say so."

"I know. And I appreciate it. I do. But…" He leaned his head back, stretching his neck to either side and hoping it would pop some of the stress out of it. "Let's just say it was bad enough that I sat outside Harp and Fiddle for a while."

"Really?" She put her sandwich down and leaned forward. "You go in?" She watched his eyes intensely.

"No." He shook his head slightly. "I ended up going to the station and poring over the files."

"Good." She sighed. Then her voice changed. "Was Molly working?"

"I said I didn't go in."

"Doesn't mean you didn't sit there and watch through the windows."

Mark looked at her for a moment. Her eyes were unblinking as she watched him. He let out an exasperated breath. He thought they had gotten past this. Apparently he was wrong. "I told you I never dated her."

"Doesn't mean you didn't want to. Doesn't mean you wouldn't still." She leaned back a little, showing off the beginning belly bulge. "I'm gonna be a whale and you're still gonna have needs."

"Is that what you think?"

She shrugged her shoulders and finally broke her stare by averting her eyes to the floor. "You used to talk about her a lot."

"Yeah, and my job and friends and a hundred other things."

"Not like you talked about her…" Her voice faded before it could crack. "And let's not forget, I'm your 'new Molly'."

"Jesus, Gina. Do we have to do this now? I've explained that a thousand times." His voice didn't necessarily rise so much as gained an edge to it and she reacted instantly as tears welled. He still blamed Kim for permanently burning a portion of his fuse, and hated the edge making its way into his voice. He and Gina were everything he and Kim were never destined to be. Gina reacted poorly to anything remotely resembling a fight. Oh she had fight in her, but she never actually wanted it called out. That broke her instantly, like a child being scolded.

Gina's glassy eyes moved back up toward him and he caught the tiniest quiver of her lip. Her posture changed. He pursed his lips, knowing he'd had enough edge to his voice to trigger her.

"You didn't go in?"

She was willing to give up the angle but not necessarily the argument, so he changed the subject. Or rather, jumped to the end of the interrogation and back into the reason he'd been there in the first place. "Squeak killed himself last night…" Mark proffered the information gently, as if it were a family member. The frustration and sarcasm removed from his voice as resignation settled in.

"What? How the…? Why?" Her eyes cleared and then filled with concern. Mark was unsure if it was intended for Squeak's miserable life or his own.

"At the scene." Mark hurriedly chewed the last bite of the first half of his BLT—amused she still cut his sandwiches for him as if he were a little kid and already forgetting she'd tried to start the Molly fight again. "The scene was a clusterfuck from the get-go. Bobby's sister was found dead. He called it in. Everyone showed up thinking he'd killed a hooker… It just went downhill from there."

She nodded silently at him and kept eating.

"I'd rather talk about your day. Or how you slept. Or anything…"

"Your sister?"

"Mmmm…" He fingered the envelope. "No contact at all for ten years and then this out of the blue?" He folded the envelope in half and stuck it in the inner pocket of his jacket. "I'll open it later."

Gina raised an eyebrow at him.

"I'm going to enjoy my BLT, my sassy little girlfriend, and a break from the rest of the world for a half hour, if that's okay with you." He smiled at her. "Then I'll let the universe have its way with me again."

CHAPTER FIVE

Mark pulled into the station cursing the traffic he found more annoying on his way back to work than it had been on the way to lunch. His anger was redirected when he saw a rookie had parked a squad in his spot.

"Sonuvabitch." He hit the steering wheel and turned it sharply to the left, heading for the side lot, knowing it would get him out of eyeshot should the rookie come back out. Today was not a good day to test his temper.

He pulled into the parking space, which always seemed available, number forty-three in the lot. It was in the sunshine and provided no shade, heating up cars in the summer. And unfortunately, directly under a broken gutter pipe that dripped incessantly on whoever attempted to exit or enter a vehicle below it, no matter the season.

He flipped his visor down to avoid the bright sunlight and took a deep breath. Squeak surely had something to do with his fluctuating temper today. Traffic and parking were just minor annoyances on the pile. The letter, however… The letter had done something to him he could neither have expected or explained. Old memories, good and bad, flooded him when he saw her handwriting, and he found himself torn between anger and joy.

Mark reached into his pocket and pulled out the envelope. He held it in his hand but didn't look at it. Instead, he noted the dust on the dashboard sparkled in the bright sunshine of parking space forty-three. He saw the car to his left was in desperate need of a wash—road salt and splashed remains of muddy snow from winter were still evident all over the vehicle. It was April. Most people had already washed the remnants of winter from their cars—erasing the memory of winter—much like a hot shower sluices away the vibes of a bad blind date. His eyes moved to the alley, clear in his view from this awful parking spot, and he watched a greasy-haired twenty-something yell at his too-thin girlfriend. The words were muffled and garbled with the car windows up but the tone was clear. The pasty girl, no doubt covered in either needle tracks or bruises from drug-induced anemia, promptly slapped the kid hard across the face.

"Good for you, honey." Mark smirked. He couldn't have cared less if they were dealing, buying or planning a raid on a schoolyard at the moment. For starters, they were both obviously white, which meant they were low-level if anything. Neither the Russians nor the Greeks allowed anyone outside of blood to rise in the ranks. Squeak had been an exception. Squeak had grown up with the kids from the family. A latchkey turned street rat at an early age, he was taken in on the premise he wouldn't betray them because he had nowhere to go. Nowhere to hide. It worked. He was loyal to the end.

"Fucking Squeak. Why the fuck did you have to go and…"

His hands registered the feeling of paper and dragged his brain out of the peripheral escape it had attempted. He eyed the sealed letter. At the *S* in Sarah. At the ragged edges and bizarrely homemade appearance of the envelope.

Sarah.

His kid sister had been the prodigy child of parents who had worked extremely hard for everything they ever had. Beautiful, brilliant and popular, Sarah was the valedictorian in high school and earned herself a full boat of scholarships to her choice of colleges. She chose to stay close to home and dove into the bachelor of music program at York College, with plans to get a master's elsewhere.

When their parents died her junior year, something in Sarah shriveled up and died along with them. She was suddenly content with finishing a bachelor's degree and finding a teaching job somewhere. A teacher like their mother had been. Like Mark's wife at the time. Mark had just made detective and his time was horribly constrained. He couldn't be there for Sarah as much as he wanted.

He still carried the guilt like a comfortable wallet.

After the fight, after Sarah left town without telling him where she was going, he held the guilt close for a time. He worked her location like a case and came up empty at every turn. He eventually gave up on it and her, replacing guilt with anger to keep him in check and out of trouble at work. He let her go.

She was back.

So was his guilt.

Mark realized he was shaking and swallowed hard, clearing his throat and his mind.

"Fuck this." He tore into the envelope, the glue giving way so easily he was shocked it had made it through the mail system without falling apart. "Whatcha gotta say, sis?" He carefully unfolded the paper—afraid it was as fragile as the envelope had been. The linen stationery covered with her handwriting felt heavy in his hands and Mark sighed at the salutation.

Sparky,

It's been a lifetime since we've talked, big brother, and I hope you are doing well. I miss you and think of you often, but I'm stubborn and pigheaded and everything else you ever called me when we were kids and couldn't allow myself to contact you and concede the battle until now. Pigheaded, ha! Remember how you were just as bad during those summers at Grandma's house. I miss her, too. You were always right about everything. I was always wrong. You used to make me so mad with that...because I was just like you.

Do you remember the last summer we spent there, before you graduated and moved out to attend the academy? I do. That was the year I learned you were afraid of spiders. You hid that very well for a long time, but I saw you react in the kitchen and everything changed. Years of chasing me with snakes, knowing I'd squeal and run and cry in a tree somewhere, came to a screeching halt when I grabbed that big brown barn spider and tossed it at you. You flailed and screamed, convinced it was in your hair. Here's a secret...I missed. It never landed in your hair, but I made you think so simply by pointing and laughing and saying nothing. I miss those days. Oma and her strict rules mixed with silliness and wisdoms. I remember how she used to ruffle your hair and say you were an old soul. I never did understand that sentiment until I began this life.

This life.

I was so mad at you when I left. You were being so overwhelmingly fatherly and telling me how to live my life, while screwing up yours. I loved Kimmy and you two were getting a divorce. In my mind, with Mom and Dad dead, you had become my surrogate parents, only to fail me. I'm sorry for that. It was selfish. Childish. But I was a child. Even at twenty-two I didn't know enough to make the decisions I was making. And while I appreciated your concern then, even your misplaced anger once I had time to calm down and realized what you were doing, I still believe you were wrong. I wasn't planning to drop out. I was really going to finish here and do everything I said I was going to do. I just wasn't going to do it under your thumb. And I was happy. I had a good life. I really did.

But I need to tell you I'm sorry. I don't know if I'll get another chance to say this and I don't want you to think I hated you. I'm sorry for my behavior then. Sorry for things I said during that last fight. Things I said about you and Kim. It was unfair of me to blame you for her leaving, I know that now. And it was unfair to take out my parental frustrations on you. I've learned a lot in a decade. Even the perpetual child can grow up. I know now how unfair life can be, and how wrongfully blaming someone can crush a person's spirit, break their soul. I've learned a lifetime of lessons in the lifetime since I've been gone.

I love you, Sparky. I always have and always will. And I'm sorry for any anger you've held for me. Bygones are just that... gone. Know I love you. I am sorry. And I'm not asking for your forgiveness... There is nothing to forgive.

Sarah

Mark stared at Sarah's signature until the tear broke free from his welling eye and hit the paper. The single drop seemed loud in the closed car and Mark drew an equally loud breath, realizing he'd been holding it for the last portion. He reread the letter and allowed several tears their unabated journey, not bothering to wipe them from his chin before they spilled over to his collar.

He shifted in his seat, overwhelmed with feelings and questions. He grabbed the steering wheel with a finger to brace himself as he adjusted his position and wiggled his toes to convince the blood to begin moving again. Pulling his hand back, he tipped the envelope and a four-leaf clover fell to his lap. Pressed flat from travel and time, the dark green shamrock lay screaming at him with memories.

So many hours at their grandmother's in the summer were spent lying and kneeling and sitting in the clover fields. At least twice a summer Mark would find a four-leaf specimen. Sarah had never found one during their childhood.

Apparently, she'd never stopped searching.

He finally blinked and a smile eased across his dry lips. He licked them and felt his chest flush with warmth. She was alive and well. He hadn't failed his parents after all. And he hadn't failed Sarah.

Mark wiped the drying tears from his face and took several deep, cleansing breaths as he pulled his composure back to the surface. He looked up and noticed the arguing couple in the alley had moved on and the sun had tipped over to the second half of the day. He folded the letter back up and tucked it into his pocket, carefully placing the shamrock into the envelope by itself and folding it over twice to keep it secure. He stretched his neck to either side, hoping it would make the lovely popping tension noise. One side rewarded him.

He got out of the car and took a deep breath of city air, calling it fresh in his mind but knowing it was far from it. The smells of Grandma's farmhouse came back to him at the thought and he remembered for a moment what fresh air was supposed to smell like. He shut the door and turned toward the garage entrance.

And stopped.

He pulled the letter back out and scanned it.

"…had a good life."

"…don't know if I'll get another chance…"

"…think I hated you."

Past tense. And Oma. And a clover. With no information about her husband or any children... Mark chewed on his lip while his mind reeled. His gut flipped.

He hadn't had a gut feeling this strong since the McKenzie case. He was a detective for a reason. He had been right then. He knew he was right now.

Mark turned back to the car, opening the door and sliding into the driver's seat in a fluid, practiced motion. "I don't like this..." He pulled out of parking spot forty-three and away from its dripping gutter pipe.

CHAPTER SIX

Mark dialed Reilly's number before he even realized what he was going to do. The great thing about technology is its portability. The worst thing about cell phones was people could always find you. The best thing about cell phones was you could find people.

Reilly Burke had been one of Mark's closest friends since the second day at the academy, when Reilly ran past him during the mile training as if Mark had been standing still. The pasty Irish kid with no muscle tone hollered something over his shoulder and spurred Mark to catch him. He did. Reilly picked on Mark's bulk. Mark tossed derogatory comments about stereotypical Irish cops. They chided each other to the end of the track, and for the next six weeks. Some would have thought they became rivals immediately, but they smiled as they fought to outdo the other at every level, and anyone paying attention saw a friendship building perfect for their field.

And it still was.

They'd had each other's back when they hit the York Police Department after graduating the academy. Mark with a criminal justice degree, Reilly with double bachelor degrees—one in psychology, one in sociology. They seemed the perfect team and worked smoothly up the ranks together.

Then the awards started to change. The direction the department wanted them to go was being coerced by higher-ups with no badges or medals or training. It pissed Reilly off and he quit the force.

Mark was stunned and hurt. Abandoned by his best friend. Mark chuckled remembering it—it was one of those proverbial moments you can laugh about later.

"I hate the fucking politics."

"Ignore them," Mark had offered at the time, unprepared for the sudden decision.

"I love the job. I'm good at the job. But I can't deal with the politics." Reilly slammed the remaining lager in his glass and nodded at Molly for a refill. "It's like being at a family reunion."

Mark almost spit his mouthful of Jack Daniels. "You hate your family."

"Welcome to the conversation, ya dumb mick."

"Please…" Mark smiled at Reilly with a toothy grin clinging to bits of barbeque wings. "My big toe is Irish. And only one of them, at that. I don't have enough of your potato blood to be called a mick."

They laughed and drank until well past midnight, but Mark couldn't talk Reilly out of it. The decision was done. Reilly gave notice the following day, and put his private investigator shingle out a month after his last day on the force. Mark had to admit, Reilly was very good at it. Even better than he'd been at being a cop. And even though he'd called him the mick dick for years, he knew no one better at finding missing persons.

He needed that right now.

The ringing on the other end stopped and a breathy "Hey brotha" filled Mark's ear.

"Hey Rye. You busy?"

"Nah… I've been sitting in my underwear all day playing video games." A two-beat pause was followed with the verbal equivalent of rolling eyes and Mark smiled at the guffaw noise. "I'm always busy. But I'm just wrapping up here. What's up?"

"I got a person for you to find."

"Yeah? Is she hot?"

"No." Mark reflexively responded and then backtracked, "Well, yeah… I mean, she was I guess." Frustration broke into his timbre. "For Christ's sake, Rye."

"Hey hey, no need to take the Lord's name…"

"Can we talk today?" Mark was in no mood for the lecture on blasphemy. "This one is important."

"Yeah, no problem." Mark could hear beeping and knew Reilly was checking the calendar on his iPhone. "I'm free for the rest of the day. Wanna meet at Harp and Fiddle in half an hour? I haven't eaten lunch and I'd kill for some wings."

"Uh…"

"Oh shit. Sorry, brotha, I forgot." Reilly clicked his tongue, the sound loud and clear on Mark's end. "Can you even be in there?"

"Well yeah, dumbass. It's not like I was kicked out. I just haven't been in there since that night."

"Yeah, that night was fun." Mark could hear the exasperation mingle with a smile in Reilly's words. "I love trying to track down friends when they go missing in the dead of night…"

"Shaddup." Mark wondered when Reilly would stop ribbing him about the DUI. It had taken every favor called in by both him and the captain to save his job. The only saving grace—he'd been off duty for over twenty-four hours when it happened. "White Rose in half an hour, then?"

"Sure. They've got great wings!" Reilly clicked the phone dead without saying good-bye, a habit that pissed Mark off to the point where he'd been known to call him back, say something minor and hang up just to do it back to Reilly. Today he didn't care.

--==●==--

"So? What's so ball-on important it's gotta be done today?" Reilly slid into the booth as the waitress refilled Mark's coffee cup.

"Sarah."

"Sarah?" Reilly looked up at the waitress. "Irish Coffee for me, please. And can I get an order of wings? Thanks." And then back at Mark. "Sarah…your sister, Sarah?"

"Yeah."

"Um, Mark… How many hours you been putting in?"

"Sixty. Seventy maybe. Not as bad as normal… Why?"

"Dude, she's been missing for almost ten years." Reilly threaded his fingers through his blood orange locks and leaned on his hand, elbow on the table keeping it elevated. "What makes today so important?"

"Got a letter." Mark stared at his coffee, stirring in the two creamers he'd poured into it.

"Really?" Reilly nodded to the waitress as she came back with his stemmed glass coffee cup. "That's awesome! How's she doing?"

"I don't know…" Mark's hand slipped inside his jacket and he fingered the paper with Sarah's words scrawled across it. "Something about it makes me worry. Like she's suicidal or something."

"What? Sarah? No way." Reilly took a sip of his Irish coffee, a low murmur of enjoyment slipped out his lips and he looked at Mark. "Sorry. Didn't mean to rub it in."

"No sweat. It's Irish coffee, not Jack." He took a sip of his coffee and thought of how good a sip of whiskey would be instead. "I wouldn't have thought her suicidal either. Especially ten years ago. But life changes people and we haven't seen her and we have no idea what's happened or going on or…well, the letter just reads weird. I don't like it. And it's the first clue we've had of where the hell she vanished to."

"Okay, okay. Let me see it." Reilly held his hand out.

Mark hesitated, suddenly unsure he wanted anyone else to hold it, let alone read it. But he knew he'd called Reilly for a reason. If anyone could find Sarah, Reilly could. He pulled the letter out of his pocket and held it out. Reilly grabbed it, but Mark didn't let go for a moment. They locked eyes and spoke in the same silent language they'd perfected on the beat years before and never lost. Mark let go and sat back, intently watching Reilly's face as he read.

"Yeah…" Reilly finally spoke. Mark had watched his eyes read the letter and then go back to the beginning and skim it. "It's been years, but this isn't our Sarah Bear." He handed the letter back to Mark. "Something is definitely up."

"On top of that, there was a four-leaf clover in the envelope."

Reilly furrowed his brows and Mark suddenly couldn't remember if he'd ever told Reilly about their childhood.

"We used to summer at my grandma's and look for them…"

"I know. I remember." Reilly took another sip. "I thought Sarah never found them."

"She didn't."

"Hmmm…yeah." Reilly held his hand out again. "Envelope."

Mark pulled it out and gently unfolded it, retrieving the shamrock and carefully folding it into the thin drink napkin on the table. He popped the wrapped clover into his pocket and handed the envelope over.

"Sarah? That's it? Oh that's fucking helpful. No wonder you called me." Reilly's left eye twitched as he narrowed it and inspected the envelope. "Homemade. Interesting. It's got a postmark though, and I can work with that."

"Find her, Rye."

"I found you in Gettysburg that night, didn't I?"

Mark pursed his lips and nodded.

The waitress arrived with the platter of barbequed hot wings. Reilly looked as if he were mesmerized by the plate of food and dug in, but his eyes told Mark he was already working through things in his head. Mark sat in silence and watched Reilly eat.

CHAPTER SEVEN

He'd called it a day after the meeting with Reilly the previous afternoon, and Gina knew him well enough to leave him alone with his thoughts all night. She went to bed early and he stared at the television without seeing it. He fell asleep in bursts, waking from interspersed nightmares of Squeak and memories of Sarah.

At three o'clock he debated going to bed but stayed on the couch. At five o'clock he glanced at the kitchen and considered breakfast. Instead, his mind drifting over his sister—from her birth, which he clearly remembered at eight years old, to the day of their last fight when she dropped out of college. Out of his life. He knew he needed work to keep his mind busy, and decided to take a drive before heading into work, sans breakfast.

Mark almost turned and left the station when he saw his desk from the doorway. This was more than keeping his mind busy, this was a small tornado of paperwork. Most likely dealing with Squeak, therefore coming with the possibility of further frustrating and angering him. Fleeting thoughts of returning to Gina and escaping in a tangle of angry sex crossed his mind, but it was wiped off his face as his eyes were drawn to the Post-it note stuck to his phone.

Squeak's supplier's name, Creeper, was clear from his vantage point. The chicken-scratched name underneath it was not. He closed the distance in two large steps and snatched the note. He didn't recognize the handwriting and immediately turned to face the shoulder-height dividers in the office, looking over the sea of heads in their cubicles.

"Who took this message?" he shouted across the room, waving the note in the air above his head. After a three-count he repeated the question, loud enough to hear it echo back from the other end of the room.

"Jesus fuck, Baker…" The captain's office door slammed open, hitting the broken bumper protecting the wall next to it.

Mark looked up and opened his mouth.

"Get in here!"

Mark rolled his eyes and crossed the short distance to the captain, already withdrawn back into his small but private room, standing behind his desk like a principal waiting for a student. "Shut it." The captain spoke as Mark crossed the threshold, and Mark pulled the door shut, tossing a smirk at the closest open-mouthed officer, feeling very much like a schoolboy.

"Do you know who left this?" Mark questioned as he thrust the note at the captain. Ray tapped the desk placard reading "Captain Ray Rickert." Mark didn't care if the man preferred to be called captain. "I need to know where the note came from. There's no phone number, no initials for who took the call, and I can't read the damn handwriting."

Ray opened his mouth just as a thought crossed Mark's mind and the detective continued without giving the captain a chance to speak.

"Is this someone fucking with me?" His tone stayed level but his volume rose. "I am so not in the mood for this shit. If one of those fucking foot punks…"

"Mark. Sit."

Mark often wondered if Ray had gotten the promotion to captain based solely on his ability to lower his voice to a baritone vibrato, which made even the mayor stop talking and listen. He did as he was told.

"How long we known each other, Mark?"

Mark shrugged his shoulders and kept his eyes on the placard. He knew damn well to the month how long. He clearly remembered their first meeting, when they'd almost shot each other in crossfire chasing the same street rat.

"Fucking long enough for me to know this isn't you." Mark glanced up at him. "I don't know if it's Squeak or Gina or the baby or what. Maybe it's a combination of it all. But you're losing your shit Mark."

Ray opened a drawer and pulled out a manila folder. It was unlabelled, but Mark knew exactly what it was.

"These are your complaints and comments."

"Yeah yeah, the yellow sheets. I know. I'm sorry."

"Don't apologize, there's a lot of good things in here." Ray fanned the stack to visually show Mark the sheer amount. "But there are some bad. And they all seem fairly recent." Ray put the folder back in the drawer and sat down. "What the hell is going on?"

"Squeak is a big part. And I'm sorry." Mark leaned back and started to relax. "You know I fucking hate it when they work the system and win. It pisses me off."

"Yeah, but now you're stalking them after they get out. Some of those comments are from criminals, Mark." The captain's voice softened. "And showing up at the scene... What the hell? How'd you even know? Are you sitting at home with the scanner on?"

Mark opened his mouth to speak.

"You are, aren't you? Jesus, Baker."

Mark noticed the switch from his first name to his surname. Ray was getting into boss-versus-employee mode. *Here it comes*, he thought.

"I'm gonna put you on vacation."

"WHAT?" Mark erupted from his chair, landing on his feet with his hands flat, palm side down, on Ray's desk. "You can't fucking do that! Not after the other night. Not after this note. Christ, Ray, I'm close. And if this name can be figured out, I'm closer than I've ever been."

"Yeah, and Stapleton's been briefed and can do the footwork for you." Ray suddenly appeared out of place without his smashed cigar in his mouth, as he chewed on nothing there and tried not to yell at a friend. "But you've gotten out of control lately."

"Ray..."

"No. It comes from the higher-ups. It came right after the reports from Squeak's death were filed and started filtering upward." Ray leaned forward. "We can do this two ways."

"Blah blah...the hard way or the easy—"

"No." Ray pulled out a fresh piece of the yellow file commentary paper. "You have six weeks built up—"

"That I was going to use when the baby is born..."

"You'll gain one back by then. Use two now."

"But..."

"If you willingly take two weeks of vacation, you're technically still active and can keep your gun and badge."

"And if I don't?" Mark felt his face begin to flush with anger and clenched his fists.

"Then you are on two weeks suspension and you turn your gun and badge over." Ray cocked his head. "And you know that, so why ask? Are you just trying to push me?"

"What can it hurt?" Mark met Ray's glare and held it for several seconds before Ray sat back.

"Get out of here, Mark. Take two weeks. Spend time with Gina before you lose your private time for eighteen years. Go somewhere. Do something. Just turn your fucking scanner off and stay the hell out of this office."

"You're really doing this to me?"

"I am."

"I thought we were friends, Ray."

"We are. That's why I'm doing this."

"Fuck you." Mark spun and stormed out the door. He scanned to the right until he found the top of Stapleton's graying head. "Paul! Put my desk the way you found it before I get back…" And added under his breath, "Fucker."

CHAPTER EIGHT

Mark drove around for several hours—stalling until he knew Gina would be gone for work and forcing an impression of the current situation into his mind to work over mentally for the next few weeks. He checked the corners Squeak would have frequented and noted who was standing in his place—partially to assure himself the streets would clean up their own mess, continue their business and fill the void, but also to reassure himself Squeak really was gone.

He drove back to the lot where Squeak's sister had been found dead. Where the dirt bag had joined her. The police tape was gone. The scene was mostly cleaned up, save for the missed cone against the side of the building.

You wouldn't know, he thought, taking inventory of the boring parking lot.

When he finally drove home, he chose to stop at Wine and Spirits. The clerk, he thought her name was Leah but couldn't remember and wondered if maybe he'd actually blocked it out, smiled at him when he walked through the doors like he was a long-lost relative.

"Hey stranger." Her hair was slightly redder than he remembered and he wondered if the auburn had ever been real or simply from a different box and brand last time he'd seen her. "Haven't seen you around these parts in for*ever*." She emphasized the second syllable of the word like a teenager.

"Yeah." He quickly walked to the left shelf and blindly grabbed a bottle. Like knowing the layout of your house in the dark, Mark could have shopped any of York's liquor stores without the benefit of lights. He put the bottle on the counter. "I quit drinking." He watched her, expecting her to make a statement, hoping she'd be sweet and let it roll without comment.

The clerk glanced from the bottle to his darting eyes and back again. "Present, huh?"

"Sure." He threw the cash on the counter and left without another word. He would have flirted with her in the past. He would have stalled for a few minutes, like foreplay to the drink to come when he got home. Now he just wanted the bottle and the solitude its amber liquid offered to his soul.

--==•==--

The house was quiet when Mark got home. The afternoon sun drifted through the lacy curtains—Gina had replaced his "man drapes" the moment she had moved in. He had to admit, the light was better. But he still felt exposed walking from the bathroom to the bedroom in his towel, as if he was on display. Until he remembered his windows didn't face his neighbor's house, but rather his garage. The alternating yard depth on his block provided more privacy than traditional rows, but Mark always thought it seemed like jagged teeth from the police choppers.

Without bothering to untie them, Mark kicked his Doc Martens into the corner by the kitchen and went straight to the living room. He set the bottle on the coffee table and plopped onto the couch like a frustrated teenager.

"Vacation." He huffed to the dust motes drifting in front of him. "Bullshit."

Mark eyed the bottle of Jack, half expecting it to vanish as if he'd only thought about buying it. He leaned forward, forearms on his knees and began a staring contest with the inanimate contestant. He let his eyes wander over the label, noting the wrinkles and imperfections in the glue underneath.

He wanted to scream or cry or punch something. He wasn't sure which would feel better. *Forced vacation because he was actually doing his job too well? Upsetting higher-ups and being on top of the case whether he was on duty or not? At least I'm doing my job*, he thought. *If the fuckers in the courthouse would do theirs I wouldn't have to work harder to unfuck the situation and bring the same bastards in over and over.*

A low growl escaped his lips and he stood, debating whether to swap his khakis for jeans. He pulled his phone from his pocket and stopped. Willing it to ring. Willing Ray to call him and tell him it was all a joke and he could return to the case. Or maybe Reilly would call with news, but he knew it was too soon. Good as the old Irish dick was, he wasn't that fast with little to no information. There was no way he'd found Sarah yet.

Sarah.

"Damn it." He tossed the phone onto the table with the bottle and headed to the bedroom. It was probably healthier to be angry with Ray than to worry about Sarah.

Mark changed into jeans and his old AC/DC concert T-shirt, pulling his socks from his feet and flinging the inside-out wads at the wall. Gina would give him shit when she did the laundry. He glanced at the socks in front of the closet and decided he didn't care. Behind the socks somewhere was a box he hadn't thought of in years.

Pushing past hangers of work shirts and suits, Gina's skirts and forgotten formal dresses were storage boxes he'd never bothered to unpack when he and Kim divorced. Among them was a white picture box with a floral print—he'd always hated the design. He pulled it from the bottom of the stack like a magician pulling a cloth from a full table. A clean patch on the top, where the box above it had rested, was framed in thick dust. *Framed*, he thought, *how fitting*.

He kicked the door to the closet shut and carried the box back to the living room, holding it out in front of him as if it were an offering. He sat on the couch sideways, leaning against the hard wooden edging on the arm and put the box on the cushion in front of him. He hadn't looked through it in so long, he wasn't even sure what was hidden inside and carefully took the top off, not wanting to disrupt anything stuck to the top from moving.

He saw the white sneakers before he saw anything else in the first picture, and his own intake of breath startled him. His parents. The photo was from the last trip they'd taken to the beach as a family. The last springtime escape before the accident. Before he'd become solely responsible for Sarah.

He couldn't handle the two-dimensional view. He couldn't be worried about Sarah and thinking about his parents at the same time. It had taken him years to pretend to be over that day. He still wouldn't go near a plane. He pulled the picture from the box and flipped it over on the table. Out of sight, out of mind.

Below it was a surprise he hadn't been aware was even in the box. Kim. The two of them were smiling from another shoreline, shoes in their hands and sun in their hair. When things were good they went to the beach often, but his bizarre ability to remember silly details told him this was Aruba, based solely on the fact Kim's flip-flops were pink. The warm fuzzy of good times ran away like a shiver and his expression and mood turned sour simultaneously.

She must have tossed all their pictures in there when he left. "Nice." He shook his head. "I meant so much… Bitch."

He rifled through the thick stack of images from a marriage that had started out so promising but ended in a battle he never expected to have, and could never hope to win. Unwanted memories floated through his mind like dust motes—uncontrolled little bits, visible only in the right lighting.

He and Kim had been in college together. He was working on his criminal justice degree. She was finishing her teaching certification. They had absolutely no classes together. But they had used the same parking lot and seemed to have the same schedule. Passing each other every day turned into waving, smiling and eventually talking.

Kim had been like sunshine itself back then. Always glowing. Always full of life. Laughter rolled through her at the tiniest things. They dated. They fell in love. They graduated. They both got great jobs. And they got married. It was exactly the plan, in the right order, as both sets of parents had told them to follow. It all seemed perfect. And it was.

Until she decided it was time to get pregnant.

They tried for two years. Disappointing as each menstrual period was, they kept their humor going and regarded the sex as practice and research and enjoyed themselves. Their lovemaking was playful, never serious. Even halfway through the second year when she'd started researching and tracking her ovulation, she giggled when she jumped him unexpectedly, declaring her body temperature was just right.

The third year with no results made Kim's sunshiny attitude start to darken. There were doctor visits for both of them. Couples counseling, at both Kim's and the gynecologist's insistence, even though he didn't think anything was wrong with their relationship. More tests. More

50

labs. Pamphlets and books and fertility questionnaires. In the end, inconclusive tests left the fault on Mark, as one doctor mused out loud how, "In my experience, it's usually the sperm not strong enough, rather than the egg or uterine wall failing after the fact." Kim didn't hear opinion or experience. She heard fault lay with Mark. Frustration turned to blame, blame turned into fights, and the perfect love turned sour.

As a secondary smack in the face, it damaged Mark's relationship with his sister. Sarah and Kim had been close. Kim was the big sister Sarah never had and Sarah was Kim's practice child. When Mark told Sarah he and Kim were divorcing, she screamed at him in ways even Kim hadn't managed—and she'd been practicing the yelling rather than the baby-making for months.

He couldn't even remember how the last fight with Kim had started, as Mark had already turned to Jack Daniels to drown the reality of his failures. No children. No parents. Soon there'd be no wife. Sarah was all he had and she was pissed at him, claiming Kim had told her about their fights. But Mark knew she'd witnessed at least one of them and Sarah knew damn well the aggressor wasn't Mark. The screaming contest always went to Kim. The judges all agreed.

The day Kim turned bright red, blaming her inability to get pregnant on his stressful job and drinking, he'd chosen to say nothing. He thought the fire would go out if he denied it fuel.

He was wrong. And while he didn't remember how it started, he'd never forget how it ended.

--==●==--

"I don't just want a baby. I want a *healthy* baby, Goddamn it. And your fucking drinking isn't going to get us there. Your sperm count is down. Your sex drive is down." She stopped, as if choosing her words, while her chest rose and fell with deep breaths of anger and frustration.

She chose poorly.

"If you could even fucking get it up at this point and manage to impregnate me, our baby would look like one of the fucking street babies with fetal alcohol syndrome or some other fucked-up deformity."

He stared at her. He knew she understood it didn't work that way. He knew she was just angry. Hell, he was angry. He was tired of the fights. Tired of the doctors and tears and the resentful blame game. He loved her. But he could feel his love getting tired, tarnished, and he hated that he couldn't just fix it. Fix her. Fix the situation. Both. Either. Whatever. He tried to calm the situation as usual, hoping to get her to crack and calm down.

Raising his eyebrows, he spoke with a smile. "You get that outta your system?"

Normally an unwilling grin would have spread across her face like moonlight across a dark room and she'd stick her tongue out at him in defeat. She'd always been a bit feistier than he in disagreements, but they'd never truly argued until they failed to get pregnant. They used to joke about the fact they didn't argue or fight. The most they did was agree to disagree on silly things. They tended to agree on the important issues. Except the pregnancy problems. This was an important issue and they were definitely fighting about it. But even that took several years to burn her fuse, which he appreciated and understood, but was still not ready to take the blame for it. The usual didn't put the fire out, it only fueled it.

"I am NOT a fucking child. And I don't want to hear your fucking condescending bullshit right now. It's not going to work." She took a step toward him, her left eyelid half-closed in an angry squint. "Just like your dick."

"Kim." He threw his hands up and turned toward their kitchen. The small A-frame was too tiny for a family but perfect for a starter house, and Kim had simply fallen in love with the picturesque white picket fence and manicured neighborhood. It took all of seven steps to get from the living room through the dining area and into the kitchen. Definitely not enough room for a family, and right now, not nearly enough room for just the two of them.

"Why are we fighting? This is silly. There are options. I don't understand why it has to be like this." He reached for the cupboard to get a glass for water. He could only assume she thought he was reaching for the Jack Daniels on top of the refrigerator.

The heavy leaded-glass ashtray from his parents' house, used as a change dish since neither of them smoked, came whizzing past his head and smacked into the cupboard next to him. The wood cracked and the ashtray landed with a thud on the linoleum. Somehow the nod to a time when smoking came with fancy accessories for the home didn't break. It lay there, waiting for him to acknowledge it. To pick it up.

He left it.

Unfortunately, a small house meant a lack of space to escape from another, which he desperately wanted to do at the moment. Mark had never been very good at fighting in his personal life. He kept the aggression in his professional life and lived like a kitten outside the badge. He didn't start fights, he didn't flame anger, and he didn't react to aggression. He was always calm, always rational, preferring to keep his tone even, his temper in check.

Until now.

"You fucking bitch!" He turned toward Kim in time for her current hardcover read from the library to catch him in the chest. He grunted as James Patterson's *Angel* briefly pushed the wind from his lungs. Kim had never been violent with him. She'd banged cupboards and doors. She'd stomped and accidentally broken a glass once slamming it down on the counter too hard. But throw things at him? No.

And to choose the ashtray—something of his parents to throw? Until that moment, Mark hadn't realized his fuse could be cut to the quick. In truth, he wouldn't realize until the next morning when he mentally revisited the fight.

"Bitch?" She glowered at him, eyes flicking around the dining room for something else to throw. "I'm a bitch?"

"What do you want from me? You think if we duke it out you'll get pregnant? You want a better word for your behavior?" Mark steadied his stance as he watched her shift her weight. He felt like a linebacker bracing for a rush by the way she stood and looked at him. "Cunt. How about that? You're being a fucking cunt."

"You…" Her nostrils flared. "How fucking dare you."

"What? It's a word. Get over it. Get over yourself. I could have just as easily called you a bucket and made it sound derogatory." He realized he was still trying to calm her down, still trying to defuse her anger. A tiny part of him wondered why he even cared anymore. Another part of him panicked at the thought. If he didn't, there was nothing left. He wasn't ready for that. He wasn't ready to call it quits on them, or their chances at parenthood. He just needed to figure out how to reason with her.

"Kimmy…"

"Don't you fucking Kimmy me." She grabbed a vase and held it high. He wasn't sure if he should duck as the target or if she just intended to break everything they had on the floor at his feet. "You heard the doctor. It's you. You read the literature. It's you. And what do you do about it? Drink more."

"What?" He cocked his head at the revelation. "You want me to stop drinking? Fine." He reached up behind him and grabbed the bottle of Jack. Was that all she wanted? Would that defuse this bullshit? Or was it just another blame-game angle? He decided to call her bluff.

"I'll pour it down the sink right now and never touch it again if you can answer this…"

She pulled the vase down from above her, placed her other hand on her hip and tilted her head. If he could read her eyes, he imagined her thoughts were something akin to "Oh *this* should be good."

"Do you want me to quit because it's bad for me and you care for *me*…" The bottle felt warm in his hand, like the grip of a parent walking to the park on a summer day. Secure and safe. "Or because you think that's why you're not getting pregnant?"

She didn't pause. She didn't hear what he was saying, what he was asking. She simply responded with a knee-jerk reaction of mixed emotion. Doctors, literature and her own doubts poured from her with anger and sadness. "You know it's why I'm not! It has to be why I'm not…" Kim's eyes softened and she looked down to the floor.

He stared at her. There it was. Her blaming him wasn't just because she wanted to; it was because she needed to. She needed *not* to be the reason. She needed to be able to blame someone else for her inability. And like many, she was the type to hurt those she loved the most. In her world, that was Mark. She loved Mark and therefore, on some bizarre unconscious level, like so many with the same habit, she presumed he could handle being the brunt of her anger, her frustration, because he loved her back and could therefore handle it and know it wasn't real.

But could he? Did he love her enough? Was love enough to get through this? They say love can get you through anything, but he was starting to wonder if there weren't occasions when love, no matter how strong, just wasn't enough.

Love, he thought. Did he mean the word as past tense or present? He wasn't sure. But the more he watched her, the more he listened to her rants and wails, the more he worried his own love was past tense. He began to wonder if he loved her, like he always had, but was no longer *in* love with her. His eyes followed the pattern on the linoleum and paused at the ashtray. Was love enough? When he looked back up to her, he feared he knew the answer and felt something inside him snap.

What if he didn't hold back? What if he had an all-out fight like she seemed to want? Would it get it out of her system? Would they go back to what they were? Would the blame ever stop? And why, in all the arguments leading to her blaming him, had he never once blamed her for their inability to get pregnant?

"What if it's you?" He said it before he thought about it. In retrospect, he did it to push her buttons, to see how far she'd go. Something in his mind turned ugly and took her there with it. If this was going to go down, then it was going to go down in flames.

"Me?" Her eye twitched again in the half-closed glare she had become so good at. "Fuck you. Just fuck you, Mark. You were at the doctor's. You read the literature." Her nostrils flared again and the vase went back into the air. "You fucking *know* it's not me!"

She released the vase with all her fury, overhand. It flew across the room like a football heading for numbers on a jersey. He dodged it and heard it smash against the cupboard behind him. His mind registered bits of glass tinkling to the floor like dainty little notes from a wind chime.

"Is this the kind of mother you plan on being?" He almost wished he could take it back once it slipped free from his thoughts and escaped his mouth.

"I…" Her lip quivered and then she stiffened. "Fuck you."

She took several quick steps and stood right in front of him. The height difference didn't seem to matter to her at the moment. She didn't even bother standing on her tiptoes to try to achieve eye level. She just barked from her natural height.

"I will make an amazing mother. I have patience and knowledge and a carefree side will make me the fun mom. What do you have? You're nothing but a workaholic drunk. You have almost no friends and practically no family outside Sarah to give you any inclination of what family is supposed to be like."

"Don't you dare…"

"You know what, Mark?" Her voice cracked as it rose in volume. Her eyes narrowed as the anger behind them pushed against her better judgment. "*You* should have been flying the plane that day, you know that? If you had been flying, your parents would be alive. Sarah would have her mother. Your father would be there to protect her like a father, rather than a big brother that doesn't have the first clue how to be anything other than a drunk!"

"You fucking bitch!" He pushed her away from him. Harder than he meant to, but he was seeing red at her words. It didn't matter if it was said in anger. It didn't matter if she knew the truth—his father was the better pilot. His father kept the plane afloat much longer than Mark ever could have. She was supposed to love him. And love meant knowing what buttons *not* to push. Love meant knowing what to never ever say or suggest because it would ruin the love. Forever.

"Motherfucker!" She stayed in a crumpled heap where she'd landed, holding her elbow. Mark assumed she'd hit it against the floor when she went down and realized he didn't care. "A drunk *and* violent? Perfect. Just perfect."

"You pushed me…"

"No, I do believe it was *you* that did the pushing." Tears welled in her eyes, but they lacked depth. They were not pain from the fall, or sorrow for the marriage, they were only self-pity.

He had no pity for her at the moment. "Fuck you, you know what I mean."

"I should just kill you." She swallowed, as if tasting the words, but didn't wince at their bitterness. "I'd be better off. Sarah would be better off. Fuck, Mark, *you'd* be better off!"

"Oh really? How? How you gonna pull that off, bitch?"

He watched her eyes flick to the countertop where the knife block sat, full of fairly new blades from the previous Christmas. He sidestepped, as if blocking her from the kitchen weapons. "Let's not forget I have a gun."

"Is that a threat?" Her eyes cleared and her head cocked oddly to one side, as if she'd just realized something. "Is that an honest threat? Would you really shoot me?"

"You just threatened me. What the fuck?"

"I'm not an officer of the law. I'm not supposed to protect and serve…"

"What? You want me to threaten seriously, and admit it so you can call the station and have them what? Lock me up? Take my badge?"

A wicked smile played across her lips. In the course of the last six months she'd become someone he didn't know. In the last ten minutes she'd turned into someone none of her friends would recognize. And just as the thought passed through his mind, he crossed a line he never thought himself capable and became a stranger to himself.

"Bitch, I wouldn't wound you if I threatened you." He leaned down toward her crumpled form, using his height and advantage to seem larger than life. The years of holding back, of being the calm one, balled up behind his temples and throbbed, begging to be let out in a show of violence meant to stop her bullshit for good.

She reached up and slapped him. Hard. The sting burned his skin and the jolt shook his teeth. He wasn't quick enough to stop her hand or dodge her, but he grabbed it on the back swing and squeezed her wrist. He moved his jaw left and right, as if testing it for damage, and wondered if she'd used a fist rather than an open hand.

"Do not push me, bitch. I'm a damn good shot. I know how crime scenes work." He squeezed her wrist until she winced in pain.

She opened her mouth to spew something back at him, her lips in a snarl.

He cut her off, "And I know plenty of places to hide your body."

Her eyes widened.

His narrowed.

And then softened as he heard what he'd just said to her. As he imagined how he'd looked saying it. Something inside him caught, his chest hitched and his stomach flipped.

"Okay…" She whimpered as her shoulders slumped and her gaze fell to the floor next to her. He felt the muscles in her arm go limp. He felt the shiver run through her body before it too felt limp, like he was holding her dead weight by nothing but her wrist. Her bottom lip quivered and her breathing began a staccato beat meant to restrain the tears he knew she refused to let him see.

When she gently pulled her wrist away from him and looked up, he saw the fire in her eyes go out.

Not just the flames fueling the pregnancy frustration or recent fighting. No. Too many things had been said in the last few minutes to go back to those problems. The problems seemed so insignificant in contrast to the words flung around in anger.

He couldn't fix this. He knew now. And he watched the tiny flame, which had begun a friendship and held fast to a relationship, flicker like a candle on its last bit of wick and die in that single beat of a moment. He watched his marriage drowned in resignation, the wick falling into the melted wax of words, which couldn't be unsaid. And felt shock and guilt as he realized he was the one who pounded the nail in the coffin.

He stood and walked to the bathroom.

He threw up until there was nothing but bile coming in strings from his throat and then took a scalding hot shower.

When he was done, she was gone.

--==●==--

That fight would never be topped. Not in a courtroom, not on a schoolyard.

A part of him was still sick it had ended that way, but life had gone on. He'd gone on. She'd gone on. Last he knew she was remarried. Occasionally, he had twinges of bittersweet sorrow, but mostly he drowned the hurt and pain and guilt underneath a mask of anger at the blame game she'd played and the way she'd let it degrade to the point of no return. Some days he clung to the anger to keep the pain away. Most days the anger survived, fat and sassy, on its own.

He put the pictures of him and Kim to the side without even noting which ones she'd given him, assuming it was whatever she didn't burn. Below them was Sarah's face, and Mark knew the rest of the box would be a combination of him and Sarah when they were younger.

He went through each picture, remembering each moment. Remembering the way she'd laughed the day she was stuck in the tree. The way she'd cried at fireworks—originally out of fear, later out of pride proclaiming, "Every spark is a soul that died for our freedoms." The fishing and camping trips when their parents were alive. The summers at their grandmother's. The school plays she was always involved in and extracurricular sports he excelled at. Pictures of trophies long misplaced or thrown away, and costumes long outgrown. His heart ached at the photos—little captured bits of a time when smiles were painted on for excitement rather than necessity.

The sun began to sink in the sky and the dust motes disappeared. He was reaching the bottom of the box but had stopped. The picture in his hand showed a gangly boy of eight, teeth too big for his mouth, eyes so wide they appeared fake. He sat in what had been his grandmother's rocking chair, scrawny legs dangling below, reaching desperately for the ground but not long enough yet to touch. A Winnie the Pooh blanket lay across his lap, folded up over the sides of the chair's arms. In the center a baby lay, curly brown wisps clinging to the perspiration on its head. Its wide eyes, large enough to rival the nervous-looking boy who held it, were dark as coal.

Mark felt the tear fall down his face as he stared at the image in his hands. He clearly remembered the day Sarah came home from the hospital. It was a day of mixed emotions and the first of several that would change his life forever.

He'd been an only child for almost a decade. Now he'd have to share his house, his parents and his life with this squirming baby who only seemed to cry and sleep. He wanted to hate her. He wanted to be mad. But as they lowered her into his protective lap, she stopped crying. She looked up at him with those dark teardrop eyes and stared. She stared at him as long as her little mind could handle and then peacefully drifted off to sleep. It had seemed forever at the time, but Mark was sure it was likely less than five minutes.

Long enough for her to sear a place in his heart. Long enough for him to become attached to the little interloper. Long enough for his protective big-brother genes to kick in.

The big brother had been to every single one of her plays, every dance recital, every game she cheered at. The big brother had continued to be part of her everyday life even after he'd graduated and left the house. The big brother became a foster father when they'd lost their own to a plane crash never satisfactorily explained. The big brother screened the boys, did background checks and shook the hands of those good enough to be around his baby sister. His pride and joy. His one true connection to life during the times when life tried to beat him down.

Mark wiped his cheek and reached for the bottle.

How could I just give up looking for her? What was I thinking?

CHAPTER NINE

Gina flicked the kitchen light on as she closed the door behind her. She put the bag of groceries on the counter and turned to the living room—the only other light in the house.

"Marco…"

No response.

She walked around the side of the couch and saw Mark sleeping against the corner of the overstuffed green sofa. A box of pictures she'd never seen was spilled across the cushions, table and floor. In his left hand was an image of a boy in a rocking chair, the eyes as piercing then as they were now and Gina knew it was Mark, and therefore Sarah in his arms. In his right hand was an unopened bottle of Jack Daniel's.

Gina swallowed and gently pulled the bottle from his hand. She put it on the floor behind her and cleaned up the photos, attempting to keep them in the order they seemed to have fallen in, and set them on the table. She pulled the blanket off the back of the couch and covered him without attempting to roust him.

She couldn't imagine what those pictures had done to him emotionally. Gina glanced at the bottle on the floor. Or maybe she could. She decided to leave him be. A hot shower and early bedtime didn't sound so bad to her aching back and feet.

CHAPTER TEN

Morning, sunshine." Gina's lilt was singsong as he walked into the kitchen. The smell of bacon filled their tiny apartment while she pulverized several eggs in a bowl. She turned toward him and pointed to the table where she'd already placed his coffee.

"You are a wonderful woman, you know that?"

"Yes. Yes, I do, and you better never forget that, mister."

He smiled at her and sat in front of the coffee, grinning over the silliness the coffee ritual had become since she'd poured the very first cup for him at Round the Clock. He'd been a cop coming off a shift and she'd been a waitress just doing her job. He imagined she'd still be refusing to let him get his own coffee when they were old and gray and had long forgotten why she did it.

He took a sip of this week's experimental brew, some off-brand breakfast blend, and remembered the bottle. He wondered if he should bring it up. He worried she would. He had purchased it under stress but hadn't opened it.

"So, rough day yesterday?"

"Uh, yeah…" He glanced around the kitchen quick, trying to spot whether she'd put it away or left it out in a conspicuous manner. He didn't see it.

"Figured it must have been bad for you to invite Jack to the party." She turned and smirked at him, one eyebrow raised in a snarky matronly motion.

Mark relaxed. He realized she wasn't going to do anything beyond point it out. He didn't know where she put it and he wasn't going to ask. If she was going to let it slide, then he was going to shut up and enjoy the free ride. To make sure it stayed that way, he began spilling the events of the previous day for her.

"Vacation?" She put the plate of scrambled eggs and bacon in front of him and sat down without a dish for herself. "He had the balls to call it vacation?"

"Yeah, can you believe that shit?"

"Trash mouth." She smiled and handed him a fork. "You have to start watching what you say…" She patted her tummy. "Little ears will be listening soon."

"Yeah, yeah." He shoveled eggs into his mouth, chewed twice and swallowed the perfectly cooked, soft yellow pillows. "I have time."

"So what the hell are you going to do for two weeks?"

"I don't know…" His eyes wandered to the box of pictures visible on the living room table.

"No." She followed his line of sight. "Reilly does not need your help. You just let him do what he does."

"I know, but babe, I'm a detective—"

"And you detect, I know. But serious, it'll make you crazi…" Gina paused and added, with dramatic flair, "…ER. And he doesn't need you breathing down his neck." She grabbed the notebook from the center of the table and flipped the current grocery list over. "I could make you a honey-do list." She spoke through a smile.

"No, no. I'm all good…" He pulled the pen from her hand. "I don't need your bizarre nesting and creativity to be suggesting I re-grout anything."

She released a full belly laugh. He smiled, trying not to catch the contagion her giggles often carried. It was nice to see her actually bubbly again. Mark had been worried the baby was making her overly cranky and paranoid and couldn't stomach the idea of them arguing for nine months over things that shouldn't be an issue. Like Molly.

"I'll work on the nursery, I guess."

"Ooohh, I've been meaning to get in there." She glanced toward the doorway next to their bedroom.

"I know. So have I." He proffered sympathy and camaraderie—still very aware he was trying to make things right with her hormonally driven agitations. "But with work and your back bugging you lately you haven't had a chance. And I…"

"Work too much…"

Mark braced himself for another unnatural episode of bitterness.

"Which I admire and adore." She grinned, her eyes sparkling at some clandestine thought. "It's a good work ethic to teach Junior."

Gina stood and pushed the chair in. "I need to hop in the shower and get out of here now though."

"So early?"

"Yeah, I need to run over to Amy's, she's got some baby things for us. And then I have a doctor's appointment before work."

"That's not until later though."

"Yeah, but you know how Amy can get. I have to pencil her in for at least an hour, if not two, just to hear all the gossip she thinks I care about." Gina rolled her eyes and Mark grinned. He loved how much she hated drama.

"You want me to meet you at the doctor's?"

"Nah. He's just going to tell me I'm not gaining enough weight. I'm going to tell him he's crazy 'coz I'm a fat cow. It's not an important appointment on any level, hon."

"You're not a fat cow…" His eyes softened as he captured her gaze. He loved the ruddiness pregnancy had given her face—slightly fuller with a healthy glow giving her the appearance of a kid who had been playing outside all day. Her tiny frame was only barely nudged out of shape by the faintest tummy bulge, as she still wore most of her pre-pregnancy pants. "You're beautiful."

"As long as you think so…" She pouted at her stomach. "I just hate this stage. Big enough to look fat. Not shaped enough to look pregnant. It sucks." She dragged the last word out like a whining teenager and headed to the shower, leaving him at the table, unaware he watched her ass the entire time with a hunger that almost made him follow her into the steam.

--==●==--

Gina, fresh from the shower and carrying the empty recyclable bags from Giant in her hand, kissed him passionately before running out the door to visit her college friend Amy. The kiss had been her way of telling him she wouldn't bring up the bottle, she wouldn't push the subject, and she desperately wanted to stay home. It left him with a slight erection and he debated whether to suggest she call in with morning sickness and they spend the day in bed. It had seemed forever since they'd played hooky and he knew they could both use it.

She was out the door and gone before he'd even had a chance to form the thought.

Mark tossed back the last swallow of his now-cold coffee and placed the cup in the sink. Turning, he saw both the couch and the nursery from his vantage point in the kitchen. He sighed, smiled at the idea of the finished product rather than the mess waiting for him, and headed for the nursery.

He stood in the doorway and scanned the room. He still needed to move his bookshelf out of his ex-spare room and move it to the living room. He could also tell he'd need to dust and vacuum before doing anything else productive in the room. Housecleaning was something he and Gina both did naturally. Not with any list or schedule, but as they noticed something needed cleaning, they did what was necessary. There were no male-versus-female chores and there was no guilt in asking the other to do something they saw but didn't have time for right now. An occasional, "Ugh, can you clean the bathroom if you get home before me," was normal. Her suggesting a honey-do list was not, and he still smiled at the idea of it. Unfortunately, neither of them had had a chance to get to the nursery, let alone start organizing it, so it had fallen by the wayside in the weekly housekeeping.

The crib, Gina's first purchase because she had always known exactly what she'd wanted for her baby's bed, was still in the box against the wall. The mattress still hermetically sealed in plastic leaned against it. A brown bag in the corner contained various decals, posters, pictures and frames she'd been gathering as she found them. But the unopened cans of paint on the newspaper in front of them begged to be first.

"I hate painting..." He spoke to the empty room and tried to imagine it full of baby smells and sounds—cooing and laughter, gently sung lullabies, and the creak of the rocking chair. The chair, he remembered suddenly he needed to fix the spoke on and oil it so it wouldn't squeak. The chair, the bookshelf and pre-paint cleaning should keep him busy, he thought, leaning his weight on the doorframe and returning to the idea of a child in his life.

He hadn't expected to become a father when he met Gina. Hell, he hadn't expected a relationship. He'd been looking for coffee and a little detox after work.

He normally would have stopped at Harp and Fiddle and ignored Molly's jolly banter, while watching her when she wasn't paying attention to him. But he'd given up drinking the night he'd run through the stop sign, crashed into a mailbox, and ended up in the holding tank of the next county. Reilly had finally found him around five o'clock in the morning, having been sent on a rescue mission by Ray, who'd watched Mark leave the station in a fit of rage he hadn't seen since their academy days. Work had been beyond stressful—he'd lost three cases in the last week to courtroom antics, loopholes and bullshit excuses provided by the defense. *Damn Lauren was good.* Kim had been gone for almost a year at the time, but was still calling him and leaving him messages of hate and anger, asking for this item or that when she couldn't find it and assuming he'd taken it with him. His life had basically crumbled around him, dragging him down with it, and he chose to drown reality in the bottom of a Jack Daniels bottle. As often as humanly possible.

Until that night.

After that night he started going straight home rather than to the Harp and Fiddle, but found he was cranky when he got home. He wasn't leaving work at the desk, but dragging it along home with him. He was physically in his living room but mentally in uniform, as he listened intently to the scanner and only half-assed paid attention to whatever channel was currently muted on the television. Reilly hit the station for a follow-up visit regarding an old cold case a week after bailing Mark out of jail, and he and Ray both suggested Mark find a release, smirking to each other and raising eyebrows.

"Get laid," Reilly said. "You're not a bad looking guy…"

"And hey, if all else fails, it's not like you don't know which whores on the street are clean." Ray pointed out through gritted teeth as he tried not to laugh at the idea of his suggestion.

"Fuck you both."

He slammed the station door on his way out and stormed to his car. He hated them because he knew they were right. He agreed with the idea, though not the suggestions. He needed something. He just didn't know what.

Chewing it over on the way home, he drove aimlessly after hopping onto Route 30 from Interstate 83, when he noticed the flashing lights ahead and knew there'd be a parking lot instead of a highway waiting for him around the next curve. Sitting at a stoplight he sighed, huffed exaggerated frustration through his teeth and took in his surroundings. The little black car in front of him, dotted in rust with fancy rims and cursive lettering across the back, "Burn rubber not your soul," made him smile. The out-of-state semitruck lurched several times next to him, as if revving his engine and waiting for some hot blonde to drop a handkerchief to signal the beginning of the drag race with the off-duty cop. Though Mark was sure the driver had no idea he was a cop, the idea of racing a rig made him smile again.

"See? I'm not all stress." He spoke to the empty stale air of the car. "I know how to smile…"

To his right was Round the Clock diner. Famous for absolutely nothing, yet reported to have some of the best twenty-four-hour breakfast choices in town. Mark knew truckers and cops alike hung there, as well as a few motorcycle clubs on weekends.

In a moment of fancy—a whim he'd never be able to explain—he checked the right turn lane next to him and his rearview mirror, saw the opening, and slid into place. He parked and entered the building before he realized and just let his mind drift and his feet lead him.

The smell assaulting him upon opening the door wasn't necessarily bad. It was just a lot to take in at once. He could smell breakfast and dinner meats—bacon, sausage, hamburger and possibly pork. The stink of sweat and feet and cleaning fluids blended in a bizarrely welcoming manner, reminding him of the out-of-the-way restaurant his parents had taken Sarah and him after church every Sunday for several years. He expected the seats to be cracked as they were in memory, even though it was a completely different time and location.

He spied a lonely booth in the back corner with window views of both the parking lot and highway. Being a creature of habit, of knowing his surroundings, Mark always faced the restaurant when he sat. He always had a view of the windows. He always knew if trouble was walking in the door or how quickly he could escort them out it if need be. He glided past families eating early with young children and older couples eating in silence, as he made his way to the back corner.

His ass had barely registered the smoothness of vinyl rather than cracked leather when a bouncy waitress appeared with a glass of water, coffeepot and menu.

"Coffee?" She put the menu in front of him.

"Umm…" Mark hadn't even fully registered he was in the restaurant, let alone he'd be expected to eat or drink something. "Sure."

"Two creams and a sugar, coming up…" She spun and grabbed a full dish of individual serving non-dairy creamers from the next table and pocketed the empty one from his table.

"Exactly… How'd you know?"

"It's a gift." She winked at him and turned, talking to the customers at the booth two over from him before she'd actually stopped in front of them.

Mark spent the next hour drinking cup after cup of coffee and watching the waitress like he had always watched Molly. She wore no nametag and he listened intently for one of the other waitstaff to call her by name. Her chocolate hair was pulled back in a loose ponytail—wisps, escapees during her shift, tucked behind her ear haphazardly. The tips of her bangs were darker and at first Mark thought it was natural shading, but as he watched her walk away after another refill of his cup, he noticed the bottom of her ponytail looked the same. She had purposely tipped the last inch of her hair black. It was subtle but still against the grain. Easily missed in the wrong lighting. Though Mark imagined it was quite striking, both in disparity and effect, in the proper lighting. Her short trimmed nails were clean of polish—Mark wondered if there was a health rule for servers—but she flashed up her hands just a touch with two silver rings on each hand. The silver matched her plain hoop earrings, appearing almost white against her hair and swinging lightly as she flitted around the restaurant. The waitress was young but not too young. He wondered if she either aged well for the life showing in her light brown eyes, or if her life had hardened her eyes before her body could catch up, and couldn't decide if he wanted to refer to her as a girl or a woman. Proper, professional, with a lilt to her voice, and a touch of spice to her personality—she was a collection of contrasts.

She was fascinating.

There was a slight bounce to her walk. She whistled while cleaning tables. Talked and cooed at everyone under ten she waited on, and flirted with everyone over fifty whether they were with someone or not. She loved her job, Mark could tell, but he could also tell by the way she spoke, by the tidbits she shared or conversations she sparked, she wasn't your usual waitress fodder. She was either working her way through college or had finished and was working while she found the perfect job.

He was wrong on both parts.

But he wouldn't learn the truth until two weeks after their first meeting.

Mark stopped at Round the Clock and drank coffee for an hour every night after work for a week. Sometime during the second week he added a burger to the routine and called it dinner. Near the end of the second week he stopped watching the waitress and started talking.

That particular night he hadn't gotten through his paperwork until almost eight o'clock and it was nearly nine before he slid into his corner booth.

"Where the hell ya been, sunshine?" She was sitting on the opposite side of the table waiting for him with a coffeepot and cup of creamers.

"Waiting, were ya?" Mark felt wrong the second he said it. It seemed dirty and flirtatious and he hadn't meant it to be either of those things. He offered a weak smile curled in an apologetic half twist from the corner of his mouth.

"Nah…" She hopped up out of the seat. "I saw you in the parking lot." She winked, menu still under her arm. "Coffee, burger, nothing, menu?"

"Burger. I'm starving."

"'Kay… Be right back." And she was gone.

He looked around the restaurant. It was far emptier than he'd seen it during previous visits. He wondered if it was a lag until the midnight rush or if the rest of the night was calm like this and figured he'd ask her to open conversation.

When she returned, he'd completely forgotten the question and his tongue took over on its own.

"So why don't you have a name tag like everyone else?"

She glanced down at her shirt, meeting her gaze with the tips of her fingers as they brushed absently at the place where it should have been.

"Oh, I had one. The great spaghetti incident of '08 was almost repeated and in a fit of ridiculous kitchen antics I lost it to the deep fryer. I haven't gotten another one yet." She held her hand out to him, "Hi, I'm Gina and I'll be your waitress tonight." Her teeth were revealed as a wickedly slow grin spread across her face and lit up her eyes. "Nice to meet you, sir."

He shook her hand. A little lighter than a formal handshake and a little longer than he probably should have. "Mark. Nice to meet you."

"That's a nice strong name. Mark." She repeated it as if tasting the single syllable and twisting it around in her mouth to see if the softness of the *M* and the harshness of the *K* blended well over her tongue.

A bell rang behind her and she spun, still smiling, to retrieve his burger from the cook.

Gina sat the plate in front of him and raised an eyebrow. He matched her brow quizzically. "You had him put the burger on when you saw me in the lot didn't you?"

"Mmmhhhm…" Her teeth were hidden in the coy, tight-lipped smile.

"What if I didn't want one?"

"Guess I would have had a burger for dinner tonight."

He laughed and she joined him. He was intrigued by her, but at the moment it was more the comfort of having achieved "Regular" status. He hadn't felt comfortable anywhere since Kim left, or welcome anywhere since the last night he stopped at Harp and Fiddle. It was nice to be both for a change.

Mark noted the remaining customers had left while he was busy trying not to flirt. "Is it always this quiet in here this time of night?"

Gina looked around behind her, up at the clock on the wall behind the register, and back to Mark. "Can be. Until the bars close. Depends on the time of month, whether there's a holiday or something going on in town or not. Lots of things. But yeah, it can get real quiet like this…" As she spoke she sat at the edge of the booth's bench, legs still out to the main floor, just resting, it appeared.

Within minutes her legs were turned inward, her elbows were on the table, and they were having a full conversation about nothing peripheral, polite or professional. She learned he was a freshly divorced detective now married to his job. He learned she was a degreed accountant who hated the stuffiness she'd found outside of college and longed for the carefree days she'd waitressed at a truck stop while paying her way through school. He found it fascinating she'd given up a decent salary just to enjoy the work she did in a menial job anyone could have done and wondered if they paid her a bit better knowing they had a treasure worth paying the price to keep.

At some point, he smiled to himself as a handful of rowdy twenty-somethings came in, obviously fresh from a nearby tavern. He sat a little taller and watched, expecting he'd need to help escort them out, feeling his unspoken vibe shooting across the room at their brackish behavior. He imagined the attitude he pushed out, something he did both consciously and unconsciously in situations where he felt the need to be on alert, was like a cone of displaced air. A spike of control he used to keep a given situation under control. It was some Zen thing he'd read about once in college and practiced ever since.

He didn't need it this time.

Gina greeted the boys with menus and coffee. Mark didn't hear what was said but smiled as he watched her slap one of them on top of the head with a menu and suggest he, "Sit down, shut up, drink coffee and sober his sorry ass up before she called the cops." The boys not only received her harsh treatment well, they seemed used to it and Mark had to wonder if they were also regulars. Familiar or not, Gina handled the situation with flair, and a smile flashed more wickedly than a young boy with a cherry bomb in his pocket or teenage girl with a secret.

That night Mark stayed longer than an hour. On that particular Thursday—because he remembered every detail, including the day of the week—he'd stayed until almost one o'clock in the morning. They had more conversations than he'd ever had on an actual date and yet never felt as though it were a date. They were just two humans talking in the quiet of a restaurant, serenaded by the sounds of the highway and smells of a grease-filled kitchen.

The next few days he stayed two to three hours every night. He debated going straight home the night she said she was off the schedule, but he stopped for coffee anyway out of habit. Round the Clock had become comfortable and comforting, and he needed both in his life.

She was sitting in the booth waiting for him. Out of uniform. Her own coffee cup half-gone when he slid in across from her. He smiled and reached for the rusty orange pot of coffee on the table and she brushed his hand away, pouring his cup for him. Neither of them spoke for several minutes. They met each other's gaze with an internal conversation, punctuated with the slightest smiles, averted eyes, and head tilts. Mark wondered if she was having the same conversation he was during the strangely loud silence. When the silence was finally broken, Mark was surprised to hear his own voice.

"You wanna get out of here?"

Giggling like schoolchildren the entire time, they went from the family restaurant to McDonald's drive-thru, a culinary downgrade in both their opinions. She ordered a cheeseburger Happy Meal and he got a Big Mac. They drove out to Lake Redman, five miles south on 83 and ate their greasy meal in the waning dusk at a picnic table under the Blue Gill pavilion. They drove around the hillside above York as the sun dipped below the late-summer horizon and watched as the city lights came on in sections to push away the falling darkness, like tiny Christmas light strings coming to life one at a time.

That was their first official date. Gina gleefully agreed to go out any night she wasn't working and he smiled triumphantly over a prize he hadn't even known he was trying to win. They enjoyed the rest of summer and the beginning color changes of fall, their emotions and physical desires strengthening with every word, look and touch. When she broke the news of her pregnancy to him, with trembling lips and a hand over the empty coffee cup in front her, reaching instead for the water, he found himself stunned and excited at the same time.

"Marry me." They dated and alternated a couple nights a week at the other's house. They had never fought. They truly adored each other's friends. He had met her family Labor Day weekend and everyone got along great. They understood the importance of giving each other private space and time, and accepted when to attack the other no matter what they were doing. They knew when to push and when to poke when the other needed to talk or act on something. It was a perfect relationship. And Mark was willing to take it to the next level. More than happy to not just do the responsible thing, but the thing that sounded as natural as breathing to him. He wasn't expecting her response.

"No." She took several gulps of her ice water.

"I…" Mark sat up. "Crap. I'm sorry. I did that all wrong!" He slid from the chair at their four-place table near the window of White Rose and landed on one knee in front of her. He looked around frantically for something that would do as a ring on the spot.

She laughed and grabbed his arm, tugging him upward.

"No, no, silly." She leaned down and kissed him full on the lips. The pressure was passionate, the tight lips were polite. "Get off the floor…"

"But…" He met her eyes and worried. *Stupid,* he thought. What if she doesn't want the baby? He had just assumed. Hadn't given her an opportunity to discuss options or plans or desires with him. He put a hand to his forehead, covering one eye and squinted at her with the other. "I'm sorry. What do you want to do?"

"For starters I want to pee. I swear it's all in my head." She sounded annoyed with herself. "Ever since I found out, I've had to go the bathroom every twenty minutes." She stood and disappeared to the bathroom by the backdoor.

Mark was so deep in his own thoughts he didn't hear her come back and didn't realize she'd both returned and started talking until she reached over and grabbed his hand.

"Hey…" She smiled. That slow, wicked smile of hers. "I love you.

Don't think I don't. And I want this baby. That's not a question." She pulled her hand back to her side of the table. "If you want to help me with it, if you want to stick around, that's great. But I'm not going to marry you just because I'm pregnant. I know too many people who've done that and are miserable."

"Fair enough…" Mark released a breath he didn't realize he was holding.

"Tell ya what." The sparkle in her eye was full of mischief and adventure. "How about we live in sin for a while and see how that works out. See how we do under one roof. And make decisions later."

"Deal." He smiled at the idea of waking up next to her every single day, having only done it a handful of times when she'd been too tired to go home, or too comfortable to tell him to go home.

"Your place or mine?" She flashed him a toothy smile and opened the menu as if they were talking about nothing of importance.

That had been five months ago. His apartment had won the coin toss, based on neighborhood rather than space, and they'd enjoyed living together every day since then. Only the occasional insecurities, which Mark blamed on the hormones, ever caused any friction, and Mark was very good at letting those moments roll off him like water from a duck's back.

Mark smiled, thinking back to the first few dates. To the months that had followed. The way her eyes lit up when she talked about the baby. The way she patted her tummy absently when he talked about the baby.

He looked at the crib waiting to be put together and the cans of paint and thought of Kim and all her hate and anger and blame.

"Fuck you, Kim." He turned from the room and grabbed the television remote as he flopped onto the couch, deciding to tackle the room after a little channel surfing. "It wasn't me that failed."

White Picket Prisons

CHAPTER ELEVEN

The ringtone startled Mark and it took him a moment to both acknowledge he'd fallen asleep and recognize the caller from the song playing. Mark had located the theme from *Magnum PI* as a joke when Reilly decided to leave the force for PI work. He fumbled in his pants pocket for the source of the ringtone and answered in a rush of air matching his instantly increased heart rate.

"Did you find her, Reilly?"

"Hey, brotha." Reilly responded as if Mark had only said hello. "I'm fine, how are you?"

"Don't fuck with me, Rye…"

"You're right. Sorry." There was a pause, a muffled cuss Mark presumed was meant for another driver, and Reilly returned to the phone. "You busy? Wanna meet?"

"Did. You. Fucking. Find. Her." Mark spat each word slowly and deliberately through gritted teeth, afraid Reilly was stalling because Sarah had been found after all. Dead.

"Yeah. I did. Relax, bro."

"Alive?" Mark heard his voice question the unthinkable and winced.

"Oh hey, dude. Yeah, she's alive. Sorry. I didn't even think to put that possibility in your head. Sorry." Reilly swore at another driver. "Wanna meet somewhere after work?"

"I ain't working…" The words twisted in Mark's mouth and the bitterness of their finality struck him in the back of his throat like bile, "…today. Just come on over to my place."

"You got it. I'll be there in ten." Reilly hung up without another word.

"Damn you," Mark cursed the dead phone in his hand. He really was going to have to beat that habit out of his best friend one of these days.

--==●==--

75

Mark was pacing the back porch when Reilly's dark blue Hyundai slipped into the driveway behind Mark's Buick LeSabre. Normally he would have ribbed his friend about the vehicle of choice, to which Reilly would have pointed out how very "fucking normal and boring" the car was, therefore perfect for surveillance. They would have bantered. It would have ended with laughing. But Mark had no funny bone at the moment. He was only interested in the manila folder he saw Reilly retrieve from the backseat.

Reilly nodded hello to Mark and headed toward the apartment.

"Why the fuck isn't the workaholic at work? Gina okay? The baby?"

"What? Oh no… I mean, yeah, everything's fine with Gina and the baby. Other than this new complaint of hers that she's big enough to look fat but not look pregnant." Mark rolled his eyes.

"Then why the hell are you home?"

"It's a long story." Mark turned toward the apartment door. "Come on…"

The story wasn't that long when Mark explained it in a frustrated rage, ignoring any and all points that could have been used against him. Reilly nodded and pursed his lips up a few times, as if trying to hold back an opinion. Mark spewed the "vacation" details as he poured two glasses of generic cola from the two-liter bottle Gina had stuck in the cupboard instead of the fridge. He dropped ice cubes into each glass and followed Reilly to the living room.

"It's all a bunch of bullshit." He dragged the first syllable of the last word, twisting it so it sounded like he said *bowl-shit*. "So? Whatcha got?"

"Some really fucked-up shit, my man." Reilly pulled a rubber band off the folder and flipped it open. "But she's okay, so stop worrying about that."

"Where is she?"

"Fucking Wisconsin. Can you believe that shit?"

"Wisconsin? That doesn't make sense." Mark swallowed a gulp of lukewarm soda and put it on the table in disgust, making a face as he did so. "What the hell is in Wisconsin besides hunters and blizzards?"

"And serial killers and cheese. Don't forget those." Reilly raised an eyebrow at Mark and Mark was glad they seemed to be on the same page.

"So why the hell…?"

"Well she's still with that guy Joshua. Or his family at least."

"Yeah?"

"Yep. In some kind of Amish community or something." Reilly pulled out a map of Wisconsin. "I tracked the postmark to Eagle River. Population 1400." He pointed to the green section of the map on the northern right side of the state. "Apparently Eagle River is considered a hopping vacation hotspot out there, but they're still small enough to be full of gossip and curiosity and finger pointing."

Mark furrowed his eyebrows at Reilly, confused by the statement as it pertained to Sarah.

"Your sister was actually quite the talk at the post office."

"What?" Mark leaned forward and studied the map. "Why?"

Reilly changed his voice to imitate a Midwestern accent. "We don't get a lot of post from those folks. We tend to remember when they bother hopping a horse to come see us."

"Horse? Sarah hates horses." Mark looked over at the shoebox full of pictures still on the end table and remembered the summer Sarah had been thrown from their grandmother's mare into the barbed wire fencing. They hadn't known at the time Fancy was pregnant, and Sarah was hurt and pissed. After they found out, she was still hurt. And it wasn't the physical wounds that kept her from climbing back into a saddle.

"Not anymore, bro." He flipped through his notes. "So apparently, she came in early morning a week ago and begged this little small-town postmaster to borrow her a stamp so she could mail this. He said he fished the change from his own pocket and handed it to her, so she could formally hand it back to him. And his voice sounded weird when he talked about her. Like sad or something."

"But she was okay?"

"Yeah yeah, he said she looked better than most of them do from Valley Mill. So naturally I looked up Valley Mill and couldn't find squat about it, so I had to call this clown back. Only now I got the other shift. I imagine they take turns covering the counter and phones with all the crazy business they're doing." His voice was sarcastic. "So this one goes off on how Sarah was real pretty and clean, not like she'd been born there. And no, before you ask, I didn't offer them a drop of information."

"Good." Mark grabbed the soda and held it, still looking at the map. "So where's Valley Mill?"

Reilly slid his finger south of Eagle River. "Somewhere between here and here." His finger stopped just over the edge of the line marking Michigan.

"Eagle River. Iron Mountain. Real imaginative out there with the town names aren't they?" Reilly shrugged at him. "You said Amish? I didn't think Joshua was Amish. He was in college with her when they met…"

"Yeah, and like we don't have any Amish here she goes and picks one from Wisconsin? But it's not really Amish. That's the part that bothered me."

"Bothered you?"

"Yeah, it's almost cultish or religious or something, I think. The second guy I talked to, the one that said she was pretty, mentioned something to the effect of '*she had all her parts*' which was just creepy."

"All her parts? What the hell does that mean?"

"Fuck if I know." Reilly shoved the papers and map back inside the folder and pushed it across to Mark. "But she's alive, somewhere in Wisconsin."

"And scared from the sounds of that letter."

"But alive." Reilly reiterated in a calm tone. "Oh, and the first postal dude mentioned she had an infant with her."

"A baby? Sarah's got a baby?"

"Dude, let's be realistic. It's been ten years and she's in Hickville with her stud. She's probably got twelve by now." Reilly offered a smile meant to make Mark smile. It didn't work. "Well, that's what I've got. Whatcha gonna do with it?"

"Get my sister back." Mark's voice was cold and calculated but his eyes shone with an edge of emotion capable of pooling over into tears at any moment.

Reilly stood to leave as the kitchen door opened and Gina came through in a blur of madness.

"Okay, Mark. The throwing up crap is getting—" She stopped when she saw Reilly standing there. "Rye!" Her face unfurled from the lines of frustration and anger. "How the hell are ya?" She rushed to him and gave him a hug, smiling at Mark over Reilly's shoulder.

"Good, good." He pulled back from the hug. "And look at you… All baby belly. You make a sexy pregnant chick, girlie." He turned and winked at Mark.

"You find Sarah?"

"Yup. Just got done giving your boy here all the details." He grabbed his cell phone off the table and put it in his front jeans pocket. "In fucking Wisconsin of all places."

Gina turned to Mark and mouthed "Wisconsin," questioning with crinkled eyebrows.

"Well, I gotta jet. I have a meeting with a hoity-toity lawyer regarding some ex-girlfriend that's becoming a problem. I love cases that smell like money." Reilly smiled and swooped out of the living room, letting himself out of the house and closing the door behind him.

"Thanks for the speedy work, brotha." Mark hollered after Reilly but didn't know if he heard it before the door was closed.

"Baby?" Gina lowered herself to the couch next to Mark. "You okay? You look a little pale."

"I'm fine. Just…" He blinked and finally focused on her. "Hey what were you saying? You throwing up again?"

"Yeah yeah. It happens. I'm pregnant." She waved a hand in front of him as if trying to physically smack the topic out of the way. "Now what about Sarah. What town is she in? Milwaukee? Madison?" She reached under the coffee table and grabbed her laptop from the lower shelf there.

"Valley Mill." His voice sounded dull. Dead.

"I can hop online and get you a plane ticket." She started typing immediately upon opening the computer. "Just let me know what the nearest airport is."

"I don't fly."

"Bah, it's cheap and quick. We'll get you there by tomorrow."

"I don't fly." His voice was a little stronger.

She stopped. He could see her gaze switching between his eyes, as if she was trying to deduce the reason for the attitude. He sighed. They'd talked about his parents, but not the fact he used to fly himself. Or the fact he'd never get in another plane again, whether he was flying it or not. He looked at the map and changed tactics.

"Baby, she's in the middle of nowhere." He circled the area Reilly had pointed out. "I'd have to rent a car once I got there and the added cost would be ridiculous. Plus, remember Sue and Darren bitching about how much their last trip cost?"

"Yeah…"

Gina looked confused. He knew she remembered the night. It was the last time she'd had anything to drink before finding out she was pregnant, and while he sipped cola all night she had downed a bottle of wine and given him a lap dance he still gave her crap about.

"Train?" she finally said and he realized she was working through the travel in her mind. It was her thinking expression, he just wasn't used to seeing it aimed at him, but rather some crazy puzzle book or mystery novel.

"I was thinking of just driving. It would be more of a straight shot." He paused, expecting her rational side to jump in with opinions. It didn't. Instead she returned her attentions to the laptop.

"Valley Mill you said?" He saw Google Maps load on her screen.

"Yeah. Wisconsin."

"Eighteen hours thirty-two minutes." Her face crinkled as she moved the mouse around and watched the blue line on the map move with it. "That's through Chicago, so it's highways and tolls the whole way. Or nineteen hours seventeen minutes up through Michigan, tolls on the turnpike and Ohio and then none. Smaller state highways instead of the interstate, but how much would you save on tolls I wonder?"

She looked at him and he could see her working something behind her eyes. The telltale licking of the corner of her mouth gave her away but she spoke again before she could ask, "Stupid question. Quicker route or cheaper route."

"Quicker." He spoke with a tone of annoyance, she knew the answer.

"Now before you jump. Look at these two routes…" She turned the laptop toward him. "Big huge monster chances for traffic issues if not jams through Chicago, Milwaukee and Green Bay. Half an hour difference with no chance for traffic issues and cheaper tolls…"

"Forty-five," he corrected.

"You know what I mean." She turned the laptop back toward him and pulled up her calendar. "You know…" She studied the colored tiles.

"I don't think so." It dawned on Mark what she'd been chewing over.

"Oh come on, it would be fun." Her eyes lit up and he could see her mischievous smile starting to curl her lip. "A road trip. Vacation. Yes, it's a serious trip with serious business, but think about it." Gina held up her hand and ticked off her reasoning, "We get time away from the world with each other. We can talk about baby names and other family stuff for us. I can drive part of the way so you don't have to stop…"

"Who says I was going to stop?"

"Mark, please." She lowered her hand and covered his with it. "I understand adrenaline and guilt and all that, but if you drive straight through, like I know you want to, you'll be dead when we get there. Useless. And rather than rescuing your sister or finding out what you need, you'll just need to nap."

"You mean when *I* get there…"

"Mark." Her tone sharpened like an annoyed teacher's but her eyes welled. "Please don't shut me out. Don't do that. Not right now. Don't leave me here alone and pregnant…"

"I'm not going to be gone long. And you're not alone. Our friends and your—"

"Fine." She leaned back on the couch and looked down.

Mark watched her face. This wasn't a game. Gina wasn't doing an annoying poor-me pout like Kim used to. She'd been genuinely interested in driving across country with him. Helping him get there alive. Helping him find his sister. *Of course, she was serious.* Mark mentally scolded himself for being stubborn and stupid.

"You know…" He put a finger under her chin to draw her head upward and catch her attention. "Driving across country, even if it's only to Wisconsin instead of somewhere fun, would definitely be more interesting with someone along to see the sights."

Gina's stubborn streak tried to keep control and remain upset with him but he saw a spark in her eye, the same spark he'd seen that night in the restaurant.

"Whadda ya say? Wanna go on an adventure with me?"

"Really? You're not just saying this?"

"Nah, you brought up valid points. And hell, if I get lost in the middle of the backwoods, I'm going to need someone to trade to the locals for passage through their land!" He smiled wide and she joined him.

"Oh Mark, it'll be fun. Just think… By the time we get there we'll be able to tell Sarah the name for her first niece or nephew. And we'll have a helluva story to tell Junior someday."

"Alrighty." He leaned in and kissed her forehead. "Print the directions through Michigan, we'll avoid tolls. And I'll start packing. You think you can get time off?"

"Fuck, Linda loves me. I'll just tell her we've got a family emergency out of town and she'll be fine. When do you want to leave?"

"Tonight?" The eagerness in his eyes was only rivaled by the bounce in his feet when he jumped up from the couch to go begin packing.

"In the morning," Gina suggested. "Then we'll be fully rested and have time to think of any details we haven't yet."

"The roads will be easier at night though. Less traffic, less headaches and assholes." He chewed on his cheek for a moment. "Call Linda, I'm going to pack and call Reilly. See if there was any other little tidbit he may have forgotten to mention that might be important. Then we'll take a little nap and leave later tonight, it's only three o'clock now… We can leave at eight and get there during the day tomorrow. Otherwise we get there in the middle of the night and that won't be helpful at all."

"Tidbits?"

"Yeah… I'm still chewing over the meaning behind Sarah being referred to as 'having all her parts.'"

"Creepy…"

"Ya think?" He nodded at her phone on the table. "Now get a move on girl. You wanna be copilot you gotta get the checklist right. Call Linda and print us a path to blaze across the Midwest."

"Roadtrip!" Gina squealed and she tapped the screen on her phone and pulled up her manager's contact info in her address book.

Mark wanted to smile at her enthusiasm, but all he could think of was Sarah, and whether she had all her parts *anymore*.

CHAPTER TWELVE

Mark pulled the ticket from the automated booth and handed it to Gina. She tucked it under the coin purse she'd filled with toll cash at the ATM and placed it in the floor console for easy access. On either side of it were large to-go cups from Rutters. Mark's with coffee, Gina's with caffeine-free cappuccino.

"Baby names, music, Sarah or general bullshit—pick your poison." Gina scooted down in her seat and lifted her feet to the dash, wriggling her toes.

Mark glanced at her mismatched socks—one lime green solid and one pink and yellow striped—and shook his head. The woman refused to wear matching socks. It was only one of a thousand little things she did that made him smile. Things she didn't think about or plan, just did. Like singing in the kitchen or talking to the plants like small children. He had once believed her quirks were from her mother, but after the Labor Day party with her family he knew better, and smiled again remembering her grandfather crossing his legs in a lawn chair to show mismatched socks.

"Baby names." Mark noticed the radio was on but turned completely down and pushed the knob to turn it off. "Family names or fun?"

"Well, what about tradition? What do you have for traditions?"

"We don't want to do that."

Gina snickered, "Oh yeah? Sounds like a story."

"I should have been named Wilfred." Mark looked away from the road to glance at her with widened eyes. "Wilfred. Can you imagine?"

"Why? How'd you get Mark?"

"Family tradition is to name the children after the grandparents. A first and middle name that works from the combination of both sides of the family. My maternal grandfather was Wilfred, Dad's dad was Raymond. I am so glad my parents decided both options were awful."

"Mark James. Your parents cheated?"

"Only a little. It's the middle name of Grandpa Raymond and Great-Grandpa Mark. Sarah got lucky. Sarah Elizabeth, both grandmothers had decent names."

"So this child would be a combination of…" Gina held up her fingers, "Christopher, David, Julie or…what was your mom's real name? I've only ever heard you say mom."

"Mary." Mark didn't look at her as he spoke his mother's name. He stared at the turnpike ahead of him and remembered the way she laughed so he wouldn't be tempted to start crying.

"Damn, none of those really go together. Christopher and David sound more like brothers than one name. And Mary and Julie are both either first names or middle names, not really a good combo." She picked at her finger and wiggled her toes for a moment in thought. "How about Mary Elizabeth—your mom and your sister—for a girl?"

Mark opened his mouth to protest and instead found himself repeating it, tasting the idea, "Mary Elizabeth."

Gina giggled, "Unless you had a nun named Sister Mary Elizabeth, then that's just out!"

Mark laughed, "No no. My nuns had horrible names. God, I haven't thought about them in forever. Sisters Louise, Ruth, Bernice and Henrietta… We called *her* Sister Hank."

"Hank? Wow…"

"Oh yeah… If we get bored on this trip I'll tell you some stories. She was hideous. And she could turn class into an hour-long lecture on the dumbest things—like chewing on your pencil or slouching in your seat. It was awful, but really easy to get her sidetracked and not have actual class that way."

"You must have been horrible…" The lilt in her voice made it sound like a hesitant question rather than a statement.

Mark grinned like a schoolboy remembering the days of raising hell in the hallways of God's school. "Oh I was… Got kicked out, didn't I?"

"You got kicked out? I didn't know that!"

"Really? I thought I told you."

"Noooo…" She pulled her legs down and tucked them up on the seat as she leaned toward him. "What did you do?"

Mark told Gina about the cherry bomb, taking the fall for Benny, and countless things they'd done before the fateful day he was tossed from their building—including toilet papering the pulpit, putting mini rubber ducks in the holy water basins, and the day they passed out watermelon bubblegum to the entire class because Sister Hank hated the smell of it. Gina alternately giggled and covered her mouth in feign shock.

"Stop. Stop." She begged finally. "No more. I'm gonna pee my pants!"

"Oh then you definitely need to hear what we did Easter service while the local bishop was in attendance…"

"Mark, please…" She wiped the tears from her eyes. "Find me a bathroom, jerk. I can't laugh like this with your lovechild doing jumping jacks on my bladder."

He pulled into the next wayside, topping the tank while she ran for the brick building and the restrooms inside. Mark checked his phone for messages and was waiting with the Explorer running when she exited. They had decided the previous night to forego the gas mileage savings on his LeSabre and chose her four-wheel drive instead, just to be sure.

Back on the road he agreed with her, "Mary Elizabeth Baker. I like it." He bit his lip and wondered if he'd jumped the gun on the last name. They weren't married yet and weren't planning it anytime soon. She could have wanted to give the baby her name. Mark waited to see if she would react, but she didn't.

"Good, now how about the boy name?"

"Christopher and David don't work, you're right about that. What about other relatives?"

Gina listed off family names like she were reading a phone book, including last names as if they were important and nicknames that would never be included in the final vote. She finally stopped and smiled. "I got it."

"Oh yeah? Cuz I wasn't really impressed with that last chunk and kinda hope Shane, Priest and Griffin are distant relatives…"

"Second cousins, twice removed…or three or something. I don't know. I only ever saw them at weddings and funerals." She waved a hand at him. "But nevermind that. How's this rock your world… Christopher Reilly?"

"Reilly? Really?" He snickered.

"Yes. Your father and your best friend. It's logical."

"But then both baby name choices are based on me…"

"So? It's your baby." She lightly punched his arm. "I think it should be named after your parents, after that, it doesn't matter. Including Sarah makes perfect sense, so why not Reilly?"

"Reilly's middle name is Thomas, can we go with that instead?"

"Christopher Thomas? Wasn't that a cartoon character or something?"

"Nah, you're thinking Winnie the Pooh, that's Christopher Robin."

"Ohhh yeah, you're right. Okay. Christopher Thomas it is." She smiled and leaned her head back. "Well that's settled. What do you wanna do for the *next* seventeen hours?"

"Drive." His acidic tone was meant to be funny but sounded mean.

"Do you want me to drive for a while?"

"No no. We just started." He put a hand on her knee. "Why don't you take a nap? I'll turn on the radio and you can drift for a bit. You've been tired as hell lately anyway and this is going to be a long trip."

"I could nap." She settled into the seat, fidgeting a few moments to get comfortable, and dreamily peeked at him through half-open eyes. "I love you, Mark."

"I know, baby. I love you, too." He turned the radio on, leaving the volume low enough to be more like background noise than a car jam session.

"Wake me up when we get to Ohio." Her breathing immediately changed into her drifting state and he knew she'd be asleep within minutes.

"Okay," he whispered, but he didn't wake her when they entered Ohio two hours later.

CHAPTER THIRTEEN

Baby…" Mark gently nudged Gina's leg. "Babe…" His voice a little louder, his nudge a little stronger.

Gina opened her eyes and looked at him without focus, then out the window, getting her bearings. Perhaps shaking the last remnants of a dream from the reality around her. She focused on him and blinked. "Huh…what?"

"Sorry to wake you up. Just a quick question…" He squeezed her leg affectionately. "How many miles can you go once the gas light comes on?"

Gina sat bolt upright, fully awake. "No no, baby, don't do that!" She leaned toward him but was eyeballing the dash. "How long ago did it come on?"

"Maybe five minutes."

She chewed her lip and looked out the window into the darkness. He was sure she noticed the blank landscape and lonely highway. "Where the hell are we?"

"Michigan…"

"Mark! I told you to wake me…"

"I know. I know. But you were sleeping and you need your sleep and it was only a couple hours." He looked at her, pleading with his eyes for the answer he wanted to hear. "How many miles can we go?"

"I honestly don't know. Sorry. I've never run it that low. It scares me to do that. Plus my dad pounded it into my brain when I was a teenager to never let it go below a quarter tank. Why… How did you do this?"

"I saw quarter tank and the Michigan border was like thirty miles so I figured I'd just get gas once we crossed the state line."

"And…"

"The first two exits didn't even have signs for gas. The next one said gas but it was closed. There were a few without anything but an exit number. And the last one had a sign for gas but the building looked like it had been closed down for years."

"And…" She looked from him into the endless night in front of the headlights and back to him. "How far until the next exit?"

"I have no idea." Mark shook his head. "This state is weird. They only have miles signs for bigger towns and there's almost no traffic…" He sighed. "Did you ever watch *Twilight Zone* or *Tales from the Darkside* as a kid?"

"Not funny, Mark."

"I'm being serious. It's freaking surreal. I mean, I know Detroit and Ann Arbor are coming up at some point but what about between here and there?"

"We don't go through Detroit…" She grabbed the Google Maps printout from the dash. "What was the last town we went through?"

"Christ, hon, I don't know… I think Toledo was actually the last town listed. Though I've seen signs for Ann Arbor and Flint if that helps. I just know I have to stay on this until it merges with 75 North." He looked at her apologetically in the dark but was certain the dash lights were not enough to illuminate his true guilt.

"Okay. This is a state highway. There has to be gas." Gina hit the dome switch and studied the map. "Have you seen any trucks on this stretch?"

"Yeah, a couple. I passed them."

"Good. Where there are trucks there will be gas stations. There have to be…"

"Exit 15," Mark exclaimed as if he'd discovered something amazing and pointed at the sign ahead of them. "Does that help?"

She shook her head and looked ahead, avoiding eye contact with Mark. He couldn't tell if she was pissed, irritated or just concentrating. Then the Gina he knew finally spoke.

"And of course I have to pee again." She smiled at him. "Take the exit."

She sounded excited and Mark looked ahead in time to note the GAS THIS EXIT sign. "Thank God."

He pulled onto the exit ramp, a slight upward slope to the overpass and came to a stop at the sign that intersected a crossroad.

Mark raised an eyebrow at GAS 8 MILES in white on an old black strip of tin, with an arrow pointing right, at the stop sign. When he turned to Gina he saw her eyes were widened as well. They looked to either side of the overpass without a word. Not a single building stood within their range of visibility in the pitch dark of Michigan's version of three o'clock in the morning. He watched her look back down the road the arrow directed them to, leaning into the window as if to see farther, and finally shaking her head.

"Get back on the highway."

"Yeah?"

"Yeah. If the ones on the off-ramps were closed, there's no way there's something open down there…" She exaggerated a shiver. "And it creeps me out."

"Next exit." He pulled straight across the road and back onto 23 North. "Okay, so worst-case scenario. The light usually signals last gallon of gas. Any idea what your mileage is?"

"Yes, actually!" Her eyes lit up like a little kid and her hand fumbled with the temperature reading dock on the ceiling. After pushing a few buttons she got it to cycle through Fahrenheit, Celsius, average speed and finally average mileage. "Seventeen miles per gallon."

"Okay," Mark thought for a moment. "We've gone maybe seven. I slowed down once I started looking for gas, inspecting all side roads and other options."

"So we have ten miles for a miracle… Great."

"Wanna have an adventure?" He tried to lighten the mood while he quietly willed an exit with a giant glowing BP or Sheetz or Rutter's or something waiting around the curve ahead of them.

"Road trip by definition is an adventure, you didn't need to push it." She smiled but sounded bitter.

"You mad?"

"Nah… I just really do have to pee now." She reached over and put her hand on his, where it was resting on the floor-mounted gearshift, and wove her fingers in between his. "Just find us gas. I can pee anywhere."

She no sooner finished her sentence and another exit sign loomed in front of them.

"Really? How many exits did you say there have been?"

"About every other mile really. Nothing on any of them, but lots of them."

They both saw the sign at the same time, with its universal symbols for hotels, food *and gas*. They shouted "Gas!" in unison, Gina pointing as Mark turned on the blinker.

The stop sign at the overpass intersection was slightly different from the last. Slightly. To the right was nothing. A road that seemed to wander off until it disappeared into a wall of blackness. No buildings, no signs, no chance of humanity. To the left was a dilapidated building that could have once been a gas station but no longer even had pumps. Gina's shoulders slumped in Mark's peripheral vision but he saw something she obviously didn't. "Buck up, kiddo. We may be in luck."

He turned while she questioned him, "Where are you going?"

"Next to that building—"

"The closed-down gas station?"

"Yeah. Maybe. Whatever. Look at the sign."

WILOX 1 MILE

"Ahhh, okay. Because they have to get their gas from somewhere, right?"

Wrong. The little town was approximately four blocks' worth of small white Monopoly houses. White with peaked roofs, all the same size and distance from each other. They drove three blocks, turned left at the end of the last house, circled the block to find another just like it behind it, and came back out to the main street. There were no gas stations, no grocery stores, no lights on and absolutely no activity. Yet Mark kept imagining the townsfolk coming around the corner of one of the houses, as a group, with pitchforks and torches. He couldn't get rid of the image and smiled when Gina verbally agreed with his assessment.

"All the little flaxen kids are sleeping."

"Exactly. Wow…" Mark turned back to the overpass and quickly got back on the highway. "Who knew Stepford was in the middle of Nowhere, Michigan?"

"You mean the Village of the Damned," Gina corrected her reference and she tossed the directions back onto the dash and reached behind her for the small lap blanket they'd brought with them for car naps.

"Yeah…" Mark slapped her leg and she spun back around to the front. As they came around a curve of tall pines and the sky broke into view, Mark smiled at the glow of lights illuminating the clouds above what had to include a gas station.

As they pulled into the truck stop the warning light for fuel began to blink on the dash. "It flashes?" Mark spoke to no one in particular. "What? To tell you it's imminent or just to make sure you noticed it?"

"Probably imminent…"

Mark wondered if Gina held her breath as he did while they pulled to a stop in front of the pumps. "Hit the bathroom, girly-girl. Then we'll switch for a few hours."

"Fill the tank. I don't want to go on that adventure again, okay?" She winked and walked quickly to the double glass doors that offered both civilization and a restroom.

CHAPTER FOURTEEN

Mark opened his eyes to Gina's frantic pleas for God to "make it stop" and looked around. He couldn't see anything. Not because it was still dark. Not because the night seemed so much blacker here, as a glance at the clock told him it was after eight and should be daylight. It wasn't black at all.

It was white.

And blurry? he thought. "What the hell?"

"I'm sorry baby. I meant to let you sleep until we got past the bridge, but I can't fucking drive in this."

"What is this?"

"God's revenge? Fuck if I know. It started as rain, turned to snow and then went into this shit."

Mark looked out the window. He could see the snow—tiny flakes falling and blowing in angry circles and clumps. The fuzz around the blizzard, which had not been on the weather forecast when they checked it, could only be one thing.

"Is that fog?"

"I don't know. It seems like fog. But I've never seen fog with snow. Snow-fog? What the fuck is that? Christ, we should have gone through Chicago. Between the lack of gas stations and the fucked-up weather, this state just sucks."

He leaned toward her and looked at the dash. "How long you been going thirty-five?"

"A good half hour. You've been asleep for almost four… Sorry it took you a while to fall asleep, you should have turned the radio down earlier than you did."

"No biggie. You were jamming while you drove. I get that. I just couldn't block it out for some reason." He looked up at the temperature gauge above the rearview mirror. "Thirty-one? Are you kidding? It was sixty-eight when we left PA."

"Oh yeah, and it's fucking cold here, too. I forgot that reason."

"Jesus…" He pulled the blanket closer around his shoulders. "Do you want me to drive?"

"You want to drive in this? Shit." She gripped the wheel and stared at the road. "I thought we'd just find somewhere to stop for a few hours."

"Like we found the gas?"

"Good point."

"Pull over underneath the next overpass, so we're a little sheltered, and we'll switch up."

"There's a gas station coming up, we can just stop there."

"Okay." Mark leaned back into the seat and watched the road.

He noticed the landscape on either side of the split highway, the depth of the shoulder when it became visible for a moment during a wind gust, and the occasional flash of brake lights farther up ahead. The swirling snow and fog thickened again for a moment and the road became a blank canvas of white. As if no one had ever driven here, walked here, visited or even discovered the land before. And then the car jostled and the road made horrendous rippling noises that startled Mark.

"What the hell?"

"Haha…" She spoke her giggle. "Welcome to Michigan pinball. I'm surprised it didn't wake you a few times. They have mini speed bumps along the centerline and the shoulder. If you hit it, you just go back the other way. It's actually kind of handy. Stay between the rails and you're all good." She smiled without taking her eyes off the road.

"Oh great. Braille for drivers."

"Basically." She laughed again, truly this time rather than spoken and added, "By the way, did you know the blind can hunt here?"

"The blind… The blind can what?"

"Yeah, not even kidding. The last place I stopped to pee—which by the way is getting really freaking annoying—the clerk told me. The place was full of trophies and heads and crap all over the walls. Very gross and creepy. And he saw me looking up at them and started talking. Saying this was a record blah blah and that was a whatever and 'This, this one was taken down by Old Man Jenkins. Man's blind as a bat, but a deadly damn shot with his laser sights.' To which I of course just stared at him. I thought he was joking but he clarified and started telling me all about how this old blind guy actually goes in the woods with a fucking gun and hunts. And he's not the only one. I told him I had a sleeping baby in the car and had to escape or that guy would have told me the story behind every dead animal on his wall." She finally pulled her eyes away from the road long enough to give him a glance of disbelief.

"Legally blind or just bad eye sight?" Mark couldn't believe what he was hearing.

"Legally blind. Please tell me we don't allow that in PA, or I'll never be able to go into the woods again."

"First of all, I have no idea, because I haven't hunted since I went with my grandpa when I was ten. Secondly, when have you *ever* been in the woods?"

"Hey, I like the woods…" They both laughed and Mark made a mental note to check the hunting regulations when he got home. He just couldn't believe they actually allowed that.

Gina pulled cautiously onto the exit ramp at Indian River and made her way to the gas pumps under the small tin roof at the locally owned gas station. A McDonald's across the street, another gas station up the road, a hotel and a small brick building declaring Hometown Insurance were gathered around the exit. It was more life than Mark had seen since they entered the state and he felt as if they had finally come out of the Twilight Zone they'd been traveling through all night.

Inside, he saw two officers near the coffee and made his way their direction as he waited for Gina to return from the bathrooms at the back of the store. In the aisles he saw snack items, trucker supplies, toys, books and magazines, and small collections of bizarre novelty items for sale, including polished rocks, Michigan coffee cups and key chains, and an entire rack of silver lights with various fantasy and horror designs that detailed dragons, skulls and more.

"Evening, Officers." Mark plucked a large coffee to-go cup from the stack and found the matching lid. "How's the coffee?"

"Fucking awful." The shorter officer spoke without remorse. Their heavy coats covered their tags and he couldn't properly address either of them, but the taller of the two offered some help.

"Jarvis…" He scolded his partner before he turned to Mark. "It's awful. He's not lying. Don't touch the regular stuff. Get the Cherry Mountain from the carafe at the end."

The cop offered the advice but looked Mark up and down, and Mark could see the officer's wheels turning. *Perhaps*, Mark wondered, *they weren't used to being spoken to by strangers. Maybe the cops in the Midwest were used to people being afraid to talk to them.*

He held his hand out to the officer. "Detective Baker, York, Pennsylvania."

The man met his hand and his eyes softened. "Long way out of your jurisdiction…"

"No jurisdiction. Family visit." He sidestepped to the end of the row and located the cherry coffee. "This weather normal around here?" Mark nodded back toward the large glass windows.

"Not really," Jarvis offered. "Lake effect does strange things to the air."

"Lake effect?"

"Yeah, some weird atmospheric pressure thing that happens when certain weather systems pass over the lake."

Mark stared at the officer for a moment, trying to decide if Jarvis was just messing with him and his partner was helping the story with meteorologist bullshit speak. He decided they were being truthful as the officer continued.

"Should clear up on the other side of the bridge. Altitude change generally kills it."

"You're serious?"

"Oh yeah. Weather, motor vehicle violations, and hunting accidents are our bread and butter around here."

"Hey, Geegs, it's not always boring. We had them two dead hookers a few months back." Jarvis spoke up and between the sheer nature of the statement and his personality so far, Mark again had to wonder if they were messing with him.

"Well, that was unusual though," Geegs offered. "And the guy was from Wisconsin. He wasn't even a local. Just got caught here dumping his bodies."

Mark's eyes lit up, hopeful the road trip was coming to a close and he'd see Sarah soon and know she was okay. "How much farther is Wisconsin?"

"Depends on where you're going. You just wanna hit the state, you can do that in about four hours at Iron Mountain."

"Eagle River? Valley Mill, actually," Mark corrected himself, since the town was before Eagle River.

The officers exchanged a glance and shrugged as the taller officer's shoulder mike squawked.

"Hey Dan, you and Greg near the bridge? We got a trailer accident at the Gaylord exit."

"We're in Indian River, Shirl… Heading up there now." The officer looked up at Jarvis who'd already grabbed lids for their to-go cups, and then nodded to Mark. "You have a good trip. The BP right on the other side of the bridge has more cherry coffee if you like it."

They spun and left as Gina walked around the end of the aisle.

"Making friends, are ya?" She smiled while shaking a single serving bottle of orange juice.

"Two dead hookers. Lake-effect snow-fog. Cherry coffee…" He snapped the lid on his coffee cup. "Pinball and blind hunters. Michigan…"

"Sucks." Gina finished his sentence, though it wasn't what he was going to say. "We're about thirty minutes to the bridge. I wanna see it, and then I'm crashing. Your lovechild mixed with snow-fog wiped me out."

"The bridge, eh?"

"Yeah, I saw a sign back a few miles for the radio station for weather on the bridge and listened to that for a few minutes. Some interesting history tidbits they throw in there between weather loops."

"If you fall asleep before we get there, do you want me to nudge you?"

"It's only half an hour, I'll be fine."

Mark smiled and walked her to the checkout to pay for their beverages and fuel. He knew better. She could fall asleep anywhere, under any conditions, in no time flat.

Gina was right about the bridge though. The Mackinaw was impressive in the middle of Michigan's nothingness. As was the coastline after it, as Mark switched from 75 North to 2 West. After that, they entered more of the nothingness he'd come to know as Michigan.

He debated waking her up to see the shore but knew she'd be mad about the bridge. He decided to just claim he had tried but she was too tired and wouldn't wake up. She could see it all on the way back home. Instead, he paused for another cup of cherry coffee, which was possibly the best damn coffee he'd ever gotten—gas station or otherwise—and was happy to find they sold the grounds in bags for home brewing. He bought three bags and two donuts from the BP station the cops had directed him to and returned to the road.

In a sense, being able to see his surroundings in the light of day, made the miles go by faster. But in another way, he felt like he'd been in this state forever and wondered if it ever truly ended or just kept going until he reached the end of the world. Or Canada.

Mark drove without the radio for over three hours while Gina made peaceful little noises in the passenger seat. He occasionally checked the temperature gauge in awe but finally decided to just ignore it. Apparently spring didn't arrive in April in the Midwest.

He passed a handful of tiny towns, Escanaba—which he imagined, based on the size, was the hub of Michigan's Upper Peninsula—and finally saw the sign for Wisconsin. He had noticed on the map Highway 2 dipped into Wisconsin and back into Michigan, but couldn't for the life of him remember what the highway was to stay in Wisconsin. The simple sound of folding the paper over the staple to read the end of the printed directions was enough to wake Gina.

She stretched like a cat and shivered as the chill of sleep caught up to the crisp air that snuck into the SUV's various air leaks. She glanced at the temperature gauge first and then at the clock before glowering at him and growling verbally. Mark immediately knew he'd made a mistake not waking her for the bridge, but he'd prepared for this.

"I have donuts…"

"You suck as a driving partner, you know that?"

"Oh yeah? I could say you have copilot fail. You haven't been keeping me awake or talking to me or staying awake when I drive at all…" He watched her face to see if she was awake enough to catch his tone and couldn't decide, so he forced the tomfoolery. "Of course, you have a good excuse. I mean, what with the lovechild and all…" He smiled.

"You suck."

"I thought Michigan sucked?"

"Oh it does. Oh God, don't tell me we're still in Michigan!"

"For about five minutes, love, then we escape to Wisconsin." He paused and laughed internally, "That sounds ridiculous."

"Or like a visitor bureau ad. Hate Michigan? Escape to Wisconsin." She finally smiled her weary morning smile and Mark knew she'd forgiven him for missing the bridge. He decided not to push his luck and tell her about the shoreline though.

Gina plucked the directions from his hand and retrieved her orange juice bottle from the cup holder, shaking it furiously while she scanned the printed pages.

"Where are we?"

"Just about to get off Highway 2. What road do I want?"

"Ah, okay. Here we are." She didn't point to the map, the directions or give any other physical clue to match her words. "You need to go west at 70."

"Seventy. Got it."

She took a few swigs of the warm orange juice and looked around for the donuts. Spotting them on the backseat, she pulled the box forward and flipped open the top. "You ate all the good ones didn't you?"

"I bought them in Michigan…"

"Glaze, powder and chocolate only?"

"Yep."

"Okay then." She pulled a chocolate donut out, put the box back on the rear seat, and put her feet back on the dash. "Holy shit." She pulled her feet away. "The window is freaking frozen. Damn." She tucked her feet under her instead and pulled the blanket around her.

As they entered Wisconsin, both of them flipping off the empty highway behind them that signified Michigan, Gina plugged in her iPod. She began scrolling through songs, singing a verse here and there between bites of her breakfast. Iron Mountain had been a blip of a small town, and they'd almost missed it as one of their markers. A few miles outside they'd seen a sign on a long strip of nothing, handwritten, crookedly, on a weathered board that may have once been white. Neither of them said a word, but a peal of laughter broke out in unison, ending with Gina wiping tears from her face and a mutual agreement *never* to check JIM'S MEATS down the desolate dirt road with no end in sight.

"I saw that movie…" Gina said between laughing fits.

"I don't care if he's got the best meat on the planet, there's no way I'd drive down there to find out." Mark gasped for breath and held his side.

The next hour was less than uneventful. Worrisome, in Mark's opinion. Following the instructions Google had given them, they questioned each other a few times, verbally as well as with nothing more than incredulous gawking looks of disbelief, regarding Wisconsin being even more barren of life than Michigan had been. Just as Mark was debating pulling over and checking the directions again, believing they'd taken a wrong turn, their destination arrived as if magically out of a crop of thick pines, in the form of a small wooden sign on a crooked post at the end of a dirt road.

VALLEY MILL
Pop. 67

The wood had been whitewashed numerous times and the smudge of a number changed as often, causing a shadow under the current number. Mark wondered if the number had been going up or down, as he turned right onto the loose gravel road that led into the dark forest between two walls of trees.

CHAPTER FIFTEEN

The road into Valley Mill turned again just past a small fenced cemetery. Six markers were scattered across the dead grass inside the whitewashed pickets—a very small population of forgotten family, shaded by ancient oaks and pines that hadn't been cleared for them, but rather, allowed their intrusion in the natural opening under their canopy. The smallest stone marked the freshest patch of overturned ground, and Mark saw Gina absently place a hand on her stomach as she swallowed loudly.

Mark and Gina looked from the graveyard to each other and back again without a chance to comment before the dense tree line opened up into a small community. Ahead of them, Mark could see several homes on either side of the road with additional buildings scattered beyond and behind.

The dirt road smoothed slightly as they slowly passed the first houses, neat ranch styles with clean, ornament-free yards with patches of sprouting green grass behind pristine white picket fences, which mimicked the cemetery boundaries. The siding appeared wood and freshly painted on both homes, the roofs crisp, tidy. There were no vehicles on either side of the street, save for an old Schwinn bicycle leaning against the fence of the right. On the left, the first home showed no signs of life at all. On the right, a teenage boy sat on the front steps, seeming to contemplate in great thought the cast on his right hand. He looked up as they drove past, furrowing his brows and hopping up to hurriedly enter the house.

Gina waved wildly as she had been throughout the road trip to truckers, children in backseats, and strangers that "looked like they needed a smile," but she was too late and the only motion she received for her effort was a screen door slamming.

The next two homes—slightly jagged and not exactly across from each other like the first two had been—were large two-story A-frames. Again, white fences marked the yards where the new spring grass was free of toys, trash or decoration. Gina raised an eyebrow at Mark, but he wasn't sure which of the several questions in his own mind she could be insinuating.

"Cleaner-looking than some of the run-down towns we've driven through." He proffered, "Though kinda quiet…"

"I'd say creepy but it seems to be a given. Where is everyone?"

"Well, it's only a little before three, they could all be at work, in school, whatever."

"Really, Mark? Where would they work?"

"Oh come on. We have people that live in the boondocks by us. They commute. Hell, some people in town commute to the next town. It's not unusual."

"No it's…"

"Let's not make assumptions, okay. I'm having a hard enough time with all of this, I don't need your imagination making it worse."

"Did you just scold me?" Gina eyed him through her lashes with a full-lipped pout.

"No. No, baby. I'm sorry." He smiled slightly at her. "Just using my cop voice, sorry. I'm just trying to absorb everything for what it is, rather than what I think it could be. It's a—"

"I know. You're detecting…" She smiled back at him. "I'm just tired and excited and worried all at once."

Mark let her apology and reasoning hang in the air and returned his focus in front of him. The A-frames were definitely older than the ranch houses had been, but the same person could have done the upkeep and landscaping. A small stretch of field on either side took up at least half a city block before they got to the final two buildings where the town opened up into a central hub of sorts, various roads shooting out in several directions.

There was no stop sign, but Mark stopped anyway, as he and Gina took in the town his sister had been living in for the last ten years. The first thing Mark noticed explained the lack of traffic signs. There was no traffic. Not that it wasn't moving, it just didn't exist. Looking down the side streets he could see and ahead of them, around what appeared to be an open-air gazebo in the center of the street, he could see no other vehicles.

The center square, or rather octagon, had eight buildings. To his immediate left was an ancient sprawling farmhouse, complete with wraparound porch and corner turret. The clean white paint was highlighted with olive green on the gables, window trim and porch rails. Not horribly ornate, but more than the previous homes had been, though the olive green matched the roof and therefore seemed muted. On the porch, an old man sat in a wicker chair, his chin to his chest, dozing with a blanket across his legs to block the chilly afternoon air.

To the right was an A-frame like those behind them, with blue trim on the front and playground equipment barely visible around the other side of the building. The first sign of children Mark had seen since the kid with the broken hand and abandoned bicycle. Mark sighed, as the sight somehow made him feel better.

Continuing counterclockwise, another sprawling country home with olive trim was followed by a very plain white building. The front of the building was taller, almost tower or turret-like, with several shallow but wide steps leading to double doors—a sign of some sort posted on the left door. Immediately behind the building were several picnic tables and more homes. Mark realized the town spread out like spokes of a great wheel and wondered if this building was the town hall.

Past the town hall was another row of homes, the first of which was another olive-trimmed farmhouse, though not nearly as large or ornate as the first two he'd seen. A smallish A-frame across the street from it had a placard next to the door Mark couldn't make out from his vantage point, obscured as it was by the gazebo. Another large farmhouse across from it, followed by what could only be a store of some sort with its large front windows.

"Should we just park here and try the town hall?" Gina spoke with a dull tone, apparently mesmerized by the simple buildings and design of the town. Mark smiled to himself, amused she had come to the same conclusion as he had regarding the building on the right.

"Sure." He put the SUV into park, rolled up his window and turned off the ignition.

Opening the door, Gina shivered. "Holy crap, it's freezing here." She turned to fetch her coat from the backseat.

They walked across the street in silence. Mark's mind working in several directions, as he watched windows for activity. He noticed the sounds of livestock coming from his right and some sort of machinery in the distance to the left. With no traffic or other city noises, and no people chatting, clomping or otherwise making their presence known, the town was quiet enough to feel like a ghost town.

They walked up the shallow steps of the hall to the double doors and Mark's shoulders slumped as his eyebrows raised. The windows on either side of the doors had crosses in the stained-glass panes, and Mark realized his mistaken identity of the building. As he started to believe perhaps a church would still be helpful for finding his sister, he read the note posted on the door.

Back at 4 p.m.

He glanced at his watch, knowing he'd just checked it and it wouldn't be any closer to four than it had been when he told Gina is wasn't quite three.

"Well…?" Gina turned toward him as he turned back toward the town square.

"There's probably someone in the store. It's a tiny town. I'm sure they know—"

Before Mark could finish, the doors in the blue-trimmed A-frame opened and a stream of children came through them, their voices preceding their footsteps. Mark watched as a foursome of late teens came into the afternoon sun with lowered heads and quiet voices, as if whispering to one another or making secret plans. Behind them a handful of younger teens broke into the afternoon with enthusiasm and Mark realized it had been their voices he'd heard, as it dawned on him the building was obviously a small schoolhouse. He couldn't make out anything they were saying until a simply dressed blonde pointed at the SUV and the group turned like a flock of birds, their excited voices raising as one. Mark didn't notice the four smaller children at the end of the pack until the older ones turned away and exposed them.

As the gaggle of children circled Gina's truck, obviously peering in the windows and pointing to the belongings inside, Mark wondered if he'd locked the doors out of habit and reached in his pocket, intending to push the button on the remote and prevent the kids from getting into the SUV. He stopped short of locating the plastic square among the coins in his pocket, as the smaller children, still on the steps, parted suddenly and an adult pushed her way past them and onto the front steps.

"Shoo!" She threw her arms out in front of her, like a magician commanding the elements. "You all have chores." Tall and thin, the brunette didn't necessarily raise her voice so much as she lowered the tone enough to make her point. A long braid down her back, twists of brown and red highlights glinting in the sun, made her appear barely older than the children she commanded. Mark wondered for a moment how a young teacher ends up in a tiny town in the middle of nowhere. *Craig's List?* He smiled uncomfortably to himself.

The children scattered down the various spokes of the square, three of them headed toward Mark and Gina. The blonde who had pointed to the SUV hollered promises over her shoulder to meet at the schoolyard after dinner and two other girls yelled back "Okay."

The smaller ones, still parted on the steps, smiled up at the young teacher. A tiny twig of a boy, no older than seven, spoke in a squeaky voice. The only thing Mark could clearly understand was the word "tomorrow" that clung to the end of his sentence and broadened his smile. The quartet bounced down the steps and headed down various spokes of roadway toward home, as the teacher quietly returned to the darkness inside the doorway and closed the entrance behind her.

The three teens, a boy and two girls, walked right past the church where Mark and Gina stood, frozen by the sudden appearance of life in the previously quiet town square. The trio didn't seem to notice the two of them standing there, as they chatted quietly and walked down the street to Mark's right. He turned and watched as the first two entered the second ranch-style home on the short street and the pointing blonde skipped the rest of the way to the third, disappearing into the front door whistling a tune Mark didn't recognize.

"Well that was…"

"Did you see her fingers?" Gina interrupted.

"Yeah, when she pointed. I thought she pointed with a fist at first…"

"Me, too, but she waved just now. She's missing two fingers, Mark." Gina's eyes were wide. "How does a young girl lose her fingers?"

"The boy had a cast on his wrist." Mark looked back at the house the children had gone into. "Maybe they were in the same accident."

"Accident? Where's a car around here to be in an accident?" Gina furrowed her brows at him, a silent version of tapping her foot.

"Farming accident, maybe?" Mark said it to ease Gina, as much as he said it to feel better about the situation himself, Reilly's words echoing in his memory.

Gina opened her mouth to speak but closed it again.

"Store," Mark stated rather than suggested, and grabbed Gina's hand, pulling her gently as he headed back down the church steps. "I need to find Sarah."

CHAPTER SIXTEEN

A tiny bell rang as Mark pulled the wooden door of the store open and held it for Gina. He let the door swing gently shut behind him as he entered the building and gave his eyes a moment to adjust to the truth around him.

Several rows of metal shelving were well stocked with canned and boxed goods, household staples such as toilet paper, and various baskets of sewing supplies. The left wall was a bank of coolers and freezers with a wide but small variety of dairy products and meat. A small wooden table near the door had a spiral notebook and pen on it, the exposed page half-full of neatly labeled lists with names next to them. Mark was struck with how very quaint it was, a lost five-and-dime store. The wooden door and sign-free front windows created an understated wall, protecting stained plank floors and a smell that was wholesome and stale at the same time. He would have believed he'd gone back in time or driven into an Amish community if not for the obvious electricity needed for the coolers and the old metal light fixtures swinging from the rafters throwing their artificial light across the country store.

A blur of pink came from a dark corner and startled Mark as his eyes focused on the shadows next to the counter where the older woman had appeared. Somewhere in her late fifties or early sixties, the woman's skin was fresh scrubbed, devoid of makeup and taut, giving her a younger appearance only betrayed by the hint of crow's feet at her eyes and smattering of gray in her otherwise red hair. A light pink sweater and deep pink skirt provided a splash of summer—the color choices gave added vibrancy to both her skin tone and hair color. A shapely leg peeked from beneath the skirt and the curve of her figure was that of a lean dancer cursed with too much cleavage. She was stunning and Mark found himself a little embarrassed to be looking at her unassuming form and thinking those things, as she was probably old enough to be his mother.

"Well hello, folks." Mark could hear the smile in her voice and was compelled to grin in response to the infectious joy. "Name's Camille Andrews, what can I do for you?" She pulled a pencil from the loose bun in her hair, a few strands pulled free with the pencil and cascaded down to her chin, which she absently pushed behind her ear.

Gina followed Mark as he closed the gap between the door and the counter, quietly shadowing his footsteps while holding the back of his coat out of the shopkeeper's view.

"Hello." Mark paused, unsure if he should offer his hand or whether the Amish found it offensive to touch their women, and reminded himself it wasn't Amish. He kept his hands at his side anyway. "I'm looking for Sarah…" He fumbled, realizing he couldn't remember Josh's last name. Introduced to him over ten years before and having not ever really thought about him or his name in the time since Sarah left.

Camille's brows furrowed and her age was suddenly apparent in the creases streaking across her face, like branches of a river creating new tributaries in a moment of spring flooding. "What has she done now?"

"I…" Mark stammered, taken aback by the stern tone and matching expression, on a face that had been previously pleasant and appealing. "I didn't tell you which Sarah…"

"I only know one Sarah. And if you're looking for a Sarah in this town, then it would have to be Sarah Andrews." Camille's lip flattened as she made what Mark could only equate to disappointment. He didn't have time to fully absorb the fact the name was the same and clarify he wasn't looking for her daughter, before she clarified both her meaning and her right to be disappointed in whatever she may have done. "My daughter-in-law."

Mark stood upright. He hadn't been expecting those words. Hadn't even considered the very real truth he'd be meeting in-laws when he came to Valley Mill and was stunned he'd never entertained the idea of the obvious. He remembered Josh's dark brown hair and forgave himself the oversight, as the woman's red hair and features looked nothing like Mark's memory of his sister's boyfriend. Husband.

"She's my sister," was all Mark could think to say. His voice was dry. Hollow. Offered neither as a defense to the shopkeeper's sudden attitude, nor an apology. He pondered Camille's disappointment, the change in her expression at the mention of his sister's name, and felt frozen in the moment, unsure what to make of the cloud that had covered the sunshine of both the woman's smile and colorful attitude.

A tall man walked out from the shadows behind Camille and Mark wondered for a moment if it was an aged Josh. The build and color matched Mark's memory, and the age seemed right, but Camille filled in the blank quickly.

"Michael, what are you doing up? I told you to stay in bed." The man opened his mouth to speak but she cocked her head like only a mother can. "You are still running a fever and you will do as you're told." He rolled his eyes and retreated back into the shadows without a word.

Camille returned her attention to Mark as if they'd never been interrupted. The silence hung as Mark and the shopkeeper studied each other, watched each other, a standoff for no reason.

"Hi." Gina stepped forward and took over, glancing at Mark as she leaned past him and offered her hand to the woman. "I'm Gina. This is Mark. It's lovely to meet you."

Camille pulled her gaze from Mark and turned to Gina, reaching out and shaking her hand. "Nice to meet you, Gina." She spoke to Gina but returned her gaze to Mark. "I thought Sarah's brother lived in Pennsylvania?"

"Oh we do," Gina replied. "We were just—"

"Visiting." Mark interrupted. "We decided it was time to visit."

"Well, the timing is perfect. She'll need family in the coming weeks."

Mark wondered if Sarah was pregnant and close to her due date. Reilly had said she had a baby but didn't mention how old it was, or even the sex, Mark realized. If it was old enough, she could be having another. Or perhaps something was wrong with the baby. Or Sarah. Mark's mind tried to spin into the world of imagined horrors but he reined it in. Neither allowing himself to create realities nor asking Camille to clarify. He'd let Sarah tell him.

"Where can we find her?" Mark questioned, while half expecting

Camille to just holler and have Sarah walk from the back shadows as she had.

Camille glanced at the clock on the wall behind her. "She should be home now." The smile was back on her face but the pleasantry in her voice sounded forced. "She and my son live in the second house behind the shop."

"Same...block?" Mark wondered what they called the patches between the spokes of roadway where the homes and yards were enclosed with matching fences.

"Yes." Camille grabbed a ledger book and flipped it open, finding busy work to bring an end to the conversation. "Last house before the fields. You can't miss it."

"Thank you." Gina smiled and grabbed Mark's hand, turning him toward the door.

"Yes, thanks." Mark spoke on autopilot. "And it was nice to meet you. I'm sure we'll be seeing each other again while we're here."

"I'm sure we will." Camille spoke without looking up.

They hadn't heard her move as they headed to the door and Mark was startled to hear the door click behind them. He turned back in time to see Camille hang a "Back in 15" sign on the doorknob and disappear into the back of the store.

"Checking on Michael's fever?" Gina offered.

Mark didn't respond. He simply walked around the building and headed toward the last house behind the shop.

"You don't want the car?" Gina stood at the edge of the building.

"Nah. See?" He pointed ahead of them. "The house is right there. Might as well leave the car for now." His rush to find his sister had been fueled by the memory of the letter, the comments from Reilly, and now the strange words and tone from Sarah's mother-in-law.

"'Kay..." Gina's voice trailed off as she hurried to catch up to him.

Mark was scanning the yard for life the moment Sarah's home came into full view. The ranch-style home was a freshly painted stark white, just like the rest of the town. The picket fence surrounding her yard was whitewashed and the yard behind it free of any type of personality. The sterile homes and yards were pristine. It made the town clean. But it was also unnerving Mark on some level. It reminded him of Benny's neighbor in a way. The older woman had more in her yard though—perfectly placed piles of polished stone and white chips of quartz with small ceramic animals, strategically placed and almost too kept. Mark and Benny would move the animals around when they were bored, switching their positions or lining them all up down the side of the driveway. When the woman noticed—and she always did, which made Mark think she sat by her windows all day long—she would come running out of the house yelling at them and hurriedly put each animal back. The same psychosis that kept her sprinting from her window perch was evident here, Mark thought, just on a more sterile level. And here it wasn't a single old woman with nothing better to do. It was uniform across the small town.

Sarah's windows each had white lace curtains. The front step had an empty pot on either side, which Mark imagined would hold flowers once the temperature allowed. No driveway. No vehicle. No bike or children's toys. It looked very much like a home that was cleaned to the point of abandonment and put on the market.

His pace picked up and he crossed the small path through the yard in a handful of steps, a finger already poised for the doorbell when his foot hit the step. No doorbell evident, Mark curled his fingers into a fist and rapped lightly on the door. Taking a step back, he glanced at Gina. Her face was pinched and he questioned her with a quizzical tilt of his head.

"Oh I just gotta pee again, that's all. No worries, baby." Gina nodded toward the house. "Knock again. Harder."

He did. After several moments without a response he looked around and noticed Gina's pinched expression again. "We could head back to the store and see if Mrs. Andrews has a bathroom you could use." He stepped down from the single step, nothing more than a pseudoporch. "Maybe she knows where Sarah would be if not home…" Gina nodded and they crossed the short path back to the street.

Walking in silence, Mark tried to ignore the quiet of the small town and crispness of the air, but was too anxious to allow himself the momentary appeal. He was so close to finding Sarah but was still chasing shadows, and it frustrated the hell out of him.

He looked up and saw the teacher from earlier walking down the road toward them. She kicked rocks on the road in front of her and paid no attention to her surroundings, fiddling with the long braid, which she had pulled forward to fall down her bosom. A lilt in her gait and a soft tune humming through her closed lips. Her clothes were much like that of the storekeeper, a sweater and skirt, though the teacher's were a navy skirt with a multicolored sweater, and where Mrs. Andrews had black flats on, the teacher's footwear was a simple white lace-up sneaker. She appeared fuzzy as she drew closer and he realized it was the sweater itself, the fibers popping free of the weave in a strategic pattern. He was debating stopping her and asking if she knew where Sarah was when she noticed them and stopped.

The humming was silenced. The braid dropped, forgotten. The teacher squinted at Mark, only ten yards away, as though the sun were in her eyes. She slowly stood taller, her eyes widening as her posture straightened. She sprinted forward and threw her arms around his neck, knocking him off balance and causing him to teeter before catching himself.

"Sarah?" He spoke into her hair, noticing a baby sleeping in a carrier on her back.

She pulled away, eyes welling with tears that juxtaposed the impossibly wide smile on her lips. "Wow, you look just like Dad."

Sarah.

He pulled her back into his arms and hugged her again, completely forgetting Gina standing there until he heard her gentle reminder.

"Ahem…"

He released Sarah with the intention of introducing her to Gina, but she spoke first, "Why? How?" She looked back over her shoulder at the SUV. "How'd you find me?"

"Reilly." He smiled, knowing she'd remember him and know exactly the skills that had landed Mark in her backyard.

Her eyes narrowed, she glanced to Gina and back to Mark. Fear crept into her eyes, drowning out the joy that had brought tears only moments earlier. "You can't be here."

CHAPTER SEVENTEEN

What?" Mark's incredulous tone was echoed in his shocked expression. "What do you mean we can't be here?"

"Well…it's not that you can't be, but you shouldn't be. Not now." Sarah looked around the quiet street. "Not now."

"Sar—" Mark started to question, to debate, but Gina cut him off, pushing herself between them and hugging Sarah without invitation.

"Hi! I'm Gina and your niece or nephew is beating the crap out of my bladder." She patted her stomach. "Is there any chance we could discuss this closer to a bathroom?"

Sarah laughed and hugged Gina back. "Congrats!" She turned back to Mark, "Is this the first? You have others with you?"

"No no, just this little surprise," Mark said winking at Gina.

"Well, you've got a few years left. There can be more." Holding Gina's hand she pulled toward her house. "Come on in."

Inside the simple one-story ranch home, Mark was surprised to find it looked and felt just like any other house he'd been in. For whatever reason, he figured the quiet life of the town and simplistic feel of the community would carry over into the private lives, but it seemed like any other house to him. Furniture, simple decorations—plants, family pictures, heirlooms—and electricity made him forget he was in the middle of a forest somewhere in the armpit of the universe. He would have forgotten completely, except for the missing television.

"No television?" He scanned the living room, centered on a fireplace rather than a box filled with sitcoms and dramas meant to entertain. Both sides of the fireplace had floor-to-ceiling overstuffed bookshelves, and Mark assumed reading was their entertainment.

"Nothing good on it anyway." Sarah pulled the straps of the baby carrier off her shoulders, as she returned from showing Gina where the bathroom was. "Wanna meet your nephew?" She looked up at Mark from her squatted position, undoing the straps and gently pulling the still-sleeping babe from the nestling material.

"Yeah…" He moved next to Sarah and bent down.

"Mark, this is Mark." She paused a moment and watched her brother's face. "You two can fight over who I said first."

"Really?" He felt his chest tighten. Several memories of Sarah as a baby flashed through his mind and he remembered how much it sucked when she first disappeared. He remembered trying to find her. And giving up.

But here he was. Here she was. Alive and okay.

"Baby!" Gina exclaimed as she rounded the corner from the kitchen, the bladder-bursting discomfort on her face replaced with glee. "Oh my God, he's adorable. How old is he? What's his name? Can I hold him?" Gina's questions came in rapid succession, her worries about the town and Sarah forgotten.

Mark smiled, wondering if this was the nesting thing she'd explained to him during the first trimester. He looked to Sarah for the answers and he realized she wasn't just showing him his nephew, she'd been about to hand him a sleeping baby. "It's okay. Go ahead…" Sarah stood up with little Mark and handed him gently to Gina's open, waiting arms. "His name is Mark, though I guess that'll be confusing at the moment, so Marky I guess. He's just shy of seven months, so he's spunky. Thinks he's strong enough to do everything but he barely sits on his own without toppling sometimes, other days he's crawling all over the place like someone put a battery in him."

Gina spun, cooing and whispering to the baby as if it were awake. She walked back into the kitchen with a slight bounce meant to rock the baby but Mark thought it would jostle him awake.

"So?" He turned back to Sarah. "What's with the letter? Why after all this time?"

"That's how you found me, isn't it? Even without a return address on it." She eyed the hardwood floor at her feet and shook her head. "Damn."

"What the hell is going on?" He looked around the house again, inspecting it for signs of something wrong, something out of place, and found nothing. "You sounded like you were never going to see me again. Ever. Suicidal or some craziness. Scared the hell out of me, Sarah-Bear."

"Oh," her eyes widened in shock. "I'm sorry, Sparky." She smiled as she used the nickname she knew he hated and waited for a reaction. He didn't give her one and she continued. "I didn't mean to scare you or worry you. And I shouldn't have written it in the first place. I'm just going through…well, a tough time, and I was thinking of you and missed you."

She stepped closer and gave him another hug, holding him tightly with her arms while her hands fiddled, almost poking him to see if he was real. Mark wondered if she worried letting go would make him disappear like a phantom daydream that was never there.

"Sarah!" The low voice boomed through the living room as the front door slammed shut. "Have you not learned? Will you learn after…"

Sarah let go of Mark and turned toward the door. "No, Josh, no. It's Mark." She walked to her husband, tentatively reaching out for his hand. "My brother. Remember Mark? You guys met a few times before we left PA and came back here."

Joshua Andrews looked Mark up and down several times, glanced sideways at Sarah and back to Mark. His face seemed to relax and a much calmer, quieter timbre controlled his voice. "Mark? Is that really you?" He closed the gap between them in several short steps and stuck his hand out to Mark.

Mark shook it and gave Sarah a quizzical look over Josh's shoulder. She answered by simply shrugging her shoulders. Mark returned his attention to Josh and saw an older but aging-well version of the boy Sarah had invited to dinner so many years before. "You look good, man." He put a hand on Josh's shoulder and they both turned toward Sarah in time to see Gina come out of the kitchen. "And the baby is adorable. Congrats."

Joshua's smile faded and he glared at Sarah. It was quick. It was meant to be subtle and unnoticeable, but Mark had seen it. He'd also shifted his gaze to Sarah in time to watch her recoil slightly at the subtle anger of Josh's expression. She quickly put a smile back on her face and turned to the kitchen, ignoring the moment Mark hadn't been meant to see.

"Well, we have guests now…" He heard a cupboard open and

close. "I'm going to have to adjust dinner plans, Josh. There's just not enough tenderloin for all of us."

"That's okay. Put it back in the freezer. We can have that another day. After Mark's gone," Josh called to Sarah and then turned to Mark. "So, how long *are* you staying?"

The smile went with the pleasant, if not overly polite, tone was perfect. But Josh's eyes gave away unease, which made Mark wonder what he'd walked into and his thoughts returned to both the letter and Sarah's comment regarding his timing. *You shouldn't be here. Not now.*

Mark turned and silently questioned Gina, still holding the baby. She shrugged and he turned back to Josh. "I don't know, really. I hadn't planned any certain length of time and I just got here so I haven't discussed it with Sarah." As an afterthought, he tried to goad Josh into explaining the looks and strange comments. "Unless it's a bad time. Then we can always adjust our plans."

Josh seemed to perk up at the idea but didn't get a chance to say anything before Sarah came back in the room. "Spaghetti work for everyone? I can make enough of that for a small army without even trying."

Mark and Josh both nodded, still eyeballing each other—one with a thousand questions, the other with an expression Mark could only equate to scrutiny and anxiety. Gina smiled wide. "Oh yes, that sounds lovely. I haven't had spaghetti since I got pregnant…" She looked off to the side and seemed to be in thought for a moment. "Probably because I always always always have red wine with spaghetti and I'm not drinking right now."

"Well, we don't have wine, so you still won't get any." Sarah winked at her playfully.

Josh broke in and turned the comment serious. "We don't have alcohol in Valley Mill. Ever."

"Really?" Mark's voice lilted in disbelief.

"We don't imbibe or partake in anything that alters the mind or clouds the conscience." His voice was monotonous, as if he were reading his response off a cue card.

"I see." Mark thought of the little church, simple clothes, lack of vehicles and Reilly's comments regarding Amish country. The town might be pristine and quaint, but there was definitely an underlying layer of something Mark hadn't figured out yet. His detective instincts were now on full alert, scrutinizing every exchange, in word choices and body language.

As if on cue, baby Mark woke with a startled cry and broke the silence hanging between the men. Sarah took him back from Gina, excusing herself to change and feed him.

"I'll come help you." Josh followed her down the hall to the last room on the right, leaving Gina and Mark in the space where the kitchen, living room and hallway intersected.

Gina turned to Mark with eyes that danced, full of thought, but only offered a weak "Well, she looks good."

"There's something going on," Mark added, glancing down the hallway. "There was more to that letter. I'm not crazy. I think she just didn't expect me to react and show up. And she had no idea how to talk to Josh about it on the spot."

"Well, there's something…but let's not assume it's bad. Maybe she really was just missing you. Maybe—"

Gina was cut off by a sharp "No" from beyond the door Sarah and Josh had closed behind them. Mark and Gina both snapped their heads down the hall. Mark listened intently but couldn't make much out, and assumed Gina was doing the same.

"Are you crazy?"

"I didn't think…" The rest of the sentence was muted and muffled.

"…next Friday."

"No one. I did it…" Sarah's voice sounded panicked and Mark fought the urge to barge into the argument, but stood his ground for a moment, still assessing.

"Eagle River?"

"Peter's horse…"

"Now you're stealing?"

"No. I brought it back…"

"I don't even know you anymore, Sarah." The door opened and closed rapidly as Josh came back toward the kitchen, Mark and Gina standing there uncomfortably watching him like children caught with

117

their hands in the cookie jar.

Mark realized his last words were clear because they were spoken right next to the door and wondered if Josh would try to explain the argument Mark and Gina had obviously overheard, not knowing they had been unable to make out most of it. Instead, he surprised Mark.

"You know, it's probably a good thing you're here right now." Josh grabbed a brown satchel from behind the corner of the living room and opened the door. "She's going to need all the support she can get in the coming weeks." He closed the door without waiting for a response.

Sarah crept back from the bedroom, sheepishly holding the baby in front of her like an offering. "Look who's awake and wants to play with his uncle while Mommy cooks dinner." Her singsong voice cracked and he knew she was doing the Pollyanna thing she'd always done as a child—pretend the ugly wasn't there and eventually it would either go away or become pretty.

"Sarah…" Mark took the baby and handed it to Gina, following Sarah into the kitchen.

"Not now, Mark. Please." She began pulling pots from cupboards. "You don't understand. I chose to live like this. I knew what I was doing."

"What exactly did you choose? What are you talking about?" Fear and worry crept past his unsuccessful attempt to shield them from his voice. "What the hell is going on here?"

Sarah spun at him. "Please don't swear here, Mark. Respect this is my house. My town. My life. And follow the rules."

"There are rules?" He looked back to Gina who was busy playing with the baby but glancing up occasionally and paying attention. "What rules? What's going on?"

"Just…" Sarah turned back to the process of making dinner. "Just visit. Know I'm alive and safe and happy. And then go back to Pennsylvania. Okay?"

"Really? You're going to just dismiss me like we visit once a year and this is normal? Are you crazy? I haven't seen you, haven't heard one word from you, in over ten years, and you expect me to just swallow every instinctual thing I've seen in the last hour and play along?" Mark put a hand on her shoulder and urged her to turn and face him. "Have you forgotten who you're talking to here? Have you truly forgotten your own brother?"

"Mark…" She turned and buried her head in his shoulder, sobbing quietly. "I'm so sorry I left. I'm sorry I didn't write or visit or say anything to you. I meant everything I said in that letter. But I didn't mean for you to come find me. Hunt me down like one of your criminals, track me to the middle of nowhere, where I never expected you'd find me, and demand answers."

She looked up at him and Mark saw his mother's eyes, except this version was full of tears and pain and something like shame or humility. She released her hold on him and twisted back to the stove, leaving him with more questions and more worry. He'd never seen anyone he loved with this expression. Raw emotion, tumbling fear and love together and pouring them out in wordless tears with no explanation, no reason.

"I have no answers, Mark."

"Sare, I don't even know the questions…" Mark wasn't sure what was happening, but he knew he didn't like it. He didn't like seeing his sister after ten years and finding her playing Pollyanna with secret tears and some bizarre hidden shame.

From the living room floor, Gina tried to lighten the situation. "Little Mark has big Mark's eyes." Her own eyes were wide and pleaded with Mark to stop the uncomfortable interrogation. Mark agreed. This was supposed to be a reunion. This was supposed to be Mark rescuing his sister from something horrible he'd thought was deep depression. But now he wondered if Sarah was ever the threat and looked beyond Gina to the door Josh had walked out a few moments before.

"Where'd Josh go?"

"His mother's. Well, the store actually. There's a light acting up he wanted to fix before dinner. It shouldn't take him long." She peered over her shoulder to Mark and then to Gina, apologetically adding. "He's actually very good at what he does. And he's a good man. A good husband."

Mark let her have the last word for now, and quit asking questions. "Okay." He went to the living room and squatted down next to Gina.

"Let me see this nephew of mine."

Mark picked the baby up and smiled at the familiar family features he could pick out. The boy smiled back at him as if he knew him and giggled softly, drool escaping the corner of his mouth in a happy bubble and exposing two viciously sharp teeth on the bottom. As Mark played with the boy, wiggling his fingers and swooping in and out at the child, he noticed a purple blemish on the boy's side when his T-shirt slipped up.

"Is this a birthmark, Sarah? We don't have those," he answered his own question. Then asked a different one. "Josh's family have those? And how is it that you only have one baby? I thought you wanted five and would have ten by now." His voice was light and jovial, meant to deflate the earlier situation with some light sibling jabbing. Her response was not jovial.

Instead of answering him, Mark heard Sarah gasp and begin to sniffle back a precursor to unexpected tears, leaving him to wonder again what he'd stumbled into the middle of and how deep in it his sister had dug herself.

After dinner, the three of them sat in front of the fireplace while Sarah gave Marky a bath and put him to bed. A low, controlled fire gave the room a comfortable glow, counteracting the strain hanging in the air between Mark and Josh. Gina managed to fill the void by talking about baby name choices and the trip through Michigan, at one point asking Josh, a smile camouflaging her snarky voice, "Does it ever get warm here?"

He laughed, "In the summer it does. Mostly eighties with a week or so of nineties. Winter just tends to be a bit stubborn about leaving on time lately, that's all."

When Sarah returned she brought three coffees and a hot chocolate. The mood lightened considerably. Sarah and Josh bounced back and forth talking about life in Valley Mill. Mark learned Josh's electrician license was utilized by the town as he was the local wire man when needed, but otherwise helped either his mother in the store or the boys in the barn with the town's livestock. Although she had quit college in Pennsylvania to come here, Mark was pleasantly surprised to hear Sarah had indeed gone back and finished her degree, returning the following year to get a teaching certificate. She now taught the local children with another woman, Naomi, who let Sarah concentrate on music, art and other creative classes, while Naomi concentrated on the sciences. He was fascinated to hear the students went off to college and returned with degrees and higher-education classes to further the community, with only two deciding not to return over the years.

The conversation continued to be polite and inconsequential. Josh and Sarah took turns explaining how the town had its own garden and farm, mostly self-sustained, and only needed the store—supplied from the outside world—for oddities and a trading center between families. The produce, dairy and meat they'd seen in the store had all come from the community itself. The clothing they'd seen was also locally made. Only the packaged stock had come from the outside world, and they rather liked it that way. They had a doctor, a minister, a carpenter, a plumber and Josh was the local electrician. They had everything they needed to survive. To survive without the atrocities of the outside world. The air was clean, the food was fresh and there was almost no crime.

"Almost," Josh had said looking at Sarah with a tender voice.

"I brought the horse back."

"I'm not talking about the horse…" Josh looked down the hall toward the bedrooms.

Mark would have questioned it further but Sarah immediately steered the conversation to Mark and what he'd been doing lately. How the boys were, if he still hung out with them, and how the job was treating him. She was thrilled to hear he'd made detective at a young age, but frowned as he vented about the system negating his hard work on a regular basis.

"I'm sick and tired of working twenty-four/seven just so the system can let them back on the streets. I'm sick of cleaning up the messes the riffraff leave behind, the lives they destroy."

"Is it really that bad?" Sarah asked the question in Josh's eyes.

Gina responded. "It's horrible. I mean, I don't run into a lot of problems at home or work, you know. You have to be in the wrong part of town, or into the wrong things. But Mark? It's horrible for him. He listens to the scanner and chases them in the dead of night.

He works all-nighters. He comes home cranky as…heck…after court goes awry." She paused and looked at Mark. He assumed she could see the anger in his eyes as he remembered the fiasco Squeak had turned the scene into and expected her to continue ranting about his behavior regarding his job, as his knuckles whitened under the pressure of the unconscious fists he was making. He was not expecting what she did.

"But he loves his job. And for as much as he complains about the bad, he's been very successful at cleaning up the streets. He's a wonderful man, Sarah. I think your parents would be very proud." She smiled sweetly at Mark, and he felt his anger subside a little.

A little.

"I just wish it was what I thought it would be when I was a kid, you know." He looked at Josh as he spoke, hoping to connect with the little boy the man had once been. "When you played cops and robbers, you caught them and locked them up and then they tried to escape so you had to chase them again. I thought I'd be locking them up. For good. I knew real criminals rarely escaped. But I didn't realize the damn system would open the imaginary door by the tree we used for the jail and just let them run free."

"I never played cops and robbers, but I get what you're saying." Josh took a sip of coffee. "It's part of the reason we live here. Why our community is the way it is. Justice should work and the more people you add, the more problems you have."

"True. Small towns do have a much lower crime rate, but even in small towns you sometimes find the ratio is actually the same."

"Not here. Here we have control. And we don't put up with it."

"You just kick out anyone that commits a crime?"

"Something like that." Josh looked at the fire, the flames flickering down to embers and coals.

"An eye for an eye, damn it. That's how it should be. Sometimes I wish it really worked like that," Mark said, and then apologized under his breath for swearing.

Sarah spoke into her coffee cup without making eye contact. "Be careful what you wish for…"

CHAPTER EIGHTEEN

Mark wasn't shocked when Josh and Sarah insisted he and Gina sleep in separate rooms. They were, after all, under a roof other than their own and would comply. But he was shocked that it was because they were unmarried. He thought Gina being pregnant would hold some sort of leverage, but Josh was quick to point out that was only a circumstance, and "rules are rules."

Nor was Mark surprised to find Sarah and Josh up at the crack of dawn. He was only too happy to be a morning person himself and not feel like he was in their way, sleeping on the couch in the middle of the living room. He folded the blankets and slipped into the shower as they busied themselves in the kitchen.

"You don't have to help on the farm this morning?" Mark questioned Josh as he poured himself a cup of coffee and joined them.

"Usually, yes, but not today. I have guests, so Petey got Thomas to pitch in." He took a sip of coffee and leaned his neck to one side, as if to crack the bones. "How'd you sleep?"

"Fine. I was actually surprised at how comfortable I was."

"Oh I'm sure it had something to do with the drive." Sarah smiled. "My goodness, how long of a drive was that? You guys didn't drive straight through did you?"

"Oh yeah, we did. It wasn't bad overall, but like I said last night, I could have skipped most of Michigan and been just fine."

"Well, if we had an airport nearby…" Sarah let her words fade unfinished.

Josh looked at her with a quickly furrowed and then straightened brow, a silent question of her intentions and insinuation.

"I don't fly, Sarah. You know that."

She pursed her lips and nodded. He understood her forgetting. After all, they hadn't spoken or seen each other in ten years and Mark supposed she could have assumed he'd gotten over the phobia. The anger. He hadn't, but he wasn't going to let it color what had started out to be a good morning.

Mark had been watching the way they looked at each other when the other was speaking. There was a bittersweet tenderness in Sarah's eyes and the same, with just a hint of something akin to frustration in Josh's expression. In the morning light, Sarah truly did seem happy, and Josh truly did appear as though he cared as much for her as she obviously did for him. *Perhaps he'd just arrived on a bad day*, Mark thought. *After all, most couples do have bad days, moments, arguments, whatever.*

"Speaking of airports and other things, I can't seem to get a signal on my phone. Are we in a complete dead zone here? I should really check my voice mail at least."

"No one here has a cell phone. Certain conveniences come with a propensity for sin, or rather, the availability to explore the darker parts of society we try to avoid. And we have to be conscious of whether the rules will be compromised—"

Sarah interrupted, "The school has two computers to prepare the students for college and such, but otherwise we don't have that type of technology here. No need for it." Sarah dumped another spoonful of sugar in her coffee cup and stirred it, looking at Josh through her eyelashes, keeping her eyes downcast.

He was just warming up to force his way into deeper questions about the way things worked around here, specifically these "rules" they had both referred to, when Sarah startled him.

"I should go rouse Gina or we'll be late for church."

"Church? I thought you gave that up when we got out of Catholic school?"

"I did. For a while." She stood and pushed her chair back in. "I gave up on church, but not on God. I've found church here is much different. Much more like it should be. I think you'll enjoy it." She turned to head down the hall to the guest bedroom where Gina had been tucked in the night before.

"*Enjoy* might be pushing it." Mark spoke under his breath. Sarah didn't hear him. Josh did.

"You still believe in God, don't you?"

"According to my old friend Benny, only when I'm pissed at Him."

He spoke without thinking, and regretted it, believing he should probably curb his opinions while in Valley Mill.

"Really? And who do you thank when good things happen?"

"Good things?"

Sarah returned to the kitchen, a groggy Gina in tow looking for milk and cartoons and only finding the milk. "Oh stop, you two. It's not the day for that kind of talk."

"What? It's Saturday, not Sunday."

"Because Saturday is church around here. Sunday is market day. So just pretend it's Sunday in your world and behave today, okay?" Sarah winked at Mark and put a tall glass of milk and piece of toast in front of Gina. "Now how about you go get dressed. There's four of us to get through the bathroom this morning and I still have to wake Marky from his morning nap and get him ready."

Mark did as he was told, pausing long enough to kiss Gina's forehead and wish her a good morning.

The church steps were crowded with people as Mark and company made their way across the center of the town square. He asked Sarah, as they passed the open-air gazebo, "What's this? You guys have a town band that plays for street dances or something?"

She looked at him a moment before her eyes fell on Josh in quiet restraint. "Not now, Mark."

Mark half expected the entire gathering on the steps of the church to turn as one and stare at him and Gina. Not because they'd done anything, but because they were outsiders. Unwanted and unwelcome in this small community made of rules and strange comments. At home, Mark was a respected albeit feisty police detective. Here, he felt like the unwashed. If he could just get a straight answer out of Sarah, or even Josh, he'd feel better about everything. But he'd been nothing but stopped, sidetracked and flat out told not to ask since he arrived. It irritated him and he expected the rest of town to behave much the same.

The crowd on the steps did turn, a couple of heads at a time. But while a few cocked their heads questioningly at the couple with Sarah and Josh, most just smiled and waved. Mark was surprised and looked over to Gina to find her smiling back at him and then waving madly at the crowd on the steps. *God, I love her insanity.* He smiled to himself.

"Morning Peter," Josh greeted the older man at the foot of the stairs. His left arm, from hand to elbow, was a twisted scar of flesh covering lumps of broken and re-broken bone. The lack of a cast told Mark the bones had knit themselves together, but done so on several occasions and had apparently given up trying to be straight. Mark nodded as Josh introduced him as Sarah's visiting brother and fiancée. Gina grinned wickedly at the idea of the title but winked at Mark to let him know she was good with playing along.

The blonde with the missing fingers from the day before smiled broadly next to another girl roughly her age. In unison they greeted Sarah, "Good morning, Mrs. Andrews," though the second girl's words were slightly garbled and Mark wondered if she was chewing gum or had a speech impediment. He decided the second was actually more likely here, since gum at church was likely frowned upon and considered some bizarre sin in some forgotten text.

He and Gina followed Josh and Sarah up the steps, slowly proceeding past the greetings and introductions. At the top, standing proudly next to the open door, stood the minister. Mark only recognized that by the grin on his face, the welcome handholding and touching to everyone passing him, and the black slacks, black button down shirt and simple golden cross around his neck.

"Well good morning, Josh. Sarah." He looked around Sarah to Gina and Mark. "And who have we got with us this morning?"

"This is my brother Mark and his fiancée Gina. They're in town for a few days." Sarah sidestepped and allowed Mark and Gina full access, or rather the minister full access to them. "This is Brother Garrett."

Garrett looked from Josh to Sarah and back again, seeming confused and a touch concerned. Josh subtly shook his head.

"Brother?" Mark questioned, believing brothers were monks with brown robes and ropes and confused by the title choice in the small-town church.

"Yes. For there is only one father, and I dare not pretend to be him."

"Brother Garrett is but a conduit for us. He is one of us and therefore a brother more than father."

"Cool." Gina smiled and put a hand forward to shake his hand. He hugged her instead.

"Welcome to my home and the Lord's temple in our fortunate village." He released Gina and swung an arm wide, inviting her to enter as his other hand went out to Mark. A firm handshake and a smile later and he found himself being ushered inside the small building on Josh's insistence.

The interior of the building didn't look like a church, but it smelled like one. Absent were the crucifixes and plaques, paintings and statues. There was no stained glass in the windows other than the two small ones to either side of the entrance, and the pews were nothing more than intricately carved homemade benches, most likely by the local carpenter. The smells however, were exactly what he remembered. Dust, wood polish and incense, though in this case he believed the incense to be the flowers at the front of the church and potpourri baskets he'd seen at the back. They settled into a bench near the front and Mark noted there were no backs to the benches, therefore no Bibles in shelving pockets in front of him. No Bibles on the seats to move before sitting down. And he looked around expecting to see the town pull their personal copies from beneath coats and out of oversized pockets. Instead, everyone sat quietly, intently watching the front of the church while the last few refrains of a vaguely familiar song echoed lightly from the left corner where several women and two men closed the opening hymn. They did not wear robes. They did not hold songbooks. They looked like everyone else—slacks or skirts and clean crisp shirts. The clothing was speckled with color and designs, and not at all the drab colors he imagined an Amish-like population would wear. But then Mark remembered the store. They were simple but they weren't without surprises.

The next of which was the older woman at the front of the choir.

As they sat down he noticed her, his view previously obstructed by the tall gentleman in front of him. The elderly woman had on a long, heavy yellow dress with green buttons down the front. Simple leather shoes like Mark remembered seeing in his grandmother's closet as a child. No jewelry or makeup, and a white cloth wrapped loosely around her eyes, making her appear as though she were in costume—dressed as the female figure of justice without the scales. He leaned over to question Sarah about the woman when Brother Garrett spoke.

"Welcome everyone and good morning."

The service was nothing at all what Mark had anticipated. He fully expected fire and brimstone, booming voices, and small-town closed-mindedness, preaching the darker parts of the Bible. Instead he found Garrett, who had a noticeable limp even with his cane, had a soft soothing voice and calming manner of teaching the day's lessons. He spoke of spring and flowers, rebirth and sunshine, and being thankful for the bounty as you begin to plant it. He smiled rather than scowled and Mark realized his last experience with any type of church had been Catholic school, to which he may have equated all other churches unintentionally. A part of him felt relief during the service. Glad Sarah was wrapped in the arms of a community that seemed to be about love and respect rather than shame and sin.

Gina squeezed his leg several times during the service and smiled at him. He saw her watching Sarah and Josh, as well as those close enough for her to watch without getting caught staring. He guessed if she had had something to write on, she'd have been scribbling him notes and comments throughout the entire service.

The service ended with a brief list of announcements from Garrett, which he read off a page in front of him—the first time in the last hour Mark had seen him read from anything.

"There is a storm coming in, and as such, we'll be cutting the picnic short today. However, Peter and Joseph have asked everyone get their market goods gathered and turned in to Camille at the store as soon as possible, and this will help facilitate that request." He nodded to someone in the front row. "Also, the council meeting regarding Andy's transgressions has been postponed until Tuesday, as the third Sunday of the month is generally the busiest at market and the members don't expect to return before dinner tomorrow."

Behind him the choir stood and began to softly sing a tune Mark knew but again couldn't quite remember.

"With that, God loves you all and watches over you. Please

remember to watch over each other as He would have you do. For we are all sheep in His pasture and must protect every member for the flock to survive. Now if you'll all join us behind the church, we'll have a brief picnic today and try and avoid the coming rains."

He stepped down from the pulpit—handmade with carvings similar to the benches—and limped toward the front of the church as the choir raised their voices and sang loud enough God Himself may have actually heard them.

CHAPTER NINETEEN

The morning air was brisk but not overly cold, and Mark found after being in the small crowded church, it was almost refreshing and his coat would suffice. Had he been at home, he would have been complaining about the cold. And if he was honest with himself, he knew he'd be complaining about it here by the end of the day. But for now, it was just brisk, and refreshing, and his mind contemplated things other than the temperature.

Examining the backyard area of the church's fenced-in parcel of land, Mark could tell the picnic area had once been very sterile and organized. If he squinted just right, he could go back in time and imagine the original pattern—five rows of three tables each, perfectly aligned, sanded and smoothed and stained against the elements. Over time, the various groups—family, friends, sects of this strange little society—had adjusted the placement of tables. Several were pushed together, perhaps for a bigger family. Three had been twisted into a rough U shape, perhaps for a meeting of sorts. But the original design was there.

Even at its inception, it had been welcoming against its own rigidity.

As Mark stood next to Sarah, not hearing what she was telling Gina in a low voice meant to pass secrets, he watched the members of the parish, the town, file out of the double doors of the church and into the backyard. The older and younger generations took seats at various tables as if they'd been assigned, or habit, like cows running as a herd toward the stanchions only to fluidly move into a single file line at the doorway of the barn and step into each of their stalls on cue.

The middle generation, Mark's generation, came single file from the back door of the church, which Mark hadn't even noticed until it opened to a parade of women and men carrying bowls, platters and baskets full of picnic goods. The three tables nearest the church, still very much lined up as originally placed, were covered in white cloths and the food was spread out across them. After the group filed through the picnic tables and sat in the openings left for them, Mark looked to Sarah and Josh and wondered where they were to sit. The minister answered his question, as well as let Mark know what the girls had been talking about while he had been observing the town gathering and ignoring them.

"The Lord has given us sunshine for the time being and we shall enjoy it as we come together under His canopy as one, united in harmony and celebrating His gracious bounty on us. But before we pray and dig in—and I must say, I do believe Andrea may have outdone herself this week, as I can smell her apple crisp from here—I'd like to introduce everyone to our visitors. This is Josh's brother-in-law, Mark Baker, and his fiancée, Gina Bennington. They have come all the way from Pennsylvania to visit and we welcome them with open arms."

A rush of whispers went through the crowd. Mark saw a few eyebrows rise and several earnest eyes note Gina's belly bulge, obvious in the umpire waist shirt she'd chosen for the day. But more intriguing was the echo of Brother Garrett's words, as he referred to Mark as Josh's brother-in-law rather than Sarah's brother. The women around him didn't seem to keep their eyes down, their heads lowered, their voices muted, so Mark had a hard time believing it was a community where men were superior. Instead, he wondered again exactly what kind of trouble Sarah had gotten herself into. Had she angered her community somehow? Was she being punished or shunned for it? The schoolchildren had been fine with her. Although, at the mention of her name, the storekeeper had definitely reacted. *No,* Mark decided, *his initial reaction, initial worries, were correct. There was something going on and Sarah was at the root of it.*

Mark was dragged from his thoughts by the pastor.

"Alright, that's enough. You'll all get a chance to talk with them and visit for yourselves, but that apple crisp is cooling off and we're all hungry. Let us pray…" In unison the town recited the Lord's Prayer. Mark noted they used the version with *trespasses* instead of *debtors* and wondered the basis of their religion. The service hadn't given anything away and for all he could figure it could be one of those new age "we love everyone and everything" churches. Until the service included snake handling, Mark wasn't going to worry about the denomination.

The pastor nodded to Sarah and Josh and they ushered Mark and Gina to a picnic table in the second row. Mark sat down across from the storekeeper, stoically watching both Sarah and the tables around her. He wanted to keep a straight face. He wanted to return the pleasant but steady stare Camille seemed to be regarding them with. But he couldn't help but smile as Gina settled onto the bench.

"Hey, Camille, nice to see you again." Her smile wide and welcoming, like a child interrupting a parental argument and forcing them to forget what the argument was about. "I love your dress, did you make it yourself?"

Camille blinked and looked down at herself then back up at Gina with a forced smile. "Actually, no. But my sister-in-law, Rebecca, did." She nodded to the woman sitting directly next to Gina, who in turn offered a hand and an equally pursed smile.

"Hi, I'm Rebecca… Becka really. No one calls me Rebecca except Cammie." She leaned to her left. "This is my husband Andrew."

Gina held out her right hand but Andrew smiled and shrugged at his missing right arm, holding out his left hand instead. "Nice to meet you, sir." Mark noted that although Gina was still smiling, and her eyes still sparkled like they did when she waited on older gentlemen at work, her tone had changed to a more cautious timbre. Mark presumed Josh noticed the change in her attitude as well and took over for his mother.

"To Uncle Andrew's right is my cousin Thomas and his wife Maggie."

Gina interrupted, "Oh hey, Maggie… How far along are you?" Only when he registered what she'd asked did Mark notice Maggie's very pregnant figure and thought back to the church steps before and after the service. He hadn't remembered seeing many infants other than little Marky. He looked around at the other tables and noted the obvious generations populating the town. He no sooner decided Maggie's unborn child and Marky were the very beginning of the fourth generation, when another infant, behind him somewhere, started to fuss and make its presence known.

Josh continued as if Gina hadn't spoken, "And across from them are their boys Rob and Tommy."

Mark nodded to each person as they were introduced, quietly taking in the family that had become his sister's and making mental note of attitude, both in general and toward him and Gina as outsiders. They all seemed pleasant enough but Thomas' wrist showed signs of scarring and he held it funny, which made Mark wish he had been seated closer to inquire, especially in light of Andrew's missing arm. The boys were in their teens and Mark wondered briefly if the pregnancy had been planned. His wondering was answered by Gina's thread of questions and Maggie's grinning nods.

"Woah, teens and a new baby? Was it a surprise or are you shooting for a girl this time, or both—a surprise you hope turns out to be a girl? And wow, that's quite the age gap, I don't know how you're going to do it. I barely have enough energy for me some days and worry I won't be able to keep up with one, let alone three with two of them being teenagers."

"Hon, you have plenty of energy," Mark interjected, hoping to take Gina down a notch. "It bubbles out of you like a geyser."

"Well, after coffee maybe." Sarah smiled at Gina, and Mark realized they'd seen pre-coffee Gina at her worst that morning.

"That's just the baby and morning sickness—"

"You mean all-day sickness," Gina cut in. "Maggie, did you have morning sickness? Was it really just in the morning?"

Gina and Maggie leaned across and continued to talk to each other as Mark watched the others at the tables around them as they started to rise and go in groups to the front where the food was spread out. Gina's normally infectious enthusiasm worried him and he was especially aware of how people watched her. They seemed to smile at her face, but frown at her belly. The expression very similar to the way some of them looked at Sarah. Something in his gut told him to take Gina aside and ask her to tone it down a touch. Just a touch. Because something here wasn't right and until he knew what he didn't want to trigger anything to make it worse.

As they ate and Gina chatted up the entire table with tales of waitressing and college and the plans for the baby, Mark continued to watch the rest of the crowd. He noted the girl from the day before with the missing fingers was sitting across from a boy in a cast. Saw scarring on the arms of several men that didn't quite look accidental or self-inflicted. They reminded him of cigar burns he'd seen on the junkies who had pissed off their dealers. A man, weathered from life rather than age, was missing a leg. And the woman with the blindfold sat next to a woman about Mark's age that seemed to seethe silent hatred toward Sarah—she watched her, unblinking, until nudged by the man sitting next to Peter, the man Mark had met outside the church with the mangled hand.

It was a lot to take in. Even for a small community of close-knit if not cross-related people. But Mark took several things away from the picnic area as they walked back to Sarah's house while the clouds darkened, the storm looming across the fields. There were more injuries in this church group than he'd ever seen in a collection of people outside a Vet hospital. And while people were polite to Sarah, they were friendly if not apologetically so to Josh. Several seemed to regard Sarah with disdain. Others seemed to force themselves to be polite.

Mark had more questions. And when they got inside the house, they were getting answered. Or he was going with his initial thought and packing up Sarah and Marky, and leaving this place as it should be. Forgotten in the middle of nowhere.

CHAPTER TWENTY

The house was chilly when they closed the door behind them and Josh went immediately to the fireplace. Gina headed, not surprisingly, to the bathroom—complaining about her bladder the entire way down the hallway.

"I'll make coffee," Sarah declared and walked toward the kitchen after hanging her coat on one of the brass hooks behind the door.

Mark followed her. His questions tripped over themselves in his mind as he watched her put Marky in the highchair and offer him a juice cup. He wasn't sure where to begin. He wasn't sure if she'd open up if he started with those around her or if he should just dive right in and ask what the hell was going on with her. He hadn't seen her for ten years. The last twenty-four hours were not enough for him to possibly know how she'd changed temperamentally or confrontationally. He knew the sister he lost would spill her guts with nothing more than a look of concern from her older brother, but this version of Sarah seemed more closed-mouthed. Tight-lipped to the point it had taken on a personality rather than a situation. The questions, the observations from today, the comments he'd heard or had aimed directly at him jumbled and he felt lost. He'd never needed a notepad to keep his thoughts straight while questioning a suspect, but he suddenly wished he had one and had been jotting down thoughts.

"Let's start at the beginning." He finally spoke his decision out loud and Sarah turned at him quizzically.

"Ooookay. Did I miss something?" She turned back to the coffeepot, which oddly looked exactly like the one she'd had back in college—covered in stickers, some fresh and colorful, others faded and torn all but off—and Mark had to wonder if she hadn't kept it as some sort of strange reminder of home.

"You missed Christmas and my birthday for the last ten years. How's that for a start?" Mark hadn't expected his snark to come out so quickly and pulled it back in, knowing he'd never get anywhere until he was calm and simply led the questioning so she'd willingly fill in the blanks. "And I missed the birth of my nephew. But those are unimportant. You're alive, you're safe. That's what counts."

She smiled at him and cocked her head, as if she knew what he was doing, and Mark chided himself internally for forgetting she was just like their mother when she was younger. Why he ever thought age would change her was beyond him.

"Why the letter? Why after all this time?" He fetched creamer from the fridge as he talked, hoping she'd see this as an open conversation while they both got the coffee ready—a normal domestic activity families do at gatherings. "Some of the word choices scared me."

"I'm sorry." She retrieved four cups from the cupboard. "I—"

"Sarah. You aced every English class you ever attended, you understand full well the difference a word choice can make."

"Mark…" She looked at him as she scooped hot chocolate powder into a cup for Gina.

"No, we're going to talk about this. Period." He stepped closer to Sarah and put a hand on the counter, blocking her inane activities from distracting her from the conversation. "Why are the people in this town all damaged? How'd you even send the letter? I haven't seen a single car and only know there's a 'truck for market' because Josh told me. You act like you're being shunned and then smile and tell me you're happy."

"I am…"

"Why did Camille clam up like she'd been kicked under a table when I said your name? Why did Josh tell me you're 'going to need me' in the next few weeks? Why do people talk to Josh and sneer at you? What have you done? What is happening here?"

"You don't understand, Mark." She looked down at the floor for a moment then back at him and Mark could see the tears threatening to spill over. "You could never understand…"

Mark put a hand on her shoulder. "Bullshit. Sarah, this is bullshit." He fought his desire to scream at her and continued to speak in a level tone but caught her frown at his language. "And fuck your Goddamn rules. Explain what the hell is going on or I'll go outside and break as many as I can figure out."

"Tell him." Josh spoke from the doorway and Mark turned to

see his brother-in-law and girlfriend watching the exchange in the kitchen, leaving Mark to wonder how long they'd been there.

CHAPTER TWENTY-ONE

Mark watched as his sister and brother-in-law stared at each other, an entire conversation passed between them through body language. Gina's gaze flicked back and forth at the couple before landing on Mark. He felt rather than witnessed Gina's stare, as he watched his sister's face slacken in resignation as her eyes continued to plead with Josh to take back his words.

"But…"

"Just tell him. Get it over with." Josh addressed Mark apologetically. "He's found us now, he'll be back to visit, he's going to find out."

"Find out what?" Gina covered her mouth as soon as she whispered the question.

"Can I put Marky down for his nap?" Sarah nodded at the baby in the highchair, completely unaware of the stress and situation around him as he shoved cookie parts against his lips and chewed the pieces managing to make it into his mouth.

"No. I can do that." Josh moved toward the baby but Gina stepped in front of him.

"If you don't mind, I'd love to take care of that for you. And honestly," she looked at each of them in turn, "I'm the only one that doesn't need to be here for this."

"Go ahead, Gina." Josh sidestepped, leaving Gina room to get through the doorway. "And thank you. We appreciate it."

Ever polite, Mark thought as he waited for Gina to leave the room. He turned to Sarah and Josh, who had walked across to stand next to his wife. "Okay then… What the hell is going on?"

"Mark, I would ask you to at least keep your language clean if not your temper down." Josh pulled a chair out at the table and nodded to Sarah.

"Fine, let's start with that. These rules. What the hell are these rules? Like Ten Commandment type shit or something else?"

Sarah settled into the chair and folded her hands in her lap, studying them rather than making eye contact with either of the men. "Something like that. Don't steal, lie, cheat, swear. You know, everything Mother would have told us when we were kids."

"But we're not kids. We're adults. And it's still a free country and if I want to swear I will."

"Not here, please." Sarah's voice cracked.

"Would you steal, lie, cheat or do anything else Sarah says your mother would have told you not to?"

"Well no. But I'm a cop. It's my job to catch those that do these things." As an afterthought he added "And even if I wasn't a cop, I'm a good person."

"Exactly." Sarah spoke so softly, it took Mark a moment to realize what she'd said.

"We've filled this community with good people." Josh reached over and placed a hand on Sarah's, hinting he handle this part. "We want it to stay that way, so we have rules. They're basic rules as far as morals and ethics go, and include the Godly orders as well."

Mark felt like a blind man with two pieces of puzzle he knew went together but without sight wasn't sure which way to turn which piece. He couldn't figure out the connection between the rules and the behavior, looks, comments and Sarah's letter. The rules. Basic rules.

His eyes lit up and Mark leaned forward. "What happens if you break a rule?"

"Punishment." Sarah swallowed hard.

"What kind of punishment? I didn't see a jail. Do you exile people?"

"We have…" Josh answered but his voice trailed off and Mark wasn't sure if it was because he knew someone who was punished or just tried to stay out of Sarah's way as she opened her mouth.

"An eye for an eye, Mark."

"An eye for an eye? So…" He thought about the rules he'd heard and those he'd imagined in his mother's voice. "So if I steal from you, you steal from me."

"No." Sarah licked her lips and looked up from her lap. Her mouth was open but Mark could see her contemplating, choosing her words. "If you steal from someone, you lose your hand."

"Well, not right away, Sarah," Josh interjected.

"Not right away?" Mark's volume increased as his brows furrowed downward.

"You lose a finger," Josh provided.

"A finger? Lose? How?" Mark thought about the girl he'd seen several times missing two fingers. "Wait a minute. What if you do it again?"

"Another finger."

"Ten times?"

"After five you lose the hand." Josh's voice was calm and rational, as if he were explaining a math problem rather than socially accepted mutilation. "Then it would go to the next hand. But we've never had anyone continue after one hand."

"You've never had anyone cont—" Mark looked between Josh and Sarah and finally landed his glare on Josh. Sarah wasn't born into this, Josh brought her here. This was Josh's world, not Sarah's and he wanted an explanation. "That girl I saw missing two fingers… You cut them off? Who cuts them off? Why doesn't she run away? This is ridiculous! What other punishments are there? My God, Sarah, why are you still here?"

"Mark." Gina shushed him from the doorway and he remembered the sleeping baby and the promise he'd made to keep his language and tone down.

"They cut those girl's fingers off, Gina. Cut. Them. Off." He stared at her, fighting to keep his voice down. She looked at him as if he'd spoken a different language and he turned back to Josh. "How old is she? She's not old enough for that."

"Yes she is. She's fourteen. The age of consent is thirteen. After thirteen they are treated as adults. Before that they are punished by their parents rather than the community."

"The community? So everyone takes a whack at a young girl's hand?"

"No, the person she wronged is the dealer of punishment." Josh looked at Sarah from the corner of his eye. "Most of the time."

"What else do you do? I saw people with casts and missing arms…" Mark thought back to the picnic. "The pastor? And oh my God, that old woman with the cloth on her eyes!"

"We didn't do that to her," Sarah spoke up. "That's not punishment, Mark. Not at all."

"No?"

"No, her horrible cataracts have all but blinded her."

"So you took her eyes?"

"No, no. She has her eyes. She just hates the idea of people staring into her whitened irises. Says they make her look dead. So she wears the scarf."

"Or dark glasses," Josh added.

"But the rest of them? I don't hear you saying you weren't responsible for the rest of them." Mark's eyes flicked back and forth, no longer caring who answered him, so long as he got answers.

"Yes, the rest of what you saw were most likely punishments."

"The guy next to Gina at the picnic, missing the arm? Andrew?"

"Yes. For theft."

"I thought that was fingers and a hand?" Mark cocked his head. The rules were rules—that changed?

"No. I mean, yes. It was his hand," Josh explained. "Ironically enough, it was for stealing from the store, run by his in-laws before they were his in-laws. But anyway, no, it was his hand. Years ago. There was an infection and it spread before they could stop it. That was before we had a doctor in town. He ended up losing the whole arm."

Mark just stared at him in disbelief. How could he talk about it so matter-of-factly? But Josh continued.

"He feels it was ironic and further punishment to allow him to marry into the family he had wronged so long ago. He's perfectly fine now. And Uncle Andy is very happy. You should know that."

"Happy?" Mark shook his head. "What about the others? The casts and pastor and there was a mangled arm and what about the scars all over the other guy's arm?" Mark stared at Sarah as he directed his questions to Josh. "And that guy's leg! What about that? What did he do? Kick a dog?"

"Did you not say you wished the system worked?" Josh answered Mark's questions with a different question. "Did you not sit in this very house and complain about the criminals getting away and the system not working? The system works here, Mark. It's worked for several generations. We have a few instances every generation and then the community on a whole is reminded and learns from the mistakes of the few."

"What. Did. They. Do?" Mark stared at Josh, unblinking, and waited.

"The scars were probably John. He used to have a mouth on him and was branded several times for blasphemy and foul language in his twenties. Again, it was years ago."

"Go on…"

"The leg is Doug. He's always had a bad temper. He went through a spout of beating Leigh. The leg was his final warning and it worked. He hasn't raised a hand to anyone since."

Mark knew parts of Josh's explanation were meant to justify what the town had done. It wasn't working. He frowned at Josh.

"The boys were fighting and had their hands smashed for their act of violence. And Brother Garrett came to us…" He looked at Sarah, his eyes in contemplation, "About five years ago or so from Black River Falls. He had a horrible habit of gossiping from living in the city and dealing with the catty way regular churchgoers tended to whisper and point. We couldn't take his tongue because he needed it to spread the good word. He suggested hobbling instead and the council agreed."

"*He* suggested?"

"Sure. You have to understand Mark. It's our town, our rules. Everyone knows the rules. If they stay, they do so understanding the punishment for breaking those rules. No one here is punished without consent." Josh looked at Sarah again.

"Even if we regret what we've done. Even if we apologize for years or fear it or whatever, in the end, we accept what we've got coming." Sarah spoke into her coffee cup.

"It works, Mark. The system here works." He took a cup of coffee and Mark sat back trying to absorb what he was hearing. He felt Gina's hand on his leg and turned his head to her. She looked scared.

"Crippling, tearing out tongues, cutting off limbs. You don't think maybe a jail cell would be more humane?"

"Perhaps, but do your criminals learn or do they repeat their offenses? Do they get away from the punishment they deserve?"

"The system is meant to provide fair…"

"You hate the system, Mark." Gina's voice trembled. "I think this is ridiculous and cruel and can't believe people choose to live like this, but don't you belittle yourself by proclaiming any dignity for the system you hate."

Mark opened his mouth to argue but stopped himself. He understood what she was saying and went back to Josh and Sarah instead. "So what rule did you break, Sarah? What body part are they cutting off? Is that why you wrote to me, because you're scared?"

"Yes…"

"Then why not leave? Come home with us and keep all your body parts…" The comment Reilly had repeated from the postman made sense now. *All their parts.*

"Because I love Josh. And I love little Marky. And my extended family, and the community, and my life here." She swallowed hard. "And I am not a coward. I have lived under these rules for ten years. I've seen tongue pieces torn free and fingers stay on the block as the hand is yanked away. I've been witness to punishments in the square. What kind of person does it make me if I run away when the rules apply to me?"

Mark couldn't answer. Somehow, he was proud of her strength, though confused by her stubborn willingness to mutilate herself. After several silent minutes of exchanged looks and a rapid firing of more questions in his mind, Mark finally focused.

"What did you do?"

Sarah looked to Josh. Her husband nodded to her, his face suddenly less political and more solemn.

"I…I couldn't…I tried and tried to have a baby, Mark. I did. *We* did. For years and years. Watching my temperature for ovulation and my diet and his diet and everything we could do from what we'd read or been told. But I couldn't get pregnant…" Sarah's voice trailed off into a sniffle and Mark realized she was looking down so he wouldn't see her cry. Her shoulders shook as the sniffle turned to sobs.

Mark watched Josh's face. He didn't know the man very well. Never had the chance before they ran off together ten years ago. But he'd been reading body language long enough as a detective to see the changes as they rolled across his eyes—pride, anger, frustration, disappointment and oddly, love. Josh put a hand on Sarah's shoulder.

"I forgave you, love."

She looked up at him with disgust in her eyes. Mark wasn't sure if it was at herself or her husband and waited for the moment to pass.

"Sarah, in an attempt to give me a child, slept with another man for his seed." Josh looked over at Mark, appearing almost braced for the response he must have expected.

"She…" Mark looked at his sister. "You did what?!"

"It was very clinical and we were never going to tell anyone…not even Josh. I just wanted to give him a baby. I wanted to take away the sorrow I saw on his face every time someone else had a child."

"You…you slept with… Who?" Mark knew he'd been out of her life for ten years, but the sister he had helped raise would never have cheated on someone. Never. She never even looked at other boys when she was in a relationship, let alone a marriage.

"My cousin William," Josh answered. "It was actually clever. We look a lot alike and he's family so the blood would be there. He was unmarried, unattached and as she said, she claims it was clinical rather than romantic."

"And you're okay with this?"

"Not always." Josh took a sip of coffee and squeezed Sarah's hand. "I had a really hard time around Marky when I found out. And it took a while, a lot of talking and praying, for Sarah and I to patch things. But we've managed to start down the road to healing and I know we'll be fine."

"So…" Mark was terrified of the question caught on his tongue, and a look at Gina made him wish he didn't need to ask it. "What do they do for adultery around here?"

Josh's eyes welled with tears and Mark feared the answer was a death sentence of sorts.

Sarah took a deep intake of breath and let it out. Her voice stronger but still soft, almost a harsh whisper, "Castration…"

CHAPTER TWENTY-TWO

No!" Mark stood abruptly, his chair slamming backward into the fridge. "Hell no. We're packing your shit and getting you out of here. Period."

"No we're not, Mark. I knew what I was doing…" She looked at him with an angry defiance. "I didn't know the punishment. I didn't expect to get caught. But I knew. And I accept my punishment."

"How?" Gina exhaled the question with a cracked shock in her voice. "How can you just accept… My God, what does that even mean? What are they doing exactly?" She looked at Josh in horror and pulled back from the table, becoming small like a child being yelled at. "Wait, the crime was against you… Are *you* doing this to her?!"

"No, no. Oh my goodness, no." Josh shook his head vehemently. "No. This has never been done before. The doctor is going to do it."

"And he's trained in this because of what bizarre medical training? My God, what the hell is wrong with you people?" Mark was pacing in the kitchen, debating whether to throw his sister over his shoulder and just go.

"He's been doing research. It's why her punishment has been delayed. So that it can be done properly without any complications. It's not about hurting the person or causing excessive pain or prolonged agony from infection or recovery complications. It's about the punishment matching the crime. It's about marking you physically so your scars keep you in line with the rules."

"It's mutilation!" Mark crossed the room and knelt down in front of Sarah. "Sarah-Bear. Honey. You can't do this…"

"Yes I can. And I will. It's my fault. My atonement."

"It's bullshit. Just bullshit."

"Mark, I understand your anger and shock, but really, please, the language."

"Are you fucking kidding me? In the middle of this and you're worried about me swearing?"

"Please."

"I don't feel so good…" Gina announced and Mark turned to her, watching her color drain from her face and her eyes get glassy.

"Oh hon, come here." He stood and pulled her out of the chair up to him. "You okay? Morning sickness? Do you need to lay down?"

"Sick, but I don't know if it's the baby this time…" She looked from him to Sarah and back. "Yeah, I'll go lay down. I…yeah…I'll go." She turned and left the room.

Mark watched her leave, debating whether he should go talk to her and tuck her in, but a heavy sigh behind him pulled his attention back to the atrocities his sister was willingly subjecting herself to.

"What of your cousin? I haven't met him. Was he already punished? Run out of town? What?"

"He was a coward." Josh shook his head as he spoke.

"He ran away after the council meeting decided our punishments." Sarah straightened a little and Mark realized she was proud of her own strength and commitment. He thought she should just be committed.

"I'm almost afraid to ask… What exactly is a female castration? What does that mean?"

"In layman's terms, they're going to clip my clitoris."

"Aaaagh…" Mark winced as if it were happening to him. "My God, Sarah. Really?"

"Yes. It was a difficult decision. As she mentioned, it has never come up before. This procedure will remove pleasure from her genitalia while not damaging her ability to urinate, menstruate or have normal sexual relations…" Josh's voice had clicked back over to the calm clinical tone and he added, "…with her husband."

"This…this is ridiculous. I'm calling the local cops in here. Maybe social services or some other agency to stop this. Child protective services would be all over the mutilation of your youth. And—"

"How Mark? How are you going to do anything? Everyone here accepts their punishments and go to them willingly. No one is injured against their will. It's a free country, as you pointed out, and people can do what they want to themselves."

"Not true. Kevorkian is in all kinds of trouble for this type of thing."

"That's different. He's killing people. We're not."

"But this…this…" Mark stormed out of the kitchen and grabbed his coat from the hook. He needed to think.

"Where are you going?" Sarah called.

"I don't know… I just can't be here right now."

"We have market in the morning," Sarah said as if nothing were wrong and she was just relaying normal activities to him. He stared at her for a moment and then turned and walked out into the dying day, slamming the door behind him.

CHAPTER TWENTY-THREE

Mark had walked through the streets watching various townsfolk deliver goods to the store by the barrel, basket and handful. He sat in the town square gazebo and watched the town close down for the night as the rains started. It took a while, but the water finally soaked through his thick coat and drenched him. He didn't care.

When the last house light went out, he found himself walking up the road he'd driven to enter the town the day before. *Was it really only yesterday?* He thought, as he walked to the curve and found himself standing in front of the tiny graveyard. The rain had stopped and the clouds cleared away with it, leaving a full moon shining through the empty pre-spring branches of the trees and lit the tiny fenced cemetery. He pushed the gate open and wandered between the handful of stones, wondering if the deaths had been natural or punishment.

When he finally snuck back into Sarah's house, he found everyone sleeping soundly, even Gina. Two tall glasses of water and a hot shower later, Mark settled onto the couch for a fitful night of bad dreams and constant interruptions in his sleep from an overworked mind and overly worried heart.

The morning sun crept through the curtains in the living room far too soon for Mark's tastes and he flipped over, slamming the pillow down on his head to block the light out. Muffled noises from the kitchen let him know Sarah and Josh were awake and he huffed into the cushion before conceding to the inevitable and crawling from the twisted blankets of his makeshift bed.

"Good morning, sunshine." Sarah greeted him with a cup of coffee, reminding Mark he said those words to Gina, just as his mother had said it to both he and Sarah as children. "How'd you sleep?"

"Not good." His head pounded behind his eyes and he found he didn't have the energy to even think about regurgitating last night's conversation. "How was Gina last night?"

"Oh she stayed in bed for most of the night. I heard her get up once and come out here, I figured it was either for a glass of milk or to check on you. I left her alone."

"What time was that? Late?"

"No, it was early this morning. Probably four-ish."

"'Kay…" Mark nodded and turned to head down the hall, calling over his shoulder with all the anger he could muster under the pressure of the budding migraine. "Is it against your rules if I wake her up?"

Sarah didn't answer him.

--==•==--

Normally, only council members were allowed to travel to market, which turned out to be several booths at Eagle River's weekly fairgrounds flea market, but because they were visiting, Mark and Gina were allowed to bring Sarah and Josh with them and further understand how the community worked. They drove in Gina's SUV rather than in the truck with the council members. The ride was silent and Mark was glad.

Market was interesting, and under other circumstances, Mark and Gina would have enjoyed it much like they did antiquing on the weekends back home. But this wasn't home and this wasn't whimsical.

Mark watched intently as Joseph, Peter, Marianne and Rebecca enthusiastically sold the town's creations and crops to the locals. Josh explained how the money would be used to purchase supplies they couldn't make or grow. Staples. And after market the council would go purchase whatever list Camille had given them for the store, as well as any special order, such as shoes in a certain size for someone. Mark heard him but was busy watching the interaction while debating the situation he'd found his long-lost sister in and what exactly he could do about it. He finally came to the conclusion he could do nothing if she was allowing it, and it hurt his chest to know he couldn't prevent her from getting hurt.

He couldn't save her from herself.

He turned his attention to Gina as Josh and Sarah droned on, knowing he was absorbing what they were saying even though his only interaction was the occasional nod or mumbled acknowledgment.

Gina was sitting next to Rebecca, wrapped in one of the handmade blankets from the town, chatting absently. Her normally bubbly self had been hit over the head in the last twenty-four hours and the dazed version of her was a bit difficult to take in. Her eyes still sparkled on occasion because of something they talked about, but her smile wasn't as wide as it should be. Her voice not nearly as boisterous as he knew it could be. He was worried about her.

At lunchtime, he and Gina went off by themselves under the pretense of checking emails and voice mails.

"I'm scared, Mark. I really am."

"I know, baby, I am, too. I'm going to talk to this doctor about the procedure when we get back to town. I don't trust these people not to fuck it up and kill her."

"I don't mean about Sarah. I mean, don't get me wrong, I'm freaked out about it and want to stop it, but I'm scared for me."

Mark looked at her, raising an eyebrow and reaching over to push a stray hair from her crop of black-tipped bangs to behind her ear. "Why?"

"Look at me? How many rules am I breaking? I have fingernail polish and colored hair and I'm living with a man in sin and carrying his bastard child. I have felt like I've been under a microscope since we got here and am worried they'll punish me, or us, or God forbid Sarah because of everything I represent."

"Gina…" He pulled her close. "Baby, I had no idea. Why didn't you say anything?"

"You were concentrating so much on Sarah and the weirdness in that town…"

"Yeah but this is you and me. We're going to go home and leave this town and it will be just you and me again. We have to talk about things like this… You should have told me."

"Can we?"

"Can we what? Talk?"

"No. Go back home and be just you and me?"

"I…" He stroked her hair as he thought. "I can't leave Sarah. Not with this knowledge. I need to be here. I need to see if there's anything I can do. If I can talk her out of this."

"How long?"

Mark pulled away and lowered his gaze to Gina. The tremble of her lip and shine of tears in her eyes made her look like a Disney character whose woodland animals had stopped singing. "Do you want to go back now? Without me?"

"I can't just leave you here. How would you get home?"

"No. I'll keep the car. We'll find a plane and put you on the first one back home if that's what you want."

"I do. I really do." She tried to blink away the tears forming but they fell free anyway. "Are you sure that's okay? I mean, do you want me to stay here with you and help? Should I stay and support you? Am I weak…?"

"No, baby, it's perfectly understandable. Come on, let's get you a ticket and get you out of here."

"I love you, Mark."

He smiled. She'd used his name rather than a nickname. Something they only did in their most tender moments, when they breathed words of love rather than speaking them.

"I love you, too, Gina Renee…Baker." He'd used his last name rather than hers to see her response. She smiled that coy grin of hers, only one side of her lip curling but her eyes sparkling full of hope and life, and some mysterious mischievous thought he could never quite figure out.

They returned to the market and told Sarah and Josh the plans. They in turn informed the council and the four of them left to go back to Valley Mill so Gina could pack. While Sarah and Gina were talking to the council members, Mark was on the phone desperately trying to find an airport and open seat on a flight to BWI. He was relieved to find one only three hours away in Ironwood. He could have her on the plane and be back before dinner.

Gina graciously thanked everyone for their hospitality as she ran into them during her escape. Fear shone in her eyes, while her sweet waitress voice filled their ears with niceties and charm. The only person who didn't seem receptive was the dark-haired girl with the eye patch that had been glaring at her during the picnic, who happened to be in the store when Gina insisted Mark let her run in and say good-bye to Camille.

"Meghan, be polite," Camille ordered with a smile.

The girl nodded to Gina and Mark and garbled, "Nice meeting you."

Mark and Gina looked at each other on the way out of the store, Mark wondered what the girl had lied about or gossiped about to get her tongue mutilated.

As she pulled the seatbelt across her, Gina sighed, "It's not too late, Mark. I can stay…"

"No. If you're uncomfortable then you don't need to be here. We don't need any added stress on Junior." Mark brushed his hand across her belly. "Sin or not, I'm rather glad for what we've done." He smiled and waited for her to smile in response. She didn't.

He pulled away from the edge of Sarah's street and left the white pickets of Valley Mill to fade into his review mirror, noting how very much like tombstones they looked like from a distance.

CHAPTER TWENTY-FOUR

Mark returned in time to find Sarah hurriedly cleaning up the dinner dishes and Josh packing Marky into his zippered full-body coat.

"Did I miss something?"

Sarah jumped and spun toward him. "Mark. Hi. I didn't hear you come in. The council meeting for Andrew was earlier. He broke the doc's fence last week and they had to decide what to do about it."

Mark cringed. "And? The punishment this time?"

"Oh nothing nearly as drastic, it was destruction of property. It's like stealing with malice. His family loses a week's worth of market goods, which they are not happy about, and he has to rebuild the entire fence by himself. By hand. No power tools."

Actually sounds fair. Mark thought, but couldn't say it out loud and risk them thinking he may agree with their crazy justice system on even the tiniest level. "Well what's going on now? We going somewhere?"

"Oh yeah," Josh interjected from the kitchen doorway. "There's a line of spring storms coming this week, so they've moved the punishment for Tommy to this evening to get it out of the way before the storms come."

"And we're going?"

"Yes. That's part of the system. The whole town gathers for support of both the victim and the perpetrator. We witness the punishment and forgive as a group under God's eye. It's what keeps our community united."

"Are you serious? What are we…" He stopped and thought of Sarah's pending castration. "Wait a minute. Are they all going to gather and watch Sarah get…" he couldn't say the word out loud, "… mutilated?"

"Yes." Sarah wiped her hands on a dishtowel and took her coat from Josh's outstretched hand.

Mark opened his mouth to resume his protest of the whole thing but decided to bite his tongue. He needed to formulate a plan, figure out the right wording to get Sarah to see what she was doing. Get her to change her mind.

"So what are we going to witness?"

"Tommy is losing an eye for spying on Dana bathing in the river…" Sarah slipped her coat on, her voice trailing off.

"He did more than just spy, Sarah. He was touching himself." Josh said it as calmly and blatantly as if he were ordering something from a menu.

"His eye?" Mark felt his headache crawl back into place, slinking up his neck and swimming through his brain to settle behind his eyes. "An eye for masturbating? The Tommy I met? Maggie's boy? Isn't that your cousin or something? How can you be okay?"

"I know you don't understand. I do. But you need to at least accept this is how it is. His generation has only had a few infractions. They're still learning. But they've known from very young the consequences of their behavior." Sarah zipped her coat and took little Mark from Josh.

"It wasn't just the masturbation, it was the fact that he was doing it while watching her in the river. Had he been in his own bedroom or bathroom, we'd never have known and as it wouldn't have affected the mental state of the girl as well as the modesty of the community on a whole. In truth, this will probably be the last punishment for that generation. They seem to learn as a group after a more serious punishment is doled out," Josh said and walked past Mark to the door. "Come on, we don't want to be late. That's rude."

Mark blinked a few times, still running the idea of local authorities through his mind, and followed the couple out of the house without a word. His world felt surreal, as if he walked in a hypnotic state to his own slaughter—drugged so it wouldn't be unpleasant. A life of believing in certain rights and wrongs was being tested. His desire for a system where justice worked was being tested. He couldn't shake the feeling, the hope, that this was all a bizarre dream and Gina would notice him thrashing in the bed and wake him any moment. But no hand reached into his dream world and pulled him from it. No amount of pinching himself on the arm changed the truth. He was willingly following his sister to witness the mutilation of a young boy.

Just as he would watch them mutilate her in several days.

Deep in thought, Mark hadn't even realized they'd reached their destination until Sarah nudged him. He looked around and saw the normally chatty crowd of townsfolk standing quietly, solemnly, in a circle around the gazebo. Most were in winter coats against the forty-degree chill in the pre-dusk air. The sun behind the group directly across from him gave them a creepy silhouette. Mark was surprised to see even the children were in attendance—older ones standing stiffly next to their parents, the younger generation hugging mother's skirt or clinging to father's pant leg.

A man he presumed to be the doctor stood at the bottom of the one-stair entrance to the town square's central piece of architecture. Next to him, Marianne stood. Sarah had told him at market Marianne was the eldest council member and unofficial town leader since her father stepped down. Mark wondered where her father was and how exactly one gets elected to the position of lead torturer.

On the opposite side of the steps was the girl missing several fingers and what Mark guessed were her parents. She must have been the one swimming that the boy had spied on, the supposed victim here. Yet she had no scars. The emotional damage to her shame and humility were nothing compared to the physical scarring the boy would carry for the rest of his life. The question of who the victim was weighed heavily on Mark as he let his gaze travel across the other members of the community he knew had signs of punishment. When he looked back to the girl, Mark's mind immediately split into opposing questions. First he wondered what the hell she was doing swimming in this temperature and how she did so without inducing hypothermia. Secondly, he pondered whether the girl would be doling out the punishment.

"Is she going to—" he whispered to Sarah but she cut him off. He could only presume his expression of horror had given away his question.

"No. The doc will."

Mark made a mental note to ask Sarah later how it was decided when the victim was the executioner and when someone else stepped in for them.

The crowd to the left of Mark parted and a couple with a teenage boy dressed all in white emerged. Mark had met them at the picnic. Had sat at a table with them and listened halfheartedly as the father, Thomas, had told him about the farming accident that caused the twisted scarring on the flesh of his right arm. Maggie, the pregnant mother Gina had chatted with regarding babies and morning sickness, had her hand on her son's shoulder. The couple had had two boys with them at the picnic, but now only walked one to his doom, and Mark wondered where the other was among the crowd.

He scrutinized the white clothing, a simple linen shirt and slacks, and wondered if it was ceremonial. He checked the crowd again, paying attention to their outfits and expecting some sort of ceremonial dress to be apparent. But they were all dressed in jeans and shirts of everyday wear.

The boy's parents walked the boy, Tommy, to the gazebo steps, spoke briefly in hushed tones and turned to join the crowd, leaving their son in the hands of those that would harm him. The boy stayed his ground, his mouth twisted in a defiant grimace of self-control and fear.

Mark narrowed his eyes at Sarah and Josh in turn, then made another sweep of the crowd, looking for pity or regret. He found nothing but sadness and pride among the expressions of those around him. Beyond the gazebo and gathered group beyond it, Mark noticed the old man he'd seen napping the first day was once again on his porch, though he sat upright and appeared to be watching. Mark wondered why he didn't come out to the center like everyone else.

"Thomas Richard Pichard," Marianne spoke directly to the boy without addressing the audience, "do you acknowledge you have broken a rule set down by our founding fathers and passed through the generations as law?" The boy mumbled something, his eyes wide with horror. "And were you tried by the council fairly and do therefore accept your punishment as declared?" He mumbled again and Marianne nodded to the doctor, who gently led the boy up into the gazebo.

"Have you anything to say for your sin?" Marianne asked the boy but now turned toward the crowd.

"I'm sorry, Dana. I really didn't know you were there and should have left immediately when I saw you…" The boy's eyes glazed over as he addressed the girl with the missing fingers, mouth agape as if he had more to say. Mark wasn't sure if it was fear that stopped his words or the inability to express what had to be going through his mind. She smiled weakly at him and then looked down to her feet.

"Proceed," Marianne said to the doctor.

Mark watched with fascination as they laid the boy on the bench inside the gazebo. A satchel he hadn't noticed was opened and various implements were set down next to the boy's head. Mark's line of sight was blocked by the posts of the gazebo, and it was only then he noticed this was the only piece of decorative wood in the town not painted white. The gazebo was a deep dark wood, black walnut, Mark thought, and stained against the elements, but left more or less in its original state. Under other circumstances, Mark would have thought it was beautifully designed, the grain of the wood highlighted against the stain and setting sun in rich hues of red and brown. But Mark couldn't help but wonder if they'd left the wood unpainted to help camouflage the blood spilled within the boundaries of the gazebo's walls and carved posts and rails.

He watched the crowd. Stoic. Silent. Those of the boy's generation fidgeted, while the older spectators were frozen, collectively holding their breath. The doctor said something and Mark almost wished they'd been closer so he could hear all the things he was missing. In response to whatever the doctor had said, the girl walked up the gazebo steps and sat on a bench next to the boy. She reached over and found his hand with hers, wrapping her remaining fingers around his in a show of sympathy and support. Mark shook his head. He would have thought there would be a few people among the crowd who were outraged at this, or disgusted, or at least quietly upset by the punishment being doled out to a young boy. He made another mental note to ask Sarah how long it had taken her to get used to this, to accept this, as part of everyday life.

A sharp intake of breath caught Mark's attention and he saw Maggie bury her face in her husband's shoulder. He imagined the parents would be proud of his sacrifice but wondered if perhaps her pregnancy didn't react well to the situation.

In the gazebo, the doctor had a wicked instrument in his hand, poised above the boy's head. "Close your eyes, son. And tell me when the numbing begins to take effect. When you can feel tingling in your toes." Mark strained to get a clear view, believing he'd missed an injection or something, and trying desperately to see the doctor's instruments on the bench to locate a hypodermic needle. It was fruitless from his position in the crowd.

The boy mumbled something and the doctor lowered the medieval instrument. The end he held was handled much like a pair of scissors, his fingers threaded through and gripping the device. An inch below the finger holes was a flag of metal on both sides, which reminded Mark of the click-and-lock clamp his father had kept in his tackle box—which he imagined was right on the nose, as medical clamps would have the same mechanics for strength and a steady grip. He shuddered at the idea of what it would be gripping. The business end of the tool reminded Mark of a tea bag caddy. The silver ball at the end was split and slotted in an ornate but most likely functional design. As the doctor lowered his hand, he used his other hand to open the boy's eyelids.

Mark winced and almost looked away, but morbid curiosity held his attention captive. The rest of the crowd disappeared. The wind building in the trees vanished. The world was nothing but a cone of tunnel vision from him to the boy on the bench. His eyes watched in horror, while his ears strained to hear something, anything, from the boy or doctor or even the girl to stop this before it was too late—like the governor calling death row at 11:59 to stop the execution at the last moment.

The doctor was speaking softly to the boy, and while Mark couldn't make out the words, he could hear the tone in the man's voice and knew he was asking questions. Mark didn't know if it was regarding pain or preparedness, his gaze flicking briefly to the girl to gauge her response to all of this. When he looked back, the doctor had opened the device and placed both sides of the open cup at the outer edges of the boy's eye. Raising his elbow for leverage, he slipped the tool into the socket, the cups cradling the eye in the dead space of their center. A twist of the doctor's wrist and a loud crunch passed across the quiet crowd as the locking teeth on the handle clicked into place. He wiggled his hand as he retracted the instrument, much like a dentist pulling a tooth will shimmy the gripped tooth with pliers. A wet, sucking sound, like a suction cup being pulled from a steamed window, was barely audible above the breeze and Mark's heartbeat.

The doctor quickly put the instrument down—its prize still locked within the cup—and grabbed gauze, soaked in and dripping yellow fluid, from a jar. He shoved the gauze into the boy's eye socket and twisted it around. Pulling it out, he replaced it and repeated the action several times. He then put a small metal rod with a bulbous end into the empty socket and ran around the edges. Mark presumed it was a cauterizing tool or some other form of blood reduction. Finally, the doctor filled the eye socket with another small piece of the yellow-soaked cloth, topped with clean white gauze from a roll he opened. He wiped the boy's face and taped a large white patch across the boy's eye. He then taped the other eye with a single piece of tape across the closed lid.

To Mark's surprise and the boy's credit, Tommy hadn't screamed or done anything more than a quiet yelp at what Mark could only imagine had felt like pressure and nothing more under the medication they'd given him. But he knew the boy knew what had happened. He imagined the boy understood the coolness on his cheek was his own blood and ocular fluids. He had to believe the boy was reacting internally, and decided he was right when the boy started to flick a foot in a nervous twitch that represented all the reaction he'd allow himself to show in front of everyone. Teenage boy or not, full of pride and purpose or not, Mark was certain Tommy would be crying like a baby later in the privacy of his home, and worried what kind of pain medications they'd give him when the anesthesia wore off. The girl was crying. The boy was twitching in imagined discomfort. The doctor's words pulled Mark from the imagined feelings of those involved and back into the reality he could verify.

"Keep them both closed for a day. I'll be over to check you in a few hours." The doctor picked his tools up, rolling the wicked instrument and eyeball—still clamped inside it—inside the towel on the bench. He tucked everything back in his bag and stepped out of the gazebo, stopping to say something under his breath to Marianne.

Marianne turned to the crowd. "The crime was committed, the punishment doled out. We learn from our mistakes and take from the past its flames, not its ashes. Thomas is now innocent again."

Mark opened his mouth to protest, unsure if he meant to do it loudly to the group as a whole or quietly to his sister's ears only. Nothing but a sharp, shocked exhale came out. He watched the crowd disperse as quietly as they had stood there. Slowly, the group became no more than him, Josh and Sarah. And the boy and girl still in the gazebo, his parents off to the side talking to Marianne.

The girl stood and bent over the boy. She bent down and kissed his forehead gently, as she placed his hand on his chest and withdrew her grip from it. "I forgive you, Tommy."

Under normal circumstances it may have been a bittersweet moment, but the words seemed hollow in the aftermath of what Mark had just witnessed. It was as if a soldier had come back from war missing his legs and his wife forgave him for leaving her for a while. It was ridiculous. Incredulous. And yet, a part of Mark was completely enthralled with the entire scene.

Boy meets girl. Boy spies on girl. Boy gets eyeball torn from head for girl. Girl falls in love with boy? Mark thought, black humor rising in his thoughts. He watched the girl bound down the steps, a bounce in her step as if she were leaving school the last day before summer vacation.

Again Mark opened his mouth to speak against the atrocities. This time his sister interrupted, "Let's go home."

"That's it? Really? Just go home?" Mark stared at her, uninterested in hiding his disgust and hoping the seething in his mind was reflected in his eyes.

"Yes. He was punished. It's over. We don't hang on the crime after the punishment."

"My God, Sarah…" Mark turned back to the gazebo in time to see the boy's parents help him to his feet and lead him down the steps.

"Take Marky home, Sarah." Josh spoke quietly, undermining Mark's anger with a rational tone. "I'll be right behind you."

"Okay, Josh." She leaned into him and gave Josh a kiss on the cheek before turning and walking back down the street to her own little picket fence.

"Is this the part where you tell me why I'm wrong and this is right?" Mark raised an eyebrow at Josh.

"Nope." Josh pulled his coat tighter across his chest against the chill the breeze had invited. "But I think it's time you met Galen."

CHAPTER TWENTY-FIVE

Without another word, Josh turned and walked toward the gazebo. Mark figured he was expected to follow, and while he wanted to protest like a child sick of getting questions answered with questions or ignored completely, he was intrigued. He smiled at the young girl as he passed her, speeding up to catch Josh's pace, and noticed tears still streaking her face. Twisted morality continued to scream in his mind as he tried to wrap his thoughts around the town's ability to live like this.

"So who's Galen?"

Josh simply nodded his head forward.

Mark looked up and scanned the area. The townsfolk had all retreated to their homes, safely tucked behind their picket fence perimeters from the atrocity they had all just witnessed. The streets were empty. The sun was beginning to dip behind the tree line to the west. The sky to the east was shaded in pre-evening darkness and gloom. In the dying light of the day, the only thing Mark could see was the old man on the porch, head lowered to chest as if he were sleeping again.

"Him?" Mark squinted in an attempt to get a better view of the man. Josh continued forward without a word.

For the first time since arriving in town, Mark took a good look at the house he'd connected to the old man. The ancient farmhouse was easily two hundred years old, with hand-carved rails and window treatments vintage enough to make him wonder if they were original. The wraparound porch ended in a turret that reached just above the third-floor gable. The tiny window in the top peak of the house made Mark think of his aunt's house. Though she wasn't really an aunt, just a very good friend of his parents, Aunt Jan, had an amazing house he had visited quite a bit when he was younger. After Sarah was born they didn't go out and see her as much and eventually he had forgotten all about her. Until now. Her house had a tiny little window up top. It had been nothing more than a small one-room attic. He had been told to be careful of slivers, but otherwise left free to roam the corners and trunks hidden up there. It was his private fort whenever they visited, and in the summer months he would open the window and let the breeze billow the dust and dirt layers settled among the attic's surfaces. Mark remembered spending an entire weekend rifling through a trunk filled with old pictures of people he didn't know and would never meet, completely fascinated by them and trying to figure out their life stories based on the photos—their clothes, expressions, surroundings, etc. He felt a rush of warmth in his jaw as an internal smile triggered the realization the trunk had likely been the beginning of his detective interests.

Aunt Jan's house didn't have a turret though. And while Mark had seen plenty of old Colonials with them, he'd never actually been inside one, and found himself suddenly interested in checking out the interior of the house. He glanced around the town again, analyzing it as he walked. Between the spoke layout of the streets, the generational building styles of the houses as you travelled each spoke, and age of the houses bordering on the town's center square, Mark could almost visualize the growth the town had seen over the years.

He almost ran right into the back of Josh, as his brother-in-law stopped abruptly and turned toward him, waiting for him to both catch up and pay attention. They stood at the bottom of the wide porch steps, thick with years of paint layered on top of itself. The man in the chair still seemed to be dozing, but Mark noticed his leg moving just enough to barely rock him in a gentle rhythm.

"Galen?" Josh called quietly, almost hesitantly, with a thick reverence in his voice.

"Afternoon, Josh." The man's eyes crept open with a slow laziness that reminded Mark of an annoyed cat whose sunray nap had been interrupted. "Got a friend with you, I see."

"Galen Miller, this is Mark Baker—"

"I know who he is…" Galen raised his head and met Mark's eyes. "You didn't need anything from me, did you, Josh?" The man's voice was commanding but kind, and Mark imagined in his younger years Galen was the type of man that walked into a room and immediately owned it.

"No, sir." Josh turned to walk away, whispering in Mark's ear, "He's very quiet and withdrawn the last few months. Brevity will be your friend while speaking to him." He patted Mark on the shoulder as a suggestion for good luck, but it came off more like congratulations to Mark. Josh walked away speaking, "I'll see you at home when you're done."

Mark watched Josh for a moment before turning his head back toward the old man, Galen.

"Come on up here and sit with me a while, Sarah's big brother from the big city." Galen smiled as if he knew something Mark didn't, showing off perfectly straight teeth that didn't appear to be dentures.

Mark nodded and climbed the steps, reviewing the comment in his head. He was unclear if the man had meant the understated sarcasm in the use of the word *big* or not. At the top of the steps he saw a bench against the rail, previously camouflaged from the street by the matching paint. He walked toward it, stopping directly in front of Galen and offered his hand for a formal introduction. Galen's smile turned icy and he reached up to shake Mark's hand. He looked frail. He looked old. But his handshake was firm, strong and anything but the weakness he portrayed from his napping position. Mark sat down. "Nice to meet you."

"I suppose they want me to tell you a story." Galen jumped right into the conversation Mark wasn't sure he even knew the topic of. "Or answer your questions?"

Mark's eyes lit up and he leaned forward, elbows on bent knees. "That would be refreshing. I've gotten nothing but the runaround and additional questions since I got here."

"So what would you like to know?"

"Lots of things. I'm not even sure where to start…"

"Then allow *me* to start at the beginning and you can interject when you see fit." Galen settled back into his chair and pulled his blanket halfway up his chest. Mark nodded, willing to listen to anything if answers were woven into the tale.

"As Josh said, I'm Galen. And I owe you an apology. It's my fault Sarah's here. It's my fault they're all here. I was the first." He looked around with sorrow in his eyes, like a parent at a child's funeral. "But before I was here, I was in Chicago."

"Chicago? How does one go from Chicago to here?" Mark couldn't fathom leaving the city for something so seemingly primitive. He didn't care if they had modern clothes and homes, there were almost none of the conveniences of the technical age and a creepiness outweighing any of the perks the town may boast.

"Well, if you let me, I'll tell you." Galen's chin down again, he looked at Mark as if he were looking over the edge of glasses he wasn't wearing. Mark took the cue and smiled a tight-lipped smile, succumbing to the suggestion and hoping to glean what he could from whatever Galen had to tell him.

"I was a cop in Chicago in the fifties and sixties. Back when we walked our beat with a nightstick and attitude, but smiled at the old women and chatted with the storekeepers. You and I actually have much in common if you think about it." He paused and Mark could almost see the gears turning in the old man's eyes. "But you don't know that yet.

"The signs of the times were starting to show themselves. Attitudes were changing. America was changing. Equal rights and freedom were just beginning to become the overused excuse of the elite they are now. The seeds of entitlement were starting to grow among the various groups coexisting in larger cities and suburbs. But you know your history, you know one war had just finished and another was looming. The Cuban missile crisis, Black Panthers, and countless other things flavored the era. And in 1962 accidental crossfire between two rival groups of self-depreciating youths caught my only son as their innocent victim." Galen stopped. Waited for something, perhaps for Mark to comment.

Mark nodded, understanding the frustration of a cop losing a family member to the very thing he's trying to clean off the streets. But he also suspected Galen knew full well Mark understood and didn't feel the need to interject or verbally agree and get chastised for interrupting, so he simply nodded.

"The funeral and months afterwards almost killed me. Almost destroyed my marriage. And did damage to my daughter emotionally. You met her. Marianne. She's come out of it. Long ago. She's stronger than whatever God can throw at her, including losing a brother, a husband and a firstborn. But at the time, when she was only eleven and on the verge of a naturally confusing time of her life, she wasn't strong enough to handle anything of the sort. None of us were.

"We initially came here because I knew the place. Had summered up here with my parents in Eagle River when I was a kid. I had hunted some of the woods, fished and swam in the waters, and knew the summers to be a rather pleasant memory. One that had never included gunshots outside of deer season. I quit my job on the force, found this farmhouse with eighty acres, and moved my family away from the city and the growing evils it seemed to be breeding." He took a deep breath and shivered. "It's getting chilly. Would you like to continue inside?"

"Yes actually. I'm not used to the chill in the air this time of year."

"I suppose not."

"It was in the seventies back home."

"Oh, you must be freezing. It won't be that warm here for another two months, give or take. Let's go in and make some hot coffee for you." Galen stood and folded the blanket before setting it on the seat of his chair. He turned and walked gracefully to the front door, floating rather than walking, like liquid on ancient legs rather than a rickety old man with arthritis and aged muscles.

Mark followed him, his eyes adjusting as Galen flipped a switch and turned on the light. The warmth of the house hit Mark like a wall and he was instantly relieved to be out of the cold. As he followed behind Galen to the kitchen he glanced around the large rooms of the house, filled with memories, photos, items children had made, beautiful quilts across the couch, and a rumpled pillow that made Mark believe Galen had been sleeping there when he wasn't outside.

Two full cups of fresh brewed coffee in hand and they were back in the living room.

"Take a seat, son." Galen gestured and Mark chose a recliner he found, although it had seen better days, was amazingly comfortable.

"Now then… Yes. So we moved here. Dorothy wasn't happy about the temperature change, but she adjusted. Tough girl, my Dottie. She was stronger than all of us when we lost Timothy, and a day doesn't go by where I don't wonder if it was her strength alone that saw us through that first year. She busied herself gardening while I toyed with the idea of farm animals. I gave that up rather quickly though. I mean, really, what does a cop know about horses?"

"I actually know quite a bit. My grandmother had horses. I've been riding since I was very small and learned to break them by the time I was fifteen." Mark hadn't even realized he'd broken in and stopped. Galen smiled at him, a twinkle in his eyes, and nodded before continuing.

The old man walked toward the mantel and Mark looked ahead of him at the items laid there. An attractive woman and a young girl in a frame, matching blue eyes, smiled at the photographer while a blazing sun made a glowing halo out of the highlights in their hair. A plaque with Galen's badge attached to it and a slip of paper Mark could only presume was discharge orders. A small frame with what appeared to be sunflower seeds against cotton. A pottery bowl, crooked and painted by the clumsy strokes of a child. A hand-carved soap or ivory pipe that appeared older than the house. Galen paused and ran a finger down the side of the frame holding the woman and girl.

"Now Marianne… Marianne was not happy about the move. She was in the middle of nowhere. Being bussed to school in town. No friends nearby. No store to walk to. All alone in the big bad woods of northern Wisconsin. She hated the smell of the horse and pig I was tending to, and only wanted to eat the vegetables Dottie planted, rather than helping with the process. So we visited friends down south rather often the first few years. And when we did and they asked about us, I always told them the same thing. The air is fresh, the water is clean, and there's no crime rate. That still holds true for the most part, but I'm getting ahead of myself.

"In the fall of sixty-five, my friend Michael thought it sounded lovely and visited us. The original land had two homes on it. Technically a carriage house, as I've been told, but it was awfully large and I always referred to it as a home in and of itself that we just weren't using. He moved his family into it the following spring. Two summers later, my cousin and his family, along with the widow of my ex-partner and her daughter, showed interest and we started building additional homes."

Galen walked away from the mantel. Appearing to pace or wander in the memories of the items on his walls, but seeming to do so with a purpose that became evident when he crossed the floor in front of Mark and stopped in front of a large framed parchment that reminded Mark of a family tree, but the branches came from the ground rather than a single trunk.

"That's how it started. Four families. Over time there was a whole new generation of families to sprout. As the years passed and we sent children off to college, we ironically began to close off more from society. We sent them out for education but shunned the idea of society touching us and created our own schoolhouse, which is governed by the state's homeschooling regulations. We kept our children safe and out of harm's way until they were ready to go off to college."

"I imagine college money is paid for by everyone in town?"

"Yes, the market proceeds go into a fund. Whatever's not used for supplies is set toward the next generation of tuitions. Of course, those of us that were first, the 'founders' as they call us, came with money and we invested wisely, so the town has a nest egg of sorts that has grown over the years for emergencies and such."

Mark nodded. It actually made perfect sense to him. The town grows a child, sends it off to learn something they can utilize and then draws them back into the fold. Mark opened his mouth to speak but Galen had been watching him intently and answered before Mark could formulate the question.

"We've lost a few over the years, too dazzled by the rest of the world to come back to our simple ways. We've had children join the armed forces for their country—I believe you met Peter—most come back, but we've got one career air force. John, my grandson. He comes and visits, and when he retires in another four years, we fully expect him to return." Galen looked over the chart on the wall, as if invisible lines were drawn across the families represented there, telling him the paths he was to speak of, and he rambled forward as his eyes skipped around the frame.

"We've got a minister and a doctor now from the outside world.

And among our own college-trained, we've got everything else we need—a plumber, an electrician, a newly graduated veterinarian, a carpenter and two teachers. What started as familial duties, with sewing, gardening and livestock, have spread and crisscrossed families. If you've had a chance to walk around town, or if Josh and Sarah have explained it, then you know we have quite a large farmyard to the south and an immense garden to the north. The river runs north to south and touches both, the animals at the bottom so they cannot contaminate the crops—Dottie's idea. God, she was brilliant."

Mark looked back to the picture on the mantel of the woman and wondered how long she'd been gone. Galen spoke so highly of her, with a glimmer in his eyes. In a day and age of broken families and twisted nucleuses, it was refreshing to see someone that had loved the same woman for several generations and beyond her death as he had loved her in the beginning. He returned his attention to Galen, a sour taste of jealousy in his mouth.

"So you have everything…"

"Almost. We don't have a fire hall and must rely on Eagle River's response time should something happen, but that's only happened once, in the early eighties. And we don't need law enforcement. We are the law. It may seem backwoods to you, or bizarre, but if you look past the situation with Sarah as it stands, because I'm sure that's the whole point to both your visit and incessant questioning, it's a very good idea. Clean air, fresh water. The children are happy. The adults are healthy. And we've even grown a few times when our children went off to school and brought friends back to stay."

"Like Sarah…" Mark thought about her meeting Josh in college.

"No, no, that was love. I mean friends who decide it sounds great to be away from the dangers and ugly truth the city offers. Friends who come and stay and marry and put down roots of their own branches."

"Really?" Mark couldn't imagine this sounding intriguing at all to someone who had grown up with television and video games and fast food and faster lifestyles.

"Yes. Depending on the person, it's surprising how much or how little they need to suffer to find solace in simplicity." Galen walked back toward Mark and stood behind the couch, one hand resting on the quilt, his fingers absently tracing patterns and feeling the softness of old, over washed fabric.

"See now," Mark started and paused, mentally removing the snark from his voice that wanted to shout out and be heard for the first time since he'd arrived. "That all sounds lovely. And everyone does seem truly happy. But the mutilations? How can you think it's okay to do that to people? What makes you their judge and jury? What gives you the right to play God—"

"Now hold up right there, son." Galen's eyes narrowed at Mark as his hand clamped down on the fabric of the quilt. "We are not playing God. We do not take or make life. We are respectful of the Father and only wish to do the best we can with the life He's given us."

"Old Testament style?" Mark met Galen's stare with a look of horror and disbelief.

"I could see how you would equate it to that. An eye for an eye. But it's not that. Not at all. It's not about the punishment itself. It's not about torture or pain."

"Well what the hell is it? A lesson learned? What lesson can possibly be learned by mutilating my sister? That boy today?" Mark stood, his voice rising in intensity but he restrained and kept the volume level.

Galen walked around to the front of the couch and sat down opposite Mark. The old man's steel blue eyes met Mark's without blinking for several seconds, then blinked in a calm, lazy fashion that matched the tiny smile at the corner of his ancient lips.

"Son… Mark… It's not a lesson learned. It's a reminder. It's a cleansing. Admitting your sin and holding the scar as a reminder. It's not only a reminder to the person though. You need to understand that. It's a reminder to those that see it, to remember what happens, but also to remember that after we pay for our sins, they are forgiven."

"Okay, you talked about God. I don't know exactly what sect of what religion you folks preach and believe here, but I heard both God and Jesus in church the other day, so I know you believe in both." Mark leaned forward and felt for a brief moment as if he were arguing with Benny, except he realized, he didn't want a drink, he just wanted clarity. "Didn't Jesus ask his father to forgive all of us before we had even committed the sin, from the cross, down the ages? Hasn't God already forgiven? What gives you the right to forgive in his place?"

"Yes, yes, you're right. Perhaps *forgive* was the wrong word. Let's call it penance instead. Equate it to the Catholics and their Hail Marys and rosary beads. They ask the priest to relay the request for forgiveness, but the priest gives them some task as penance. We don't give a task, we give a punishment."

Mark sat back and chewed on the idea, swirling the beliefs and process around his mind. "Okay. I get the logic there, twisted as it may be, but you're still doling out in His name. And not just Hail Mary repetitions. You're maiming and mutilating."

"The truth? It wasn't intended to progress to the level it's at now."

Mark cocked his head. "What?"

"When it started…" Galen's eyes glazed over in thought for a moment and he glanced at the family tree on the wall. "We lived for quite some time with no problems, but the bigger any town gets, the more problems it has. When Andrew stole from the store we had set up, we needed to do something about it. That was when the council was created.

"It started as the four founding members, the founding fathers as they call us now—Me, Michael, Thomas and Andrea. We included Gail, Michael's wife, to make it an uneven number for voting and such. We talked for days. Andrew was twenty-one at the time and actually courting Rebecca, whose family ran the storefront. If we had reported him to the local authorities, he faced the possibility of going to jail, and we didn't agree with the way the system worked, putting a thief in with murderers, and the way jail time had somehow started to make repeat offenders of criminals who were not deterred by the rather blasé punishment three square meals and cable television provided."

Galen stood again. His calm demeanor was a bit more agitated now and the pacing was just that, rather than the casual strolling through his own house he had been doing earlier.

"We decided to punish him ourselves. We held a meeting with everyone and discussed it at length. Everyone was happy with the town the way it was. Even Andrew was okay with whatever punishment we thought would best suit his crime. Cutting off a finger was actually his idea." Galen stopped pacing and turned to Mark. "It was *his* idea. And they all agreed. We uniformly saw the Old Testament and modern-age validity of such a punishment."

"He suggested it? Really?" Mark thought back to the picnic table he'd shared with the family. "But he's missing a whole arm, not just a finger."

"Yes, but that wasn't us. That was before we had a doctor here and we made the mistake of not checking it religiously for infection. He ended up losing right past his elbow to an infection we noticed too late to stop. But the arm was taken in time and the infection did not go beyond that."

"And who cut that off?" The incredulous timbre returned to Mark's voice as he asked a question he dreaded.

"Oh not us. We went into the Eagle River for that."

"So how do you get from a finger to an eyeball?" Mark wanted to stand and join the man pacing the room, but kept firm to his seat out of respect. "How exactly does one get from there to here?"

"Again, that was decided on by everyone." Galen returned to his perch behind the couch and began fingering the quilt again. His eyes were filled with regret and sorrow. "Before we took Andrew's finger, we did a lot of talking. We came up with a list of rules for infractions. They made sense. A finger for stealing, a small clip of your tongue for gossip, et cetera."

"Sure, I can see that. But an eyeball? Castration?" Mark swallowed over the lump in his throat, torn between a desire to save his sister from humility and pain, and a sudden understanding of how and why the system was the way it was.

"Well, not all of those were on the original list. Things happened over the years we weren't prepared for, crimes we'd never had in town before. And when those happened, the council—now made up of the firstborns of the founding four—decides an appropriate punishment."

Mark opened his mouth but stopped—he wasn't ready to accept the fact he understood the logic. While he may not agree with everything they were doing, he could at least understand how, in their twisted ways, it made sense. *The community liked life the way it was and agreed to these terms. It was no different than many situations where you agree to do or not do something in order to receive something in return, whether it be a no-compete agreement for a job or a specific list of rules set down by a home owner's association. Granted, this was a bit more strict, a touch* Twilight Zone*, and definitely less forgiving…*

"What about warnings?" Mark looked up at Galen. "Is it first offense or are there warnings? I mean, that boy was what? Josh said fourteen."

"He is fifteen." Galen's eyes flitted around for a moment as if he was questioning himself. "Yes, fifteen, next week. And an adult as far as the rules go. Once a child turns thirteen, they are considered old enough to know what they are doing, and therefore old enough to be punished for their wrongs. Before thirteen, they are disciplined by their parents. And only twice have there been repeat offenders to the point parents came to the council for advice."

"Thirteen? Adult?"

"King Tut was ten."

"King Tut lived three thousand years ago."

"Joan of Arc was only twelve when she started having visions, and still a teen when she led soldiers in battle."

"Again, ancient history. We've learned since then."

"No, we've decided to coddle our young and let them get away with more." Galen raised an eyebrow. "And look where it's gotten our youth today?"

"But…" Mark sighed and a thought came to him. "Okay fine. You're not playing God and you're not punishing. You're offering atonement. But your crimes are based on basic morality, the Ten Commandments with a modern twist. But what about other things? Where do you draw the line of what is a crime and what isn't? The woman with the scarf on her eyes? That's vanity. It's a deadly sin. Keeping the Sabbath holy? You celebrate church on Saturday because you're at market on Sunday, trying to make money—which is worshipping another God before God. Money is the modern golden calf, but you do it every week with no shame."

Galen nodded slowly as he listened to Mark, as if making bullet point responses in his mind. His response startled Mark.

"You're right." The man stood and looked from the portrait on the mantel over to the family tree and back at Mark. He walked around the couch and sat back down, his mouth twisted in thought.

"I'm right?" Mark tasted the words and watched Galen's face. The man's eyes were full of his own questions.

"Yes. You are. Gail's blindfold is vanity, a deadly sin, but we allow it. I never looked at it like that." Galen folded his hands in his lap, the fingers lacing and interlacing repeatedly as if trying to get comfortable while his mind spun. "The rules work though, Mark. Sure they've seen evolution and sudden jumps when necessary, but they work. We are crime free for the most part."

"How often—"

Galen cut him off, "Not often at all. We have a handful of punishments that have been doled out. A very small percentage really. It just seems like a lot to you. A couple per generation, because that's how it works. Each generation has to learn the hard way. But usually, after an infraction or two is dealt with in the gazebo, the generation on a whole learns."

"Josh said something like that…" Mark remembered the calm way Josh and Sarah had discussed punishments, as he watched the man's fingers fidgeting among themselves. Only then did he notice Galen was missing an index finger. "So what did you do?" Mark pointed to the man's hand.

"Ah this. Nothing. Everything." Galen held his hand up in front of him and looked at the missing finger as if it were a fresh wound. "When Andrew was punished, I had this done. First. I told them all I couldn't allow a punishment system across the board like that, couldn't be considered their leader, without going first. I volunteered my finger to match his punishment. Mine was for all past sins and future responsibilities."

"Noble." Mark heard the word and meant it, but it sounded hollow. His anger and confusion at the town and their ways, the situation with his sister, the mutilation he witnessed earlier, all fought the logic and he heard it in his voice.

Galen's lips curled in a tight smile as he pulled up his sweater sleeve. "Let me show you something…"

The man's arm was thin, covered in age spots and loose skin, and somehow slightly tanned in the dead of winter due to years in the sun that changed a tan to a weathered look. From wrist to elbow the leathery skin was marred with long lines of bright white scar tissue. If Galen was a teen from the city, Mark would have assumed he was a cutter. But he wasn't a teenager and this wasn't the city. Mark remembered the list of crimes and punishments Josh had rattled off and questioned Galen.

"So you have a foul mouth?"

"No. Not at all." Galen ran a finger across each line on his arm. "Every one of these represents a punishment doled out to someone else in town. These are the marks I take onto myself to allow punishment to be handed to them. It's my fault they're here. They are my responsibility. And I take damage whenever they do something. It is not only a reminder to myself of what we've created here—the genesis and evolution of just wanting to keep my family safe and away from society's evils—it's also a secondary deterrent I hadn't planned."

Mark tilted his head quizzically at the old man as Galen pulled his sleeve back down.

"They all know I take a line for each of their sins. They don't want to cause me pain for their indiscretions any more than they want their own pain, so they keep to the straight and narrow." He met Mark's gaze. "Did you think I only punished and accepted no responsibility for what I've raised, trained and preached for forty years?"

"It's not that... It's..." Mark was at a loss for words.

Galen nodded. "You can't know what goes on behind closed doors if all you do is stand outside the fence."

Mark's mind reeled with new questions, new thoughts, and settled on one he hadn't even expected. "Josh said you've been quiet and withdrawn lately. You've been anything but that since I walked in here..."

"No I haven't, but Josh was not wrong." Galen looked up at the portrait on the mantel again. "I suppose I've been a bit quiet since Dottie passed last fall." He looked at Mark and for the first time appeared weak, vulnerable. "I miss her."

"Understandable, and I'm sorry for bringing it up."

"Don't apologize." Galen took a deep breath and pushed it out through his nose. "Was there anything else I could help you with?"

"Just one. How do I save my sister?"

"You don't, I'm afraid." Galen shook his head slightly, as if subtly scolding a child. "She's an adult and it's her decision to accept her penance and stay in the community. William fled. She could have. What she chooses for herself, what she accepts, is her choice. We call it free will." Galen smiled at the last part.

"Who will do it? The doctor? Will it be public like this was? And how... Did she confess or something? I mean, from what she said it was only to get pregnant, not an affair or anything."

"Oh no, I completely believe her on that regard. But it is still a sin. And quite frankly, the biggest we've had. It was very difficult to decide how to deal with that one. Again, the sinner was included and made her own suggestions."

"She didn't come up with this one, did she?" The horror had returned to Mark's expression.

"No. She'd suggested hobbling and limbs. Marianne vetoed those because it would reduce her capacity as a mother and she still had that responsibility to both the baby and Josh. Brother Garrett suggested a hysterectomy after the birth of the baby, to more directly relate to the sin. Considering how long she'd tried to get pregnant, that was a pretty good slap in the face. But the doctor suggested we do castration instead, as it would still allow for sexual relations and not punish Joshua, but it would remove her clitoral pleasure during intercourse."

"But it's... It's barbarian. It's something they do in Third World countries, deep in the hills, among tribes still in the Stone Ages..."

"It is. I'll grant you that. But it was discussed, decided on, and your sister accepts her penance." Galen spoke matter-of-factly, as if discussing police procedure and Mark's mind split between the next question and a nagging thought.

He chose the thought.

"How can you do this as an ex law enforcer? Serve and protect. What about all the good you wanted to do on the streets?"

"I still am. I hold the laws and am final veto on anything that happens with regard to the rules. Nothing in this town happens without my say. Nothing."

"How you are any different than a dictator then?"

"More like a judge. There is a community worth of jury members, officers of the court in the council and I hold the gavel. It works, Mark. Look around you and tell me it doesn't."

Mark relived his experiences since arriving in town. Ran a mental checklist of attitude and aptitude. He couldn't argue that the system worked. But he still wanted to argue the severity of the system, especially where it concerned Sarah.

"So how did you find out? How did she…"

"A little birdie, so to say." Galen took another deep breath and exhaled through his nose, making Mark wonder if his breathing was labored or just frustrated. "Meghan saw them and told her mother and cousin. Her mother suggested she come talk to me. She did, sort of. More like she came storming into my house screaming about how we needed to kick Sarah out of town."

"Kick her out?"

"Sure, exile is a possibility. But that's generally for someone that doesn't learn and is a repeat offender to the point of exhaustion. Sarah had been a perfect citizen."

"And how did Meghan…"

"Did you meet Meghan? Short, dark black hair…eye patch?" Galen's eyebrow rose as he finished with the defining characteristic.

"Yeah. Well, we didn't meet her, but I saw her. She was busy glaring at Sarah throughout the entire picnic…" Mark nodded as it dawned on him. "She's the one that told."

"And she lost her eye for spying. Two bits of her tongue for gossiping about Sarah after that."

Mark was suddenly confused on the timing of everything. "Wait. When did she tell? When did she see? The baby is six months old…"

"She didn't see the first time. She saw the second time."

"Second time?" Mark's voice raised in anger. Not at Galen, but rather at Sarah, as she had left out that tidbit when telling Mark what she'd done.

"She didn't tell you…" Galen paused, waiting for Mark's anger to come back down and his eyes to refocus. "The first time had been successful, so she and William thought they'd do it one more time to try and get Josh a family of four rather than an only child. They were interrupted and did not commit the act the second time. Though they confessed to everything once brought to council. That birthmark on little Mark? His father has one exactly like it. There was really no way they could deny it—family similarities aside. And around these parts, when questioned you come clean, because it's always easier that way in the end. They didn't bother lying."

"So when…when was this?" Mark was doing the calculations in his mind. "And why has Meghan received her punishment already but not Sarah. Not that I want you to mutilate my sister, but I'm trying my damnedest to understand all this craziness."

"No no, I understand. It happened in early February. William ran right after the council meeting deciding their fates—his was to be castration as well, in the removal of one of his testicles. We spent some time trying to find him before doling out punishment to her, while the doctor researched the procedures. In the meantime, Meghan's mouth had been getting the best of her, so we bumped her punishment up to make a point. She received both penance and forgiveness in mid-March."

"You've given up on finding William? And now it's Sarah's turn?"

"Not to put it bluntly, but yes. It's time." Galen absently rubbed his arm where his sympathy scars were hidden by his sweater sleeve. "She's scheduled for Friday, though with the storms, we may do it Thursday."

"Thursday." It wasn't a question. It was an acceptance, the truth as it finally started sinking into Mark's reality.

Mark didn't notice Galen watching him as he ran through the situation in his mind. The birth of the rules made sense. The birth of the town itself was innocent, logical. Mark had to admit to himself, the end result, if you could stomach small towns, was actually quite pleasant. He finally looked back up to Galen.

"I…uh…" He stood and offered his hand to the old man. "Thank you. Thank you for your time. I understand why Josh thought I should talk to you."

"You have no more questions?" Galen stood and shook Mark's hand.

"Oh I have plenty of questions. But I think I need to process all this…"

"Well, I have an open door. Anytime you want to chat, just come on over." Galen picked up both coffee cups and walked Mark to the door.

"There's really no way I can save her?" Mark's expression was resignation but his voice pleaded like a child wanting a treat.

"Only she can 'save' herself, and in her mind, that's exactly what she's doing by accepting her punishment. Remember, we don't hold grudges. After your punishment, you are forgiven. Clean. Innocent again. You have to understand, Sarah's been the target of scrutiny and subtle looks for months. She's been shunned in a sense because she hasn't been punished yet. Until she is, she's a sinner in their eyes. I'm sure she'd like to get back to her regular activities."

"Activities?"

"Well, she doesn't sew or anything, but she did do a lot with the children after school. Most of the parents aren't allowing their children near her outside of school until she's punished appropriately."

"Wow. Okay." Mark hadn't even thought about what Sarah had been going through, only what she was going to go through. "Wait, did you say sewing? Sarah never could sew."

"She still can't. Though the knitting circle tried to teach her." Galen smiled. "Dottie did her best, but in the end Sarah just went to spend time with the girls, especially my Dottie. She used to tell me Dottie reminded her of your mother."

Mark could completely understand Sarah latching onto anything or anyone that reminded her of their parents. But the bittersweet thought was overridden by the city cop's snark so comfortably living inside him. "Of course you have a knitting circle…" He smiled at Galen.

"Oh no. Not anymore." The old man looked around the dark town from the doorway, as if making sure they were alone. "They were nine shades of crazy and becoming quite a little circle of bitchy gossip. Two lost tongue parts and we broke up the party shortly after Dottie passed."

Mark laughed quietly and turned to the dark streets. He heard the door close softly behind him as he descended the porch steps. He looked to his left, down the spoke of street that would bring him to Sarah's house, but walked straight instead. He needed to contemplate everything Galen had said. What he did and didn't understand still. And how he felt about it all. He still had a few days to talk sense into Sarah.

CHAPTER TWENTY-SIX

Mark wasn't sure how long he'd sat in the gazebo. He contemplated whether they'd cleaned the tiny unseen spattering of blood from the wood or left it to soak in there—absorbing the blood of the sinners and making the town stronger in a bizarre sense. He was careful not to sit on the benches the blood would most likely have spilled onto earlier that day.

That day. Today. It was still Sunday. My God, what a day it had been.

It felt like he hadn't seen Gina in ages, rather than only a handful of hours ago. It seemed like a blur of motion, activity, revelations had come slamming down on him, and his body—his conscience—just wasn't big enough to take it all in. To organize it. Label it. Know how to deal with it.

He'd left the gazebo a while ago and wandered forward down the spoke past the doctor's office, only identifying it by the moonlight shining on the plaque out front. Past several houses he found himself at the edge of a thick forest. He walked into the shadows of its canopy in a daze while his mind continued to roll the realities around like a kaleidoscope, different reflections of different pieces making designs twist this way and that, hoping one of the combinations would make sense to him.

He'd been wandering most of the night when he both noticed the crack of predawn light and realized the sound he'd been ignoring for several hours had been running water. He presumed he was near the stream Galen had mentioned and headed toward the sound to find his bearings in the woods.

Breaking through the thick pines, Mark found the stream to be an understated river that hadn't quite grown up. A good thirty yards across, Mark could see the water tumbling over large boulders and swirling in the eddies of their shadows. Tall dead reeds and brown grass had been pounded flat by the weight of winter on both sides of the river. Mark imagined it was plenty big enough to support life and wondered if the town fished or trapped in the running water so convenient to their lives. If it had been summer, he could imagine children swimming in the churning waters, clouds of insects above their heads. For a kid, this would be a great place to hang out, or hide from your parents.

Bent over on this side of the stream, at the edge of a row of planks covering the muddy shore, a woman bundled in a long quilted coat held fishing line in one hand and stared intently into the waters below her. He turned to leave and crunched a dead twig—its echo seemed to boom across the predawn silence of the woods. The woman jumped and turned toward him, dropping the fishing line.

"Sorry, didn't mean to startle you." Mark held a hand out in front of him apologetically. She brushed her hair from her face with a hand and Mark saw the eye patch. Meghan. He wanted to ask her why. He wanted to ask her what she got out of it besides her own mutilation. But as he had walked throughout the night and twisted things around, he was starting to understand the logic and natural progression the town had taken, even if it had taken it too far. Meghan's actions were still an anomaly and he thought he'd be more comfortable with everything else if he just pretended that little hiccup in the logistics didn't exist.

But his mouth opened anyway.

He heard his own voice before he realized he was even talking.

"Why were you spying on my sister? Better yet, why did you tell knowing what would happen?"

She stared at him for a moment, glanced around as if to see whether he was alone, and stood to face him. She opened her mouth to speak and closed it again. Her head tilted as she cocked both physically and mentally at him and his question. Then she took several brisk steps toward him, stopping at his feet and looking up at him.

"How dare you question me." Her speech was just slightly tweaked, as if she had a new tongue piercing she wasn't quite used to yet and Mark remembered she'd lost several pieces of tongue for running her mouth about Sarah. "You are an outsider. You do not understand. You come storming in here like the white knight and demand answers and audience, but you don't know anything about what you're asking. You don't know us, as a community or as individuals, and you have no

White Picket Prisons

right to anything within our boundaries."

Meghan made a proud grunting noise, as if she'd said the final word and Mark should just tuck his tail and leave. He wasn't going anywhere.

"Actually, I understand quite a bit." He met her single staring eye with his own unblinking attitude. "I spent last night with Galen, learning all kinds of things. I do understand your community, your ways. And because I do, it only makes me question further. You *knew* what would happen to you. Why would you willingly risk that? Twisted loyalty or jealousy or just childish behavior?" He almost regretted his last words.

Almost.

"You spoke to Galen?" He saw her visibly pause, both her attack and approach, briefly before shaking it off.

His calm demeanor—that had been wandering the woods and working things out in his head—was slipping away. His frustration was coming back into focus, and he felt it building like heat behind his eyes.

"It didn't matter what happened to me. It only mattered *she* be punished. The golden child that isn't anyone's child. I waited. I watched. For years. I knew she'd eventually fuck up, no one is that perfect, but I never dreamed it would be on such a grand scale." The snarl on her face curled into a cruel smirk of self-imposed grandeur.

"Years?" Mark looked down at the woman. "Why? What did she ever do to you?"

"You don't know, do you?"

Her smirk became something undefined as the glimmer in her single eye caused Mark to take a step back. He had spent years on the street. He had seen a lot of expressions meant to intimidate, terrify. But he'd never seen a stink-eye so perfectly crafted to raise every hair on his body. He shook his head and narrowed his eyes, requesting she fill him in without uttering a word.

"Josh was mine." She spat the last word and took a step forward. "I lived the first twenty-two years of my life expecting to marry Joshua. Planning our wedding and our babies' names. My life mapped out. And then he comes back from college with *her*." She blinked several times and stood a little taller. "It took years to get over. To try and move on. And I was just beginning to be okay with the idea I would still be part of his family when his aunt Rebecca tried to get me to give my attention to her son William. William. Josh's cousin. Your whore sister's lover."

"Oh," was all Mark could manage. He could actually understand this woman's anger. She felt she had been wronged. Though Sarah likely didn't know about her when she met Josh in college, and probably wasn't aware of the William connection, but Mark couldn't be sure of that.

"Did Sarah know about William?"

"She didn't need to. She was already married. It was none of her business and no reason for her to be involved…or so I thought." She looked to the side and Mark watched her focus flit off into a thought before coming back, her eyes returning to his with a new vigor in her intensity. "In a sense it's really all your fault."

"My fault? What the hell did I do?"

"You let her come here. You should have stopped her. You should have fought her until she caved. You should have sent Josh away, unwanted, unwelcomed." She took another step toward him. "*You*," she poked a finger into his chest with angry force, "should not have let her come here."

"Are you crazy? You can't blame me for that. She was an adult, making her own decisions. I didn't exactly throw a party and celebrate, you know. But I couldn't stop her any more than I could have made the sun stand still."

"Fuck you." She pushed him away hard and he stumbled to keep his footing. She lurched forward and pushed him again, knocking his already unbalanced form to the forest floor. "Fuck you and your sister. She's ruined my life and now you're here to try and save hers? Bullshit. This is all bullshit!"

Meghan leapt on top of him, sitting on his chest and began screaming as she pounded her fists against him.

"Perfect fucking bitch. Everyone loves her. Everyone thinks she's the best thing to ever happen to this town. They don't care about me. They never cared about me. The only thing that was ever going to make me worth anything in this town's eyes was Josh. And she fucking stole him!"

Mark used his left hand to shield his face from her wild swings, his right to try and push her off him. He was taller than her by at least five inches and guessed he was a good fifty pounds heavier, but her rage was that of a crack addict on a bad day. Her knees were clamped into his ribs and continued squeezing, pushing against his midsection like a rider spurring a horse forward. Her fists were a nonstop barrage of years' worth of hatred coming out against him, just because he was related to Sarah. He fought against her as she continued to scream and finally stopped blocking long enough to grab both of her wrists. He squeezed them hard to get her attention, her shocked expression made worse by the fact he now noticed tears streaking down her face, from both her good eye and behind the patch as well.

"Get. Off. Me. Bitch." He pushed her with everything he had and she toppled to the side.

A primal scream escaped her gaping mouth as she grabbed a stick and immediately came back at him. Swinging haphazardly, she hit his ribs, head and arms.

"She stole Josh. She fucked William. And now you're here to make sure she's not punished for it?" Her slight lisp from the missing tongue pieces, combined with anger equal to a pissed-off badger, caused spittle to fly from her lips as she screamed at him. "Just take her home. Fucking leave. Both of you!"

The stick in her hand swung down at an angle he wasn't quick enough to block and it connected with his collar, jabbing the flesh and tearing it open as it slid across the bone. He felt the searing pain in a flash of intense heat. He felt warmth spread across his shoulder and neck and instinctually knew he was bleeding. A quick mental calculation of the area and the arteries she could have nicked sent him into a panic and he reached around him blindly for something to strike back with.

"She was so fucking perfect but couldn't get pregnant. Bullshit. She lost one right after they got here but wouldn't admit it. Claimed they hadn't had premarital sex. Claimed it was just a bad period. Bullshit. She lost his baby because she wasn't supposed to have his babies. She wasn't supposed to have him. Josh was mine, damn it!"

Meghan continued to swing with both the stick and free fist. She connected with his jaw, his ribs, and narrowly missed his eye when he snapped his head to the side. Reaching behind him, his hand found purchase on a fist-size rock. His fingers curled around it and his survival instinct swung it up at her. He connected with the side of her head. Meghan's eyes went wide for a moment as she was jolted to the side, her mouth open as if she was going to continue to rant and scream at him. Her face went slack and she slumped to the side, sliding off him in the process.

Mark lay there for a moment, catching his breath. He reached up to his shoulder and gently touched the wound she'd made with the stick. The skin was tender, pulsing in beat with his racing heart, and his fingers were instantly coated in blood. He pushed down on the wound and tried to prop himself to the side to check on Meghan.

She lay crumbled on her side, stick still in her hand. Her eyes were closed, her lips slightly parted. He reached over and pulled the stick from her grip. He fumbled with her sleeve to move the heavy coat out of the way and checked her pulse. He felt nothing at first and panic crossed his expression—what would be the punishment for this? Then he felt it. Weak, but there. Skipping and sporadic, but there.

He needed to get back to town and get the doctor.

Mark pushed himself up to his feet, his head swam and his vision blurred. He felt every bit as awful as he was sure he looked. His ribs hurt, and when he realized he was wincing with each breath, he feared she might have actually cracked one or two. His face felt like he'd walked into an automatic car wash and been whipped with spinning rubber tentacles. He hadn't been battered like that since he was a rookie and wondered if it was his age that made it seem so bad. But he had seen large men taken down by tiny angry druggies on the street. Rage is a powerful conduit for power, and this little woman had a lot of it. He grunted and headed away from the river, hoping town would be right through the trees.

He used the trees to brace himself as he walked. Squinting through the branches, he hoped to see some sign of town in the early dawn light. He doubled over coughing. His ribs screaming at the brutal force of the jagged hacking. He spat blood and wiped his mouth with his hand. He tried to stand upright again but the world tilted on its axis and he landed in a pile of dead leaves, wet from the recent rains, and smelling of death and decay.

CHAPTER TWENTY-SEVEN

Mark felt his ribs protest his breathing before he realized he was no longer on the forest floor. He blinked several times and winced, holding back a cough tickling the back of his throat. He felt the weight of blankets and the softness of a pillow behind him, but didn't recognize his surroundings.

The small room was painted white with a single window framing a dim sky, making Mark question whether it was morning or evening. The walls were plain except for a rather generic painting of a field of flowers with the blur of children playing in the distance. There was a small table near the window and a chair at the side of the bed, but otherwise the room was bare of any type of furniture or decoration.

Mark struggled to sit up and flopped back down onto the bed. The ribs on his left side pinched, making it difficult to breathe. He lay back and tried to relax, to regulate his breathing. After a few moments he felt his chest and found it was tightly wrapped and he wore no shirt. His hand rose to his collarbone and felt a large patch of cloth and tape and he realized he'd been found and patched up by someone. *The doc?*

As if on cue, the door to the small room opened and the man from the gazebo walked in.

"Ah, I see you're awake. Welcome back, Mr. Baker." He smiled and sat down on the chair. He grabbed Mark's wrist and felt his pulse, nodding to himself. "How are you feeling?"

"Where am I? Your place?"

"Yeah. Both to keep an eye on you and as a neutral location until we figure out what happened and what to do about it."

"What happened? What do you mean?"

"Well, you're recovering. Meghan is in the gazebo being laid out for her viewing. She didn't make it." The doctor watched Mark for a few moments and then smiled widely. "I'm sorry. Where are my manners? I'm Dr. Evan McCloud. My father was the town doc for years, but I'm taking over. You're in my house because it's easier to keep an eye on you than if I leave you at the office."

"Meghan died?" Mark spoke as if he hadn't heard anything else the doctor had said.

"Unfortunately, yes. Before we found her…and you. And had we not found you for another few hours, I'm not sure you would have made it either. You lost a lot of blood from your shoulder there."

Mark's hand was still on the bandage there and he pulled it away. "My ribs?"

"Cracks, not breaks. Which is good, but will hurt like crazy for a few weeks." The doctor's brown eyes were soft, caring, and perfect for his profession. The lines in his face appeared to be from worry rather than age, as Mark didn't think he was even in his forties yet.

"Meghan…"

"Let's wait until you're on your feet." The doctor stood. "You should feel more yourself in the morning. I'll go get you something to eat and be right back."

"Morning? How long ago…"

"We found you yesterday morning. You've been in and out for two days. It's just past eight o'clock at night now."

"Oh, okay." Mark felt strangely relieved he hadn't been out for very long.

"No worries. You haven't been gone for weeks or anything like that." The doctor smiled as if he could read Mark's thoughts and disappeared through the door, closing it softly behind him.

--==•==--

Mark wasn't in any shape mentally to attend anything remotely close to the wake or funeral for Meghan the next day, but watched for a bit from the little window. He knew after the funeral he was to meet with the council to explain what happened, and he turned away from the solemn words he couldn't make out anyway to try and struggle into the fresh change of clothes Sarah had brought him earlier.

The hot shower he'd managed had made him feel a hundred percent better, but his body still protested at the smallest things. A sneeze almost sent him into screaming tears of pain but he managed to choke them back. The button-up shirt and jeans were easy enough, but after the struggle to get his socks on he knew there was no way he was going to be able to bend down and tie his shoes. He sat on the edge of the bed contemplating this when the doctor's wife walked in. "They'll be here soon." She stopped at the doorway and looked at him for a moment. "Do you want help with those?"

"Please." Mark smiled weakly. He didn't like feeling helpless and hated needing this tiny little blonde woman to tie his shoes for him.

He wondered why she wasn't at the funeral and looked out the window to find everyone had dispersed and the proceedings were evidently finished. He shook his head as he realized how long it had taken him to accomplish the simple act of getting dressed.

"There you go." She stood and offered him a hand to help him stand.

He waved it away and pulled himself to his feet, checking his footing against the dizzying pain that raced through him whenever he exerted himself or just breathed incorrectly. He felt sturdy enough.

"So, where to?" He turned back to the bed to gather his wallet and watch.

"I'll take him," came a voice from the doorway behind him and he turned to find Josh standing there. The doctor's wife nodded and left the room.

"Josh," Mark said as a salutation with no feeling attached, wondering if the man had a new reason to dislike him.

"How ya feeling, Mark?"

"Like I've been run over."

"Did Doc give you anything?"

"Yeah, I have some Tylenol with codeine for later, but I didn't take it. I want to be clearheaded for whatever they're about to do to me." He looked up at his brother-in-law and saw sorrow in his eyes. He had to wonder if it was for Meghan, or whether it was just pity for Mark. "What exactly are they going to do to me? Do you know?"

"Sorry, I don't. The council will decide. Come on, they're waiting." Josh turned and walked out of the room, his pace slow enough for Mark to catch up.

Mark expected Josh to lead him to the church or some other

official building in the town for the council meeting. He was more than a little stunned to find Josh head straight for the gazebo. Mark could see several people sitting there.

Josh stopped and waved Mark forward. Mark walked up the steps and nodded to the council members. He had met each of them previously and gone to market with most of them. Marianne, Peter, Joseph, Andrew and Camille sat along three of the benches quietly. Mark recalled the family tree on Galen's wall and remembered the council was the four oldest children of the founding members. He decided Camille must have been the fifth chosen to create an odd number, just as the first generation of council had needed to do.

Marianne gestured for Mark to sit down. "How are you feeling?"

"I've been better." He spoke as he watched a smattering of townsfolk begin to gather around the gazebo. He looked back to Marianne questioningly.

"Yes. You're an outsider. You don't know how this works." She smiled. "They can gather and watch. They are allowed to listen. But they are not to interject or interrupt. They will only be involved if we request a vote from them or something else. But they are here as witnesses. This is the way it's always been done."

Mark nodded. "Okay. So what do we do?"

"First." Marianne lifted a coffee cup Mark hadn't even noticed from the bench and held it in her hands as if for warmth. "You need to tell us what happened."

Mark told them about the evening chat with Galen and wandering town. He explained he was tired, he'd walked all night, and hadn't wanted to argue with Meghan when he ran into her that morning. He described her rage and language, much to their surprise, and the attack as he remembered it. He made a point of telling them she was alive when he went for help and they all nodded as they glanced at one another.

"Well…" Peter spoke first. "Do you feel you could have saved her?"

"Oh absolutely." Mark nodded earnestly. "I hadn't intended to hit her that hard, it was just reflex and panic." He was ashamed on some level to admit that. He was a cop. He wasn't supposed to panic. He'd been trained for years not to panic. It was the number-one reason innocent civilians were wounded and he had refused to be responsible for an accidental death. And here he was, just that.

Andrew piped up, a slightly cynical expression pre-coloring his question as he leaned forward and rested his arms on his legs. "Do you think it could have been avoided had you not questioned her. If you had just gone home rather than wandering about?"

Mark felt his defensive survival instinct kicking in and bit his tongue to prevent his words from being filled with anger. "I don't think that's a valid question. I didn't go looking for her and I would have never tracked her down to ask her those things. It just happened that way."

"Why did you ask that, Andrew?" Camille questioned him.

"I was wondering what kind of temper we're dealing with here. After Galen told him, was he angry at Meghan rather than his sister, displacing the blame for the situation he has such a hard time accepting?" Andrew looked from Camille to Marianne. "I think we need to establish his personality and proclivity for violence. To see if there's any familial similarities."

"Similarities? Sarah is gentle as a mouse," Joseph jumped in. "I don't think we can judge like that at all. We must judge Mark for Mark's actions, not by his relationship to someone else."

"True. Okay." Andrew sat back and left the floor open to whoever wanted to question Mark next. Mark was surprised at the result.

"I think we can all agree it was obviously involuntary manslaughter at best." Camille shook her head as if scolding a child.

"We've never had anything like that before though," Joseph added.

"And he's not one of us," Marianne concluded. "If he were it would be different. We'd then have to decide how he could atone for it. But he's not. So the decision becomes, do we deal with this in a fashion he will agree to, or do we turn him over to the state authorities?"

"We can't bring Meghan back," Camille said, her voice soft and unsure. "And it was an accident…" She looked at Mark. "In your world, what would happen? Would this ruin your career? Your livelihood?"

"Absolutely…" Mark was unsure why he lied. He knew it would be an investigation into the situation but never go to trial. It was self-defense and accidental, nothing worth losing his job or even paid time for, though they'd probably want him to talk to the station shrink. He didn't want to admit their ways had its merits, but for whatever reason, he'd rather they deal with it than report it and he let the lie hang in the air.

"Meghan is dead though." Joseph looked to his wife. "He can't just get away with that."

"No. I know…" She looked across to Marianne for help.

"What would you have us do, Mark?"

"Uh…" He hadn't been expecting that question and his mind reeled at the possibilities. His detective self wanted to do things by the letter. He knew it was an accident and he wouldn't see jail time let alone the inside of a courtroom. But did they have the equivalent of jail here? Gina suddenly came to mind and a new worry came with her. *Or missing the birth of my son because I'm sitting in some hickville jail for killing a bitch that deserved it.*

He chewed on the scenario and its various outcomes, and finally came up with the right way to word things. "What would you do if it was someone just passing through that wasn't related to someone here? If it was someone not visiting, with no ties?"

"We would turn them over to the state or local authorities." Marianne spoke without hesitation.

"And if it were one of your own?" Mark watched her eyes.

"We would have to settle on atonement and punishment." Joseph spoke before Marianne could answer.

"And what would be a happy medium? Or rather, something that would fall between the two? Exile?" A part of Mark was hoping they'd just choose to exile him. Ban him from returning. And if they told him to take his sister with, then he'd save them both.

"Bring him to me." Galen's voice broke through Mark's thoughts and he looked around, startled. He didn't see the old man and looked up to his house, finding him on the porch there, and wondering how his voice had been so clear. Joseph pointed to a speaker under the railing next to Andrew's leg and Mark nodded.

Marianne twisted around in her seat to face her father. Mark imagined they were having a silent conversation such as family members are able to do with nothing more than a look or body language. She turned back around and scanned the other council members briefly before settling on Mark's waiting face.

"Do you want me to walk over with you?"

Mark looked over her shoulder to her father and shook his head. "No. I'll be just fine."

"That remains to be seen." Andrew raised an eyebrow at Mark and nodded, indicating he should leave now.

CHAPTER TWENTY-EIGHT

I've thought about this for a few days." Galen's words were still running through Mark's head Thursday morning. "And I think you should do the same."

The conversation replayed over and over, as Mark weighed the consequences of both his actions and Galen's words. The way the old man had spoken calmly, but with authority, and asked Mark to put himself in their position. The bizarre way the situation had been twisted around and the suggestions Galen had presented. Mark had spent most of the night tossing and turning to either his overworking mind or dreams he could not control. He'd been alternately castrated and celebrated in his nighttime wanderings, and woke in a sweat more than once. But this morning he would have no time for thought, no time for contemplation on his own fate.

This morning his sister's was in question.

He watched her busy herself with household chores, the baby and small talk, as she tried not to think of where they'd be heading off to at noon. Perhaps it was her way of ignoring her own atonement, perhaps just curiosity, but Sarah took the conversation exactly where Mark wasn't prepared for it to go.

"So? What did Galen decide?" She brought the coffeepot to him and filled his cup. "The suspense is killing me. You're not one of us and that worries me."

"Worries *you?*" Mark stared at her as if she had spoken another language. "Considering what will be happening soon, how can you possibly be worrying about me?"

"Well yeah I'm worried about you, silly." She sat down on the coffee table in front of him. "Like I said, you're not one of us. I don't know what they'll decide and how it will affect you once you leave here. I'd hate to think an accident would destroy your career…"

"Actually, they're considering that carefully." Mark took a sip of coffee. "I'm still absorbing most of the conversation, but that was one of Galen's worries. He was a cop and he understands, but there's also something else…"

"You like Galen."

"Yeah, I do." Mark set the coffee down next to her on the table. "Oddly enough, I like most of the people I've met here."

"Yeah?" Sarah smiled knowingly.

"Yeah. I mean, I won't lie, I wanted to hate everyone after you explained how things work around here, but they really are very nice. I'm still having problems with the way you deal with things. With what they're about to do to you…"

"Well, I wouldn't expect you to be okay with it. I'm just glad you've finally come around to accepting you can't change it." She stood up and grabbed the coffeepot. "Speaking of which, I should probably go get ready. I need to stop by and see the doctor before we go to the square, and I have a few more things to do here. I don't know when I'll be up on my feet again."

"Yeah, about that…" Mark grabbed her arm gently and stopped her from walking away. "They've never done this? Do they know what they're doing?"

"Oh yes. Doc has been busily researching and speaking to other doctors about the procedure."

"Other doctors? Really?" Mark could only imagine the horror that conversation would cause in the medical community if they knew why the doctor was asking.

"Sure. Of course, I don't think he's said why, probably just claiming to be doing a research paper or out of curiosity after seeing some documentary or something. Who knows…" She pulled free from Mark. "But I know him and trust him, and the point to atonement is not pain, it's punishment. I know he'll do a good job and I'll be fine."

Fine. The word echoed in Mark's head as Sarah vanished into the kitchen briefly and then down the hallway without the coffeepot. When he heard the shower come on, he was still struggling with the question of which was more disturbing—the fact that they were okay punishing one another so severely, or how they accepted their own punishments as easily as if it were a simple household chore.

--==●==--

Mark accompanied Josh to the square. Sarah had gone ahead of them to the doctor's for some preparations, and Camille had come by just after to gather Marky. The town had gathered already by the time Josh and Mark arrived. This time he noticed the looks were aimed at him, rather than at Sarah, as they had been previously. He could only presume she was about to succumb to her atonement and Mark's punishment was still undecided, his crime still unanswered for. The crowd parted and allowed Josh and Mark to walk to the front, near the gazebo, where Josh stopped and Mark followed his lead. Mark turned toward the corner the doctor's office was located and waited for his sister to appear with her executioner.

He didn't wait long.

The crowd parted and Sarah came through in a white dress, like a bride walking to meet her fiancé at the front of a church. The doctor followed directly behind her, but he neither held her dress off the ground nor threw flower petals. This was not a wedding. Not a happy occasion at all. And Mark remembered the boy had worn white when they'd taken his eyeball. *A symbol of innocence?*

She stopped at the steps of the gazebo and looked at both Mark and Josh in turn, without a word but with plenty of communication with her eyes. She appeared terrified but pleased. Her chocolate eyes, a shade more orange than Mark's, were full of anxiety and something else.

Hope? Mark thought, but shook the idea free.

Mark jumped when Marianne addressed the crowd, as he hadn't even seen her approach the gazebo and hadn't noticed her there when he and Josh arrived. A glance over his shoulder confirmed his suspicion and he nodded quietly to Galen, sitting stoically in his rocking chair on the porch.

"Sarah Elizabeth Baker Andrews." Much like the last time, she addressed Sarah as if the crowd wasn't there. "Do you acknowledge you have broken a rule set down by our founding fathers and passed through the generations as law?" Sarah nodded mutely. "And were you tried by the council fairly and do therefore accept your punishment as declared?"

"Yes, ma'am." Sarah's voice cracked and Mark could only guess at what could possibly be running through her mind. He panicked and began to frantically recant everything in his head, to see if there was some way he could stop this. But he knew he couldn't. He knew this was Sarah's decision.

"Have you anything to say for your sin?" Marianne asked Sarah but now turned toward the crowd.

"No, ma'am." Sarah's voice was weak, like a child who'd been caught doing something wrong and was afraid to speak and make things worse.

Marianne nodded at the doctor and Josh nudged Mark. As the doctor and Sarah walked up the steps to the gazebo proper, Mark looked at Josh questioningly.

"Do you want to stay here or come up with me?" Josh asked in hushed tones.

"Come up?"

"Yes, you can come up for support if you'd like. I already cleared it with the council."

Mark was about to decline when he caught Sarah's gaze over Josh's shoulder. Every time she'd needed him—because she'd fallen and skinned a knee, had her heart broken by a boy, or suffered from the childhood twinges of self-deprecation—he'd been there for her. Every time. And there was no way he could sit by and watch this happen without her knowing he was there for her. Even if he could do nothing to protect her. To help her. To stop her.

Mark nodded silently to Josh and followed his brother-in-law up the steps to join Sarah. Unsure what to do, and muted by anxiety, he stood and waited for direction. The doctor waved Josh to the bench the girl had occupied a few days beforehand, holding Tommy's hand for support while they tore his eye from his head. When the doc turned to Mark, Mark could see him considering things. He finally pointed to the bench beyond Sarah, which would put him near her head once she laid back.

Marianne looked beyond Mark to where he knew her father sat on his porch, watching the proceedings and, as he learned the other day about the speaker in the gazebo, listening. She nodded at the doctor and left the gazebo area, joining the crowd around it.

Mark noticed the crowd, while still gathered en masse, were farther back than they were the other day. He wondered if it was respect for Sarah's privacy or a desire not to see this particular procedure up close. He agreed with both options and was relieved the doctor had put him behind her.

Sarah lay back and looked at Josh, holding out her hand for him to grab. Then she turned her tear-threatened doe eyes up at Mark and smiled weakly.

"Are you sure?" he whispered, giving her one last chance to change her mind and force him to make a run for the both of them out of town. She reached up a hand and cupped his face, smiling at him. She looked years older suddenly and as she pulled her hand away he grabbed it and held it. He wasn't sure if it was to soothe her or himself.

"How we doing, Sarah?"

"Oh, I'm all kinds of happy. Whatever you gave me is clearly working."

"I gave you a muscle relaxant and a sedative. I see the euphoria has kicked in. You should be feeling very groggy soon." He looked up to Mark and Josh. "When you feel her grip loosen, let me know." Both men nodded at the doctor.

Mark watched, this time with a better view, as the doctor began to lay out his instruments. Any questions Mark may have had regarding sanitary measures in the open air of the gazebo were answered as he watched the doc unroll freshly sterilized tools from clean white towels and spray them anew with a bottle clearly marked as alcohol-based antibacterial solution.

The towel contained a suture kit, still in its prepackaged surgical pouch, and Mark realized the doctor got his supplies from a legit source, rather than just backwoods implements crafted by the locals. A scalpel, several clamps, and what Mark could only assume was the tool designed for the mutilation itself. Similar to a single-handed garden sheer, the handles were thick and covered in gripping rubber. The clipping end was very narrow and curved up at the end, like it had been bent against something, but Mark was positive it was meant to be shaped that way. The shiny stainless steel was unmarred and Mark had to wonder if it had been a special purchase for this procedure.

Surely they've never had a reason to use such a tool, and Mark couldn't imagine they'd use it for any normal procedures.

He was at a loss, taking in so many details and avoiding the woman lying in white in front of him. He looked out the open areas of the gazebo and studied the crowd. The women all seemed to be there, supportive, but less stoic than they had been when Tommy had been up here. Mark presumed the whole idea of what they were doing was affecting the women of the community just like a room full of guys will wince and protect themselves if they see another guy get hit in the balls.

Mark felt Sarah's hand relax just as Josh spoke, "Baby?" Josh looked to Sarah but her eyes were unfocused, as if she were in a daze. "Her grip is limp, Doc."

"Okay then." Doc Evan turned to the white dress she'd chosen and began unbuttoning the bottom. Until then, Mark hadn't realized it had buttons all the way down the front as closures. The doctor undid the dress to Sarah's navel and pulled the two sides apart, covering her legs with the flaps as if they were operating room cloth meant to shield the surrounding tissue during procedures. She was naked underneath and Mark averted his eyes, though not fast enough, and noticed she'd been shaved bare—recently, he gathered from the red skin—and assumed it was part of the preparations she had to have done this morning.

The doctor turned toward the towel and chose two small silver clamps with scissor handles, unlike the simple alligator-style clips he'd used on the dress. Sarah murmured something and Mark watched her eyes for fear or pain. He saw neither and assumed the noise had been a dazed response to the cold as the dress had exposed her flesh. Mark looked up at Josh, feeling it was the only safe place to leave his gaze and still know what was going on. He was right.

Mark could tell by Josh's expressions certain things were likely happening. He imagined the clamps were to hold her labia out of the way, so the doctor had a clear view, clean line of sight and attack, to her clitoris. He presumed correctly moments before the doctor reached for the wicked-looking sheer implement. He returned his gaze to Sarah's face, stroking her face with his free hand. "It's almost done, sis…"

"Shhh." The sharp admonishment came from the doctor and Mark wondered if there was some bizarre protocol regarding speaking during the procedure they'd forgotten to tell him. He opened his mouth to apologize but stopped himself, realizing the apology would only be more of what had gotten him scolded in the first place. If it weren't for the gag order, he'd have expected the doctor to say something comforting or warning to Sarah, such as "you'll feel just a pinch now" and found himself wondering exactly how much pain would be involved. He knew she'd been drugged, because as they had all repeatedly told him "it's not about the pain but the punishment." But he also knew there were a hell of a lot of nerves gathered in that little bud of flesh. Perhaps it was nothing more than getting a piercing—after all, people did pierce their clits and they didn't die from it. But again his mind scolded him. This was not a piercing. This was a removal. There would be blood, on some level, and if she weren't doped up, there'd be pain. And perhaps there would be pain afterward.

He looked up at the crowd again, sensing a shift, and saw the circle had become a half moon instead. They were still there, still standing tall and showing support, but they had all moved to the sides. Just as they had seemed farther away, Mark assumed this was a small but appreciated show of respect for Sarah's privacy, as she was exposed to both the elements and the people she spent her life with.

The combination of the instrument's natural *snip* noise upon closure and popping of tender flesh interrupted his thoughts and he instinctively looked to the source of the sounds as Sarah's fingers flinched in his grip. A small spray of blood spattered the white dress on Sarah's right thigh. Thicker blood drooled down the edge of the instrument still positioned in front of her vagina, a small angry piece of flesh pinched in its blades.

Again he was glad for his position in the gazebo, as he couldn't directly see the wound itself, but his imagination filled it in. The purple of rich blood and recently torn flesh would have replaced the nub where her clit had been. It likely throbbed, dripping or spitting blood with each pass of her pulse through the base of the missing nerve bundles. He had seen enough wounds to know the surrounding tissue would appear pale due to blood loss and the body's natural response to send more blood there to fix whatever was wrong. Except the body couldn't fix this. No one could.

He couldn't save her from herself, and now he'd become party to her mutilation.

"When one of us sins, we all sin." Galen's words rolled across his memory and he felt the overwhelming urge to cry for Sarah. Instead he gazed down into her eyes. Love and respect and adoration shined back at him. Even in her drugged state, he could clearly see the expression he'd seen a thousand times throughout their younger years. The big brother. The protector.

The failure.

I could have stopped this, he thought. *I could have overtaken the doctor and Josh without any problems. I could have taken down much larger men in much worse situations.* Mark's jaw tightened with stress, he could feel his skin tingling with adrenaline. *I could have thrown her over my shoulder and run to the truck. The keys were in my pocket. The escape was right there.*

He looked over at the SUV he'd left parked in front of the school. The Pennsylvania license plate a beacon as the midday sun shone off it.

But I didn't. I let them do what they do best—clean their own dirty laundry. They sin, they atone, and the outside world knows nothing of either.

In a sense, it was the way it should be. There was no gossip or speculation, no national headline to drag someone through the mud long after they'd paid their dues. There was a problem, it was dealt with, and they moved on. In the midst of Mark's emotional tornado, the guilt he now felt for being a part of what he'd come to stop, he found himself respecting their lifestyle.

He managed a weak smile at Sarah, as he watched the doctor clean up both patient and equipment peripherally. The clipper, clit still firmly gripped in its closed blades, was put onto a white towel and wrapped up. *Just as Tommy's eye had been*, Mark realized, and wondered if they saved the parts somewhere.

"Sarah?" he whispered to her, rules be damned.

She looked up at him, still weakly focused in her drugged state. He thought her the most amazing woman in the world for allowing this, for holding her head high while they destroyed her most private parts—exposed for the world to see. But he saw the deep brown doe eyes lighten to the caramel they turned when she was upset. He saw the tear roll down her cheek unchecked. He saw her lip quiver.

And felt his own tear leave a shadow of wetness in its wake as it rolled to his chin and hung there precariously. He let go of her hand, but did not wipe his own tear. He left it. He didn't need to hide his emotions. Instead, he wiped her tear. He didn't want any of them to see her weakness. Didn't want her internal child, the young woman he'd known and loved to be upbeat even in the face of disaster, to be exposed.

Sarah flinched a tiny bit when he touched her face. She smiled up at him, more with her eyes than her mouth, and he bent down and kissed her forehead.

"I love you, Sarah-Bear."

In a voice so quiet, so weak, so afraid of the answer, she responded. "Is it over, Sparky?"

He nodded as the single tear called forth all its relatives and he openly wept. The doctor's voice interrupted their conversation, both verbal and silent sibling speak.

"We'll get you back home and settled. You rest for a few days and I'll check on you." Mark noticed the doctor wrapping up a used suture kit and realized he must have stitched the area rather than just cauterized and cleaned.

Marianne appeared on the gazebo steps behind the doctor, addressing the crowd, "A crime committed, the sin atoned. We take from the past its flames, not its ashes. Sarah is now innocent again."

Several of the community's men appeared with a stretcher and the doctor motioned them up onto the gazebo. He turned back to Sarah, "You did good, kiddo." And nodded to Josh.

Josh moved out of the way. Under the direction of the doctor, the men transferred Sarah from the bench to the stretcher and took her away, Josh in the lead. Marianne and the rest of the crowd dispersed without a word. The doctor stood, packed bag in hand, and looked at

Mark, eyes full of sorrow.

"I don't necessarily like doing this, you know. It's in the job description though." He paused, watching Mark's reaction. Mark felt numb. For the first time since he'd arrived, he had nothing to add or question. "It really doesn't happen often. You should know that…" He turned and walked out of the gazebo, leaving Mark there with his thoughts.

The town seemed to go on about its day as he sat there. In a surreal way, it was almost as if he had peripheral time-lapse vision. He didn't notice any details. He didn't recognize any faces. He only acknowledged movement around him.

Mark had no idea how long he'd sat there, feeling his sister's tears drying on his fingertips as he watched her blood dry on the stained wood of the bench. The speaker under the railing pulled him from his state.

"Do you want to talk?" Galen's disembodied voice was quiet and far away.

CHAPTER TWENTY-NINE

Galen's home didn't seem as warm and comforting as it had the last two times Mark had been there, and he thought perhaps the old man had turned down the heat. Mark sat in the chair across the coffee table from the couch and stared at the rumpled blankets, as he waited for Galen to bring the promised coffee. The room was dimming as the afternoon waned into evening, and Mark had to wonder how long he'd sat in the gazebo.

"I don't sleep in the bed anymore." Galen's voice startled Mark and he looked up, confused at the statement. Galen settled onto the couch, pushing the blankets to the end and tossing the pillow on top of them.

"Ever since Dottie died," he continued, staring down at the floor. "I just toss and turn. Too many memories—long languorous discussions, caring for each other when sick, the children and grandchildren coming in giggling and jumping on us. That bed has seen a lifetime of happiness outside marital relations. It hurts to lay there alone, in an empty house."

Mark nodded, allowing the man his rant to see where it was leading.

"The sheets have been washed, obviously, but even the pillows have lost their scent. She's gone. And the desperate act of spritzing the pillow with her favorite body spray wasn't enough to trick my mind."

Galen looked up at Mark, eyes wet with tears that threatened to destroy his persona. Mark was reminded of his grandmother and what she'd gone through when Grandpa died. But he'd been a child then. He hadn't understood the emotions involved with a partner rather than a grandfather. Mark slowly nodded to Galen to urge him forward.

Galen complied. "My life ended when Dottie died. She *was* my life." His gaze swept around the room, past furnishings but pausing on memories.

"My life—your life, any good life—is made up of the little things. The smiles you remember, the tears you hold dear, the laughter and learning, the sharing of excitement and hope with another person. What you garner from the world around you. And what you leave behind in your wake. It is not that I skinned my knee when I was small. It was that my mother decorated the wound with paint. It was not that my own Marianne started the kitchen on fire cooking too young. It was that she was trying to make us breakfast in bed. Sometimes it's the reason. Sometimes it's the result. But it's never the cause. Never the negative in and of itself. Listen to someone tell you about something bad that happened…" He stopped and looked Mark in the eye. "They don't remember the pain of it. Pain is only a memory of an emotion. A shadow of the event. They remember what got them there or where they went from there. It's not the pain of childbirth, it's the joy of the child. Not the cast on your arm, but the excitement of making it to *that* branch in the tree."

Mark nodded, his own lump forming in this throat as Galen's words reminded him of his mother. *She'd always said things like that. She'd always laughed at the bad and found the good. She'd always…* Mark's thoughts halted. *Sarah was just like their mother. Always had been.* He opened his mouth to speak but Galen cut him off.

"We have an awful lot of good things here. We have memories that carry over and cause laughter long after the event. We have flaws, like any group, but we have a unity you don't see anymore. We care about each other, we help each other. We play together and we cry together…"

"And you atone together?"

"Exactly." Galen raised an eyebrow and one side of his mouth in a crooked smile. "We may remember what happened today, but we'll never discuss it. We'll take from it Sarah's bravery and passion. Sarah's strength, in a bizarre twist of irony, will actually heighten our love for her. And you should know, Sarah's always been loved. Since the first day Josh brought her home. Dottie adored her beyond anything you could imagine from someone that wasn't actually her mother or grandmother. Camille usually calls her daughter, not daughter-in-law, and the children think the sun rises and sets on her. I wish you understood how very much she is loved here…"

He picked up his coffee cup but didn't drink from it. He just held it while he looked from Mark to the picture on the mantel and back.

"Today was unfortunate, and if I could have spared her, I would have. But the rules are the rules for a reason. And she accepted it when she joined us with as much vigor and determination as she accepted it today. We did not hurt her. We did not wound her personality or her passion for life. We will continue to adore her." He smiled as if he knew something Mark didn't. "And Camille and Marianne will continue to train her."

"Train her?"

Galen looked at him and Mark could see the wheels turning. It was as if he could see the man deciding whether to tell him the secret to the universe. He was apparently deemed worthy, as Galen continued.

"The council will be passing the torch to the next generation soon. With the death of Marianne's James, the transition began. The next generation has many firstborns and true-bloods to choose from, but there's a level of responsibility that goes with being on the council. A level of respectability necessary for the town to look up to them as authority. When James died and Marianne came to me about the next group of councilmen, she immediately suggested Sarah be considered, even though she's married in. Camille concurred, based solely on the sheer amount of adoration this community has for your sister."

"Does Sarah know?"

"Sarah's a smart girl, Mark. I'm sure she figured it out fairly quickly. And she's up for the task. What we did today—what she did today—will have no adverse affects on that. Only positive."

"That's why she wanted to stay and go through with this?" Mark's week worth of questions and confusion started to sort itself out internally as he spoke.

"Oh no. Even if she weren't being groomed for the position, even if she were planning on moving back to the city with you, she would have gone through with today." Galen finally took a sip from his cup and put it back down. "She's strong, much stronger than I think you realize. After all, you've been out of her life for the last ten years, and she has grown immeasurably as a woman, a human, an adult, in those years. She would have taken her atonement anyway, out of a sense of duty and loyalty to all of us. The shame she had for disappointing us, especially Josh and Camille, is erased by her acceptance of punishment. You heard Marianne. Her words were true. Sarah is innocent again."

"And your suggestion for my atonement the other day?"

"Oh, you have no loyalty. You can leave and take the easy way out and the council won't stop you. They won't blame you or hold it against you." Galen leaned forward and held Mark's gaze. "But I meant what I said. I see me in you. I know you're as good a person as Sarah. And the council agreed without much discussion at all."

Galen looked up to the mantel again. Mark let the old man drift while he did his own version and considered everything he'd seen and heard. Everything that had been said to him. He felt his chest tighten with pride for his sister and was surprised when it replaced the pain and fear he'd been holding on to so tightly since he learned what they were going to do to her.

"You know," Galen interrupted his thoughts, "I'm going to be gone soon. I feel it in my bones and hear it in the whispers of my Dottie's memory. The offer stands. If I died tonight, the offer would stand and the council would support it. But you need to decide for yourself."

CHAPTER THIRTY

Sarah didn't need nearly as much help over the next few days as Mark had presumed she would. She was out of bed by the time he returned from Galen's that night and was caring for the baby as if nothing was wrong. Mark, on the other hand, required a bit of assistance while his ribs healed, though he tried to pretend he was tough and didn't need help and instead worried about Sarah.

"Just think of it as you would any stitches," she told Mark after dinner. "Sure it hurts, it's a wound, but it's nothing Tylenol can't deaden. And as long as I'm careful going to the bathroom, it's sterile and covered and there's almost no chance of infection."

"Can you move around okay, really?"

"Well, bending down pulls on certain muscles and skin, but otherwise, I'm fine. Really." She smiled at him.

"You amaze me, you know that?" He helped Josh pick up Marky's toys in the living room and put them in the chest at the end of the couch. He caught Josh's smile at their conversation, and saw the twinkle in his eye when Josh glanced at Sarah.

"I know. You've been telling me that since I was eleven." She smiled at him. "So? You're killing me here, you know that, right? What exactly did Galen decide to do about the Meghan thing?"

Mark stood and turned to her, confused. He'd assumed the whole town knew he'd been given a choice, an ultimatum of sorts. "You don't know?"

"Oh no, there's been no public meetings on it."

"Won't you get in trouble for gossip if we discuss this?" Mark questioned Sarah but looked at Josh.

Josh answered, "Actually, no. This is immediate family. We're allowed to discuss the situation, the circumstances, whatever. Now if we were to talk outside this circle, that would be a problem."

Mark nodded and pondered Sarah for several beats. "I was given a choice. It's a pretty heavy decision, really. And one I don't think I want to discuss…" He was startled by his own words. "Sorry. I love you,

Sarah-Bear and I respect your opinion, but I think you would color this decision and it really needs to be mine alone."

"Much like mine was when I left you and came here…"

"Yeah, sorry about all that back then. I get it now." Mark smiled at her as if she were a small child who'd done something adorable. "Some things have to be your decision, and your decision alone. I get that now."

"About time you caught up." Smiling, Sarah adjusted her position on the couch with only the barest hint of discomfort on her face.

"So, Mark…" Josh sat at the end of the couch, lifting Sarah's feet and putting them across his lap. He absently stroked her ankle and foot, much like someone would softly rub their partner's back while standing in a group talking. "Do you hate me and the rest of us for what we did to your sister, or do you get that finally as well?"

"Oh no, I get it. I just don't know if I want to get it." Mark settled in the chair by the fireplace. "I still have a lot of questions, but they're not things anyone can answer. It's more how to mentally catalog things for myself. And thank you, Josh, for introducing me to Galen. He's really been helpful, and is quite the old man."

Josh laughed. "Oh he's quite a character alright." He looked up at Mark and furrowed his brows for a moment. "Matter of fact, from everything I've seen and what Sarah's told me about you, you're a very similar character…"

"Yeah, I've noticed that myself. I think it may be the police work or training that skewers our sense of humor and strengthens our loyalties to things we love or believe in." Mark's own words echoed in his mind and he almost heard something in his brain click. The puzzle was working itself out.

"You know, I think I'll go for a walk. Give you two some alone time."

"Planning on running into anyone at the river?" Sarah snickered.

"No. And Jesus, Sarah…" He scolded her, only to receive a silent chiding back for his language.

"Josh, can I?" She looked at her husband with a glint in her eye.

"Yeah, it's just us."

"You really shouldn't feel too guilty. It was an accident…" A cloud of emotions swirled in her gaze and Mark couldn't tell if she was upset or happy, hurt or angry. "She was mean to me, hated me really, for Josh—"

"And we were never promised to each other. She'd just decided that in her head. You should know that," Josh interjected.

"But she was mean to everyone. She was slightly crazy I think." Sarah's eyes flicked to Josh for a moment, then back to Mark. "Not JJ crazy, but almost a rational crazy. A scarier crazy."

"Who's JJ?" Mark cocked his head.

"Oh, you probably saw him at the picnic—"

"No hon, remember, he was sick on Saturday."

"Oh that's right. Well, at the gazeb…" Her words faded for a moment. "No, you wouldn't have seen him there. He's not allowed. Well, anyway, JJ—Justin Josiah—is Randall and Naomi's son, you know Naomi and I'm sure you saw Randall. Unfortunately, he was born with a form of retardation. He's twenty and acts about four. We all keep an eye on him because he has absolutely no judgment, good or bad, when it comes to anything. And his mouth would get him in trouble constantly if we didn't try and keep him in check. He runs Naomi to the ground on occasion, as he's quite a handful. I mean, it's a medical condition and we all know that and love him regardless, but if you didn't know you'd think he was one of those crazy men you see on the streets. Do you remember the guy we used to see on the boardwalk when Mom and Dad would take us to the beach? What did you used to call him?"

"Boardwalk Elvis." Mark laughed, remembering the well-dressed but tattered man constantly strolling the boardwalk singing songs without ever actually begging for change.

"Yes, him!" Sarah giggled. "But we try not to laugh at him. And we don't really mean to. I mean, it's a condition, but sometimes what he does is actually funny. But if we laugh at him then he continues to do it and that usually leads to bad decision making on his part."

"Anyway…" Josh steered her back.

"Meghan was crazy, Mark. You're lucky she didn't kill you as an avatar of me. You really are." Her eyes glazed over for a moment. "I'm lucky she didn't kill me."

"She's always been like that though. No medical excuse, just, for whatever reason she's always been mean and spiteful. Cruel in a sense you don't usually see in adults but might in children. She lived in her own reality," Josh added, pausing before continuing. "She was caught talking to baby dolls not long ago, referring to them as her children. Children she believed she had with me…and then with William."

"She was a troublemaker and always in trouble, Mark. She was part of the community though, and accepted as such. But in all honesty, I imagine there's much relief at her being gone. Unfortunately, it's because she's dead rather than just run away, but regardless, she's gone. So please, please don't hold any guilt."

Mark could tell they were both holding back. Biting their tongues rather than getting them snipped for gossip, but he'd gotten enough information. More from their expressions than their words.

And it only confused things again.

"I think I'll take that walk now…" Mark finally spoke as he stood up.

"We leave the door unlocked." Sarah smirked and Mark grinned back at her, knowing full well they never locked the doors around here.

CHAPTER THIRTY-ONE

Mark tossed his bag in the SUV and shut the rear door. The morning sun was a gentle warmth against the chill of Wisconsin's April air, but as he slipped into the driver's seat, the wave of artificial heat from the dash vents hit him, feeling almost muggy in comparison.

He sat in the running truck for a few moments and watched as Joseph packed the last of this week's market goods into the back of the town's old pickup. Joseph turned and nodded to him. He nodded back, respectfully, as if he were addressing a veteran or elderly family member.

Mark put the SUV into drive and did a U-turn around the gazebo, slowly, as to not gun the engine and wake anyone who may still be sleeping. He headed back down the road he'd used to enter Valley Mill over a week beforehand. His head full of an entirely new set of emotions and thoughts.

He passed the little graveyard at the curve and thought of Galen—knowing Dottie was one of those stones, and the old man would be making his daily trek down the road to visit her after his breakfast. He smiled a bittersweet smile and returned his focus to the road. He broke out of the tree line and onto the small state highway that would lead him back to Michigan, and eventually to Pennsylvania. To Gina.

God, he missed her.

Without cell service, he'd had no chance to talk to her over the last few days. He'd been so wrapped up in Sarah's situation and his own troubles, he hadn't even driven over to Eagle River to grab a signal long enough to let Gina know what had happened. He hadn't discussed anything with her. But he wasn't worried. They were a team. They worked well together for a reason. And they could overcome anything the universe decided to throw at them.

The universe didn't put us together just to tear us apart.

He turned the radio on but didn't pay attention to the rhythms it provided. His mind was making its own music, as his thoughts swirled and pulsed across everything that had happened, everything he'd seen and heard, and what the future held.

He thought of Squeaky and the corners already filled with new dealers. New dealers to get caught and slip through the system—the revolving door of catch-and-release criminals. He thought of the small crimes and larger crimes. He thought of the influences the outside world had on itself, and how he had thought Galen's rules were tough, but they evolved just as those in the real world did. And in both—in a parallel he hadn't been willing to acknowledge right away, neither was perfect—neither was without its over-the-top accidental developments. But one was far more logical than the other. One worked.

He heard his own voice, in a memory asking some thug that wanted to get off without a scratch, "What makes you so special the rules don't apply?" and realized he'd tried to do the exact same thing when it came to Sarah's punishment.

The walk he'd taken had led to the river. To the same spot where he'd run across Meghan and accidentally taken her life, trying to save his own.

Trying to save his own. That's all he'd been thinking when he'd wanted to save Sarah from herself. But she wasn't above the rules. And community member or not, neither was Mark.

He passed vaguely familiar signs and sections of land, as he drove. Yearning to return to Gina's laughter and passion for life. The drive was different alone. There was time to think. Too much time to think. And he didn't want to change his mind.

Galen's words rolled over themselves in his mind, writhing like snakes that won't sit still long enough for you to count them. He respected the old man. Much like he would have respected his father if he were still alive. Much as he continued to respect the memory of him. He was wise, beyond even his considerable years. Galen had seen much, before and after he'd established Valley Mill. He'd lived a long, full life, and he'd taken from the past its flames rather than its ashes. He'd buried a son and a wife. He watched his daughter grow into an amazing woman. And he could fall asleep at night knowing he'd created a community for his loved ones that was safe.

Galen had made a lifetime of memories, and acknowledged his story was almost finished.

Galen's proposal had both shocked and frightened Mark. The reality of what the man presented took days to truly sink in. At first Mark believed it was Galen's love of Sarah that had offered Mark an out, but he knew better now. He knew Galen saw himself in Mark. Knew Galen respected him on a level only another cop could understand, just as only another parent can truly appreciate the pain a parent feels when their child is hurt or lost to them.

Mark could go home, return to Gina and work and life as usual, and Valley Mill would hold his secret along with their own. They would tuck his sin behind their little white picket fences of projected perfection. He would not be allowed back into town proper, but if he wanted to visit Sarah, she could meet him in Eagle River.

The option was more than fair, more than Mark could have hoped for. It gave him a new outlook on the community and their rules. Not because he was being given the chance to literally get away with murder, accidental or not, but because their forgiveness was all encompassing. It was true, in a sense the word was lost over time in a society filled with media exposure and a constant need for entertainment and drama, real or imagined. As Mark himself had witnessed, even when a jury declared someone innocent, they were never truly forgiven and believed to be so.

And Mark would have immediately packed his things and headed home, if it weren't for the second option. The option that intrigued him.

Galen had offered Mark his job, his life, in either world.

He could return to Pennsylvania unscathed. Or he could stay.

"I'm old. I'm tired. And I miss my Dottie." Galen had spoken in a broken voice, which became stronger when he looked up at Mark from the couch the day of Mark's judgment meeting with the council. Still in pain from Meghan's attack, he'd been unprepared for the man's words.

"The community needs someone to keep the laws. Not in the city sense, but in a moral sense. A watcher, like I've become, that keeps the records of the families," he'd glanced at the family tree on the wall, "and acts as judge to the council's jury."

Mark couldn't speak and let the man continue uninterrupted.

"I do not believe it coincidence at all that fate brought you to us. Only a trained lawman would ever truly understand the need for an unbiased examination of the situation, the crime, the sin. Only someone with a lifetime of experience in the outside world would understand the importance of keeping it at bay from what we've created here." Galen sat silent and let Mark absorb the words, both spoken and unspoken.

Mark had opened his mouth several times to speak, to question, with both conviction and confusion, but couldn't force his myriad thoughts to transform into speech.

"Of course, it wouldn't come without cost..." The man had lowered his head, looking at his lap and the gracefully folded hands there. Nine of ten fingers interlaced. "You would have to take on all my duties. Including the shared scars as a show of unity and penance, and the initial payment of one finger."

Mark was honored Galen thought so highly of him. He tried to think of who gave him that much respect in the real world. Outside of friends and family, he could think of no one. Galen had gone on to explain how the houses were built for each generation, but he was offering his own. Mark could move his family right in there, take care of Galen in his fading years and have hands-on transitional time.

Mark looked at the road in front of him, his fog of thoughts clearing as he passed the WELCOME TO MICHIGAN sign. He checked his gas gauge, remembering the difficulty he and Gina had finding fuel in the state that seemed to go on forever—he was good for a while. He hoped the weather would hold while he drove by himself, but otherwise wasn't bothered by Michigan this time. He knew it wasn't the destination, only part of the journey. He smiled and turned the radio up, catching the tail end of AC/DC's "Highway to Hell." He drove toward Gina and drummed his fingers on the steering wheel.

Nine of the ten—a bandage marking his payment for entrance and innocence.

ABOUT THE AUTHOR

Born and raised in Wisconsin, Kelli Owen now lives in Pennsylvania. She's attended countless writing conventions, participated on dozens of panels, and spoken at the CIA Headquarters in Langley, VA. Visit her website at kelliowen.com for more information. F/F

Made in the
USA
Middletown, DE